WITHDRAWN

FULL CLEVELAND

Les Roberts

ST. MARTIN'S PRESS

NEW YORK

FULL CLEVELAND. Copyright © 1989 by Les Roberts. All rights reserved. Printed in the United States of America. No part of this book may be used or reproduced in any manner whatsoever without written permission except in the case of brief quotations embodied in critical articles or reviews. For information, address St. Martin's Press, 175 Fifth Avenue, New York, N.Y. 10010.

Library of Congress Cataloging-in-Publication Data

Roberts, Les.
    Full Cleveland / Les Roberts.
        p. cm.
    "A Thomas Dunne book."
    ISBN 0-312-03349-4
    I. Title.
    [PS3568.023894F8 1989]   89-32759
    813'.54–dc20   CIP

First Edition

10 9 8 7 6 5 4 3 2 1

To JUDITH GARWOOD,
who convinced me to go for it,
and

To DR. TOM JOHNSON,
who taught me how to keep it.

FULL CLEVELAND

1

In blue-collar towns such as Cleveland you don't often run into guys with names like Richardson Hippsley-Tate. It isn't the norm. There are plenty of people named Annunzio Napolitano or Bernie Feinberg or Leroy Washington, Jr. Or even names like mine, Milan Jacovich. That's Yugoslavian—Slovenian, to be more precise—and in my old neighborhood on the east side, or in Bernie's or Leroy's or Nunzio's neighborhoods, a guy with a hyphen in his name had better be either pretty good with his fists or damn fast on his feet.

On this particular afternoon, one of those oppressive August days in Cleveland when the air clings like wet cotton and beer sales hit an annual high, I had just finished a big job for an electronics firm in the eastern suburbs and written them a thirty-six-page report on implementing security procedures, preventing industrial espionage, and keeping the ribbon clerks from stealing paper clips. It's not the most exciting type of job I get, but it was a nice change from spying on errant husbands and wives, or having guys with bent noses try to make mine look like theirs. The president of the electronics company had given me a little bonus and a glowing letter of reference, my bank account was healthier than it had been in a while, and I was feeling pretty satisfied with myself and with life in general. From past experience, I should have known that someone was going to rain all over the picnic—someone always does. But even if I had thought about it, I wouldn't have figured it to happen that day. It was just too hot and muggy to start stirring up any shit. That's when my telephone rang and I first heard of Richardson Hippsley-Tate.

You'd expect a fellow with a hyphen to have a stuffy British accent, but this guy sounded more like New York than New Hyde Park. He was the general manager of the Lake Shore Hotel, a huge new resort-and-convention-center complex that had been completed just the past spring, with all the attendant hoopla, grand opening visits by show business and sports celebrities, and a ribbon cutting by Governor Kinnick capping a boring and windy speech. The Lake Shore had been built, after an internal battle in the city council chambers that had left several members either politically dead or mortally wounded, atop a landfill on the west side overlooking Lake Erie. It catered to fast-track business executives, *Fortune* 500 corporations, the local fat cats, and the out-of-town idle rich who were perverse enough to want to spend their precious vacation time in Cleveland.

When Hippsley-Tate called, he told me he needed to see me on "a matter of great urgency." That's what he said, a matter of great urgency.

"Could you be a little more specific, Mr. Hippsley-Tate?"

"It's not something I can talk about on the phone," he answered, "but this hotel has been ripped off for a great deal of money, and I need you to help me get it back."

2

I run a private security agency from my apartment in Cleveland Heights, so I assumed he'd gotten my name from the classified directory. For someone like myself with an independent bent, self-employment seems to work out a lot better than punching a time clock and trying to look busy when the boss walks in. I never bitch about the boss, because I am he; I never have to worry about layoffs, because I am the sole employee of Milan Security, as well as the entrepreneur. So I didn't have to check with anyone before arranging a meeting with Hippsley-Tate that evening. And since I get to the west side all too infrequently, I decided not to waste the trip. I invited my lady, Mary Soderberg, to join me for the evening and dinner at Johnny's.

I picked her up at her place in Shaker Heights and we headed out the Shoreway to the west side. In a pair of black slacks and a shiny green blouse that did funny things to the normal blue of her eyes, she looked merely sensational, causing heads to turn everywhere we went. She knew the outfit was one of my favorites, and I was touched that she wanted to wear it for me. In fact, just about everything Mary did touched me one way or another. I was getting scared about Mary—she was beginning to mean too much to me.

Mary regarded the rough-hewn scenic wonders of downtown Cleveland as we swung by Municipal Stadium and approached the bridge. "This isn't going to be one of those deals where you get hurt again, is it, Milan?" she said. "I hate it when you get hurt."

"I'm not real fond of it myself," I told her. "When it comes to that, the whole idea is to hurt the other guy."

"Didn't General Patton say something like that?"

"He never said it to me."

The big-shouldered silhouette of the Lake Shore Hotel rose against the darkening sky on our right as I pulled off the Shoreway and started down the access road. It was a beautiful hotel, some fourteen stories high, covering almost two hundred acres of prime lake frontage. Beautiful, that is, if you like stark modern architecture done in grays and muted pinks. Me, I prefer the solid buildings that have been around for a while—the ones that proudly announce they're from the Midwest: Terminal Tower, Gray's Armory, St. John's Cathedral, and the old Deming Mansion, which climbs the bluff just a few blocks from my apartment at the intersection of Cedar Road and Fairmount Boulevard. Then again, I like big band music and American cars and Beeman's gum and day baseball on grass, so you can't go by my tastes.

The entire effect was as cold and emotionless as the eyes of a doll. Glass elevators climbed up the outside of the building like glossy-backed beetles, mirrored glass reflected the colors of the evening sky as though bent on improving them, and there was a too noisy waterfall in the lobby. For the life of me I couldn't find a ninety-degree angle anywhere in the hotel. The walls of the lobby were covered with a kind of carpeting, and curved, as if they had been photographed with a fish-eye lens. The only thing square was the Muzak chirping merrily from hidden speakers all over the place. I asked at the desk for Mr. Hippsley-Tate. The clerk, a perky nineteen-year-old girl wearing a gray blazer with the hotel's name and crest on the pocket, pointed me across the lobby to the executive offices.

Mary said, "I'll meet you in the cocktail lounge, or whatever they call that place with the tables by the waterfall. I don't want to sit there in the office like a camp follower while you play detective."

"I hate to tell you this," I said, "but I'm not playing."

Mary didn't understand about my work sometimes. Our relationship, now six months old, was basically hassle free. We hardly ever argued about anything, and when we did it was more of a spirited discussion than an argument. But she didn't always understand about my work, and it troubled me. One of these days I felt it would cause a problem.

Richardson Hippsley-Tate's secretary was supercilious and curt, as if I were a pencil salesman come to foist some low-priced soft-lead specials on her boss. I guess when your hairspray is laid on as thick as hers was it cuts off circulation to your head, and you tend to snap at people as a matter of course. Eventually she relented, performed some sort of mystical ritual with the

4

intercom system, and the man himself came out of his office to greet me. Hippsley-Tate was a stocky five foot eleven, and affected a dashing Continental-style Vandyke that matched his sandy hair. His expensive three-piece suit was of the same shade of gray as the carpeted walls. It must have been the corporate color. His handshake was firm and hearty.

"Come on in, Mr. Jacovich. It's so nice to meet you," he said, seeming almost puppyish in his desire to have me like him. "How about some coffee? A drink? Name it."

"Nothing right now, thanks," I said, "I'm on my way to dinner. How can I help you, Mr. Hippsley-Tate?"

"Richie," he corrected me, indicating a comfortable chair for me to sit in. "My last name's too much of a mouthful." He sat down behind his desk and folded his hands very correctly in front of him. "I'll get right to the point. Does the name Gregory Shane mean anything to you?"

I frowned. It did ring a bell somewhere, but I couldn't place it at first and told him so.

"How about *North Coast Magazine*?"

"I seem to remember them," I said. "They're new, just starting up. In fact, they called me for an ad about four months ago, but I wasn't interested. The guy I talked to—was that Gregory Shane? A hell of a salesman. He said he'd write a small article about my business and do a quarter-page ad for two hundred dollars."

"Two hundred dollars," Hippsley-Tate murmured.

"It seemed like a good deal at the time, although now that you mention it, I haven't seen the magazine anywhere."

"There is no magazine," he said.

"What do you mean?"

"I imagine that Shane told you the magazine was designed to highlight members of the business community here in the Cleveland area, right? And that instead of simply buying ads, the businesses were, in effect, buying editorial space: the stories that would be written about them would be twice as efficient as just an ad."

"Something like that."

5

"That's what happened to me," he said. "It was about two weeks before our grand opening in May. I'd had meetings with the financial interests in this hotel, and it was my idea to bring some of the local people in here to dine and drink and dance, to attract business meetings and conventions from the immediate area as well as the out-of-town trade that obviously will keep up the occupancy rates. I'm not worried about the transient business, but it's very important to me to keep our banquet and F and B divisions in the black."

"F and B?"

He smiled. "Sorry. Food and beverage. So anyways, I was making that a priority. And when Dan Mulkey called to ask for an appointment and told me about his magazine, it seemed to be just what I was looking for in terms of local publicity."

I took out my notebook and jotted down two things. One of them was *Dan Mulkey* and the other was *Anyways????* I said, "Who is Dan Mulkey?"

"He was involved with the magazine somehow. He set up an appointment with me. They promised me that for the first three issues they wouldn't accept any advertising from any of the other hotels in town, like the Hyatt or the Hollenden House. In other words, the Lake Shore had an exclusive with *North Coast*, for the back cover, which is the most desirable place to put an ad, as you know."

I didn't know. I'd never advertised in my life. I said, "And the cost of this ad?"

"Forty-two grand." I noticed that he was perspiring. General managers of luxury hotels weren't supposed to sweat. Under my other notations I put *42 Grand??*

Hippsley-Tate ducked his head. "It was quite a price, but it was a new magazine and it was bound to get a lot of attention. I figured it was well worth it. Three-color printing, and they'd do all the layout and typesetting."

"What did they tell you in terms of readership?"

"They said they were aiming for a circulation of a hundred thousand. I mean, they were going to do a print run of twenty thousand, but he figured at least five people would see each issue. In doctors' offices and hotel rooms and places like that, he said. And of course on the racks in all the markets and discount drug outlets and the bookstores." The perspiration had begun to collect over his eyebrows and he wiped at it absently with his hand. "And they promised to give good reviews to our restaurants and to mention whatever entertainment we had in the lounges in later issues."

"And you gave them the entire fee up front?"

He nodded.

"With amounts that large isn't it customary to spread payments out over longer periods?"

"Usually, sure. But when Dan Mulkey came to pick up the money he said the only way he could give me such a good rate was if he got a lump sum in advance." He pounded his desk gently with a knotted fist. "I realize now what he was up to, but like I said, it seemed like such a good deal at the time."

I scribbled *Like I said??* Richardson Hippsley-Tate was beginning to interest me. "When is the last time you heard from them?"

He held his hands up in a gesture of supplication. "The day he picked up the money."

"Did you get any sort of a receipt?"

He got up and went to a file cabinet in the corner. Ruffling through the folders for a moment, he came up with a piece of paper, which he brought to me. It was a standard receipt form, printed cheaply on thin paper, with Dan Mulkey's signature scrawled almost illegibly across the bottom. It said, "Three issues, back pg., 3-color," and the date and the dollar amount. Across the top of the receipt was printed the name of the magazine and an address in Ohio City.

"Listen, Mr. Jacovich," he said, going to sit at his desk again. "Can I call you Milan? Jacovich is almost as much of a mouthful as Hippsley-Tate."

I nodded.

"The owners of this hotel are very upset about this, and I'm kind of on the line about it. I mean, I cut this deal without going to executive row for approval. You've got to help me."

"What do you want me to do?"

"Find Greg Shane and get our money back."

I noted the use of the plural and lit a Winston. I didn't ask permission, because he was puffing away like mad on a cigarette of his own. He said, "We'll give you a quarter of all the money you recover, with a minimum of five thousand dollars if you find Shane and don't recover the money right away."

"And if I come up empty?"

"We'll pay you your standard daily rate and cover all your expenses for a week just for you to look. Is that fair?"

It was more than fair, and Richardson Hippsley-Tate knew it. But it didn't smell good to me. "If you can't get the money back, why is it important for you to find Shane?"

He shrugged his shoulders. "Everyone has assets that can be converted to cash. We'll get something out of it. Mainly, we don't want to look like a bunch of patsies."

I wrote down *patsies* in my book. "It seems to me that these people are bona fide con artists. Why don't you just put the police on them?"

"They came around and they took statements, but they are short on manpower, as usual, and right now they're looking into a real estate rip-off in Parma, where the sting is well over six figures. This case will die in the files, I'm afraid."

He removed a wallet from his pocket and extracted a number of crisp one-hundred-dollar bills. It was the kind of flat wallet that didn't fold or crease the money inside; Benjamin Franklin was young and unwrinkled—all fifteen of him. "This should cover you for the first five days," he said. "You can invoice me personally for the expense money."

I took the money as though it might burn my fingers and put it in my jacket pocket. It felt bulky and unnatural there, like a tumor. "Okay," I said. "Tell me where to start."

"There on the receipt is Shane's address. It's a house in Ohio City, and I can tell you right now that it's empty. He cleared out of there lock, stock, and wife." Hippsley-Tate pushed a piece of paper across the desk at me. It was a list of names and addresses.

8

"Who are these people?"

"They're the so-called staff of the magazine—or they were. I've heard of Leonard Pursglove before; he used to work for several local ad agencies. If you have connections in the ad business you might want to check up on him. Dan Mulkey used to have something to do with a record company. Greg Shane I never heard of until I got involved with his magazine."

"Okay," I said, and put all the papers in my pocket with the money. "Tell me, how'd you happen to get into the hotel business?"

He shrugged. "It's as good as any other," he said. "I managed a place in Manhattan Beach out in L.A. for a while. A small, European-style hotel with very expensive antiques in every room. The money was good, and it was a fun job, so I stuck with it. I've never handled a place as big as this one, though. It's a hell of a lot more hard work."

"I've always found that anytime someone gives you money to do something, it's more work than fun. Otherwise they'd make you pay them."

He laughed, ducking his head in agreement. "Milan," he said, "it's really important that we get some action on this. I mean, the owners of the hotel are holding me responsible, and forty-two Gs is a big bite out of anyone's paycheck."

"That's more than I make in a week," I agreed.

I went back out to the lobby to collect Mary. She was seated at a table near the waterfall, working on a glass of house Chablis, looking bemused as a paunchy middle-aged man in a blue suit stood over her giving her the rush of her life. He looked as if he was a regional sales manager in town for the annual corporate meeting of a bathroom accessories manufacturing firm. I sighed. When I had started seeing Mary several months before, I'd come to uneasy terms with the fact that such a truly beautiful woman is going to get a lot of attention from other men, but I've never quite accustomed myself to it happening in front of me.

I put on my best glower and stalked up to the table. " 'Scuze me, ma'am," I drawled, "is this fella here botherin' you?"

9

He looked up at me, the color leaving his face via express. "No," he said quickly. "No problem. Just . . ." He didn't say just what but beat a hasty retreat to the other side of the lobby. Maybe the fear of scandal getting back to his boss and to his wife at home in Columbus or someplace changed his mind about pursuing his line of inquiry. Maybe it was because when I was at Kent State I was a first-string defensive guard, and I look it.

Mary watched him go and sipped her wine. "It's getting so a girl can't turn an honest buck around here," she said. "He wanted to know what he could get for a hundred. Look, Milan, I'm getting hungry. Are you planning on buying me dinner? Because if not, I can earn my own, right here."

She stood and I took her arm. The regional sales manager was glaring at us from across the lobby. He thought I was the house detective.

"I don't know," I said. "What can I get for buying dinner?" She put her mouth very close to my ear and told me.

During the day Johnny's is a shot-and-a-beer bar, its clientele mostly unemployed steelworkers who sit hunched over their drinks in a cloud of cigarette smoke—plaid-shirted in the winter; muscle-shirted in the summer, so their tattoos show— for upwards of seven hours each day, ignoring the game shows and soap operas flickering on the TV, talking in rumbling monotones about the fates of the various sports franchises in town and about the weather and about their cars and about women. The smells of the beer and the smoke and the sweat seem to have been soaked up by the walls. There are ten thousand such neighborhood taverns in a hundred industrial cities, and almost all are interchangeable, except that one might trade talk of the Browns and Cavs and Indians for speculations about the Lions and the Pistons and the Tigers.

But along about six thirty or seven in the evening a strange thing happens to Johnny's. The unshaven steelworkers at the bar are displaced by yuppie lawyers in three-piece suits and their tall, elegant women in clinging jersey dresses and full sets of acrylic nails, trailing clouds of Enjoli and waiting not always pa-

10

tiently for a table. The daylight odors of Stroh's and Lucky Strikes are overpowered by those of beef en croutade and veal marsala and fusilli in a pesto sauce served on a bed of radicchio. The bartender, a hard-looking young woman in a well-filled T-shirt, spends more time selecting the right pouilly fuissé than she does drawing beers, and suddenly a maître d' appears to recite the specials. He looks like a former welterweight contender, but that doesn't take away from the fact that for good, fancy cooking, Johnny's is one of the best restaurants in Cleveland.

Mary ordered roast quail with sherry lime sauce, and I had pasta with walnut sauce. We split a bottle of California grey Riesling. As we were preparing an assault on our goat cheese salads, Mary said, "Well, how did it go with Mr. Stokeley-Pipps?"

Mary had come into my life at just the right time. I had been divorced from my wife Lila for almost a year and was missing the hell out of my two sons, whom I see less and less frequently as they get older and busier with friends their own age, and who seem to be spending a lot of their spare time with my wife's new friend, one Joe Bradac from the neighborhood. Joe had evidently worshipped Lila from afar since she and I had been a steady item in high school. To give him credit, he never made any sort of move in her direction while I was still in the picture, but as soon as Lila and I separated he moved in like a hermit crab, to inhabit the shell I'd left behind. In the meantime, my life had become as bland and flavorless as yesterday's chewing gum; I had been turning into a lonely, cranky old bachelor, drinking beer at Vuk's Tavern in the old neighborhood on St. Clair Avenue and watching the game on TV by myself every night. I always figured that when I got married it was going to be forever, and the fact that Lila had filed divorce papers on me didn't change my gut feelings that she was still my wife, still the only family I had, and that somehow I had failed, screwed up, taken a wrong turn somewhere along the line. But when I met Mary it was like the sun coming out after a long winter of gray.

"I got the job," I said. "He seems to be a scared little man who's gotten in too deep."

11

"And you're the life preserver?"

"It's what I do."

"Is it going to be dangerous? Rough stuff?"

"Not at all," I said. "He's been scammed, that's all."

She reached over and put her hand on my cheek. "I hope you're right," she said. "I'd hate anything to happen to this gorgeous face."

I don't have a gorgeous face. If you stretched real hard you might say that I'm okay-looking. But Mary makes me believe, for a few seconds at a time, anyway, that I have a gorgeous face. Relationships have been built on a lot less.

I looked up toward the front door as the noise level intensified a few decibels. Making a rather grand entrance was an old high school chum of mine who had gone through the police academy with me but had stayed on the force and earned his gold shield. Marko Meglich, now a homicide bureau lieutenant, had dropped the *o* from his first name and was called Mark by everyone, except those of us who knew him back on East Fifty-fifth Street. He was wearing expensive tailored sharkskin suits now and got a manicure once a week, but I could remember when he had the best hands of any wide receiver in the East Side City High School League. I'm told he often uses those hands to bounce recalcitrant witnesses off walls, but I couldn't substantiate that. He was with another couple in their late thirties and a flashy-looking redhead, who I don't think was of legal drinking age. Marko's marriage to a neighborhood girl had, like my own, recently caved in—his under the pressures and exigencies of police work—and now he was most often seen around town squiring some pretty young thing like this one, with a body built for the fast lane and a vacant stare. Most of them were too young to be classified as bimbos; privately I referred to them as Marko's Bimbettes.

I rose as he approached our table. "Milan!" he said. "You're moving up in the world, my man, coming in here. I've never known you to eat anything more exotic than klobasa on rye bread." He ignored my outstretched hand and hugged me.

There was still that much Slovenian left in him. I could feel the gun nestled beneath his left armpit. Regulations.

"And this must be the magical Mary," he said, taking her hand and kissing it gallantly, then preening his drooping black mustache. "You're Milan's only topic of conversation the last few months. I feel like I know you already."

"Wouldn't it be awkward," I said, "if this weren't Mary?" For a moment I thought Marko was going to wither away with embarrassment, so I quickly bailed him out. "Mary, meet Lieutenant Mark Meglich, Cleveland PD."

Mary gave Marko one of her more dazzling smiles. "I've heard a lot about you, too, Lieutenant."

"Mark, please," he said. And then as almost an afterthought, "Oh. Everyone say hi to Brenda."

The girl smiled faintly, her red hair in a wild, trendy perm framing her pretty, empty face.

"What brings an East Side Kid like you west of the Cuyahoga?" Marko said.

"A case."

"Naturally," he said. "Anything you want to talk about?"

"Nothing that would interest homicide. Have you heard about *North Coast Magazine*?"

"I'm not really familiar with it," Marko said. "If I recall rightly, they went around selling advertising to a bunch of mom-and-pop businesses and then disappeared before the magazine ever hit the stands. Small-time bunco stuff."

"Do the names Greg Shane and Dan Mulkey mean anything?"

"Not Shane, but I can look it up for you. Mulkey, the last I heard of him, was a record company executive, a little on the shady side. Is that your case? The magazine?"

"Yeah. One of the scam-ees is bellowing."

"Poor baby," he said. "When will people learn that everything's a scam? Religion, politics, television, football." He took Brenda's arm possessively. Maybe she was a scam too. "Listen, I'm with some people, I gotta run. Don't be such a stranger,

Milan. Quit keeping this beautiful creature all to yourself. Maybe the four of us can go out sometime." He turned to Mary. "Make him call; all right, Mary?"

She smiled. "I'm not sure anyone makes Milan do anything."

Marko scowled. "That's his damn trouble!"

"Let's just say I'll suggest it," Mary offered. "It was nice meeting you, Mark."

I noticed that the broken-nosed maître d' made a bit more of an obsequious fuss over Marko's party than he had with us. A gold shield comes in handy sometimes, and one of Marko's favorite pastimes is chiding me for not staying in the department and earning one of my own. For two people who've been friends for almost thirty years, he and I have definite communication problems. I've never been able to make him understand that I left the force because I'd had enough saluting at Cam Ranh Bay to last me a lifetime.

"So that's the famous Marko Meglich," Mary said as I sat back down and rearranged my napkin on my lap. "When should we get together with him and Brenda and all of us go out for some fun?"

"I can hardly wait."

"I hope he won't keep her out too late for her to finish her algebra homework. She's certainly pretty, but your friend Marko seems better than that, somehow."

"It's his postdivorce play time," I said. "She's the flavor of the month. All divorced men go through it. Some take longer than others."

"Did you, Milan?"

I thought about lying for a moment; then I said, "No."

"Why not?"

"I don't know. Just needed to lie back and lick my wounds, I guess. Spent a lot of time alone, getting in touch with my own feelings. Is this conversation going to get heavy?"

"We haven't talked much about Lila. Maybe it's time we did."

"Why?"

"I don't know," Mary said, "maybe because we've been hanging out together for a while and it might be helpful to define the relationship."

"I'm nuts about you," I said. "You're very important to me, and I don't know if I could make it without you. How's that for a definition?"

"Right out of Webster's," she said as the waitress brought our dinners. "The silver-tongued devil strikes again."

The walnut sauce was delicious, and Mary and I, as is our custom when we come to Johnny's, tasted each other's dinner. I'm not an authority when it comes to roast quail with sherry lime sauce, but the sample I had was spectacular. We discussed the food and the wine for a minute, easy once more after a few moments that had been less than comfortable. That was what was so good about Mary—the comfort level was remarkable. We are so often chameleons with other people, role-playing and trying to keep our dialogue and our scenes straight, it's rare and very special when we find someone with whom we can relax and be ourselves. Woe to whoever lets such a person get away.

After dinner, instead of taking the Shoreway back to the east side, I drove on surface streets past the old recently restored houses of Ohio City on the west bank of the Cuyahoga, which had once sheltered the families of European immigrants and now were the abodes of upwardly mobile young executives, and stopped at the address Hippsley-Tate had given me, the last-known residence of Greg Shane. Mary and I got out of the car and walked up the stone steps to the front porch. The house was dark. A few cobwebs were strung across the upper corners of the doorway, and there was no sound coming from inside. I peered in the windows, trying to see through the lace curtains that covered them, but I wasn't too successful. From what I could make out there wasn't much to see; a few cardboard boxes on the floor, a cheap aluminum chair in the middle of the room. An empty house isn't all that fascinating.

Mary hugged herself. "It has a spooky feeling about it. Do you suppose they sneaked away in the dead of night?"

"I'll find out tomorrow." I wrote a reminder to myself in my notebook. Then we drove back to Mary's house, and for quite a while I didn't think about Gregory Shane or Richardson Hippsley-Tate.

2

It was a terrific night—it always is, with Mary—but when I got back to my own apartment in the morning it was time to go to work. I consulted the list Hippsley-Tate had given me, beginning with the suckered advertisers. A lot of people in several different types of enterprise had apparently been pretty gullible, although from the kinds of businesses listed, none had been in for as much as forty-two thousand dollars.

The logical place to start would be with the magazine's staff, the people who had worked closely with Greg Shane. After depositing most of Hippsley-Tate's money in my bank account, I looked up Jay Adams in the phone book. According to the papers I had, he had been *North Coast's* first editor in chief. He was listed in University Heights, close enough to my own apartment that on the drive over, the air conditioner in my oversize Chevrolet station wagon didn't cool off the interior in time for me to be comfortable. My shirt was sticking to the small of my back. The Midwest can be just as rough in the hot weather as it is in the winter.

The apartment building where Jay Adams lived was at the crest of a small hill, an old stone relic from the twenties, massive like a king's fortress, with several different age-faded colors of brick and masonry forming an eye-pleasing pattern in the hot, bright sunshine. Midwestern to its foundations, it was frankly a dinosaur, but beautiful in its very ugliness, with walls thick enough to keep out the heat of August and to shelter its inhabitants from the northerly winds that whip their Canadian-born blasts of ice so wickedly off the lake in the wintertime. Inside the foyer I detected the layered odors of fifty years of cooking— chicken and onion and hard-boiled eggs and garlic and klobasa sausage and cabbage. People had lived in this building for forty years at a stretch, raised children and grandchildren, and died, leaving their smells and their auras behind in the foyer and hallways, along with the ghosts of their dreams.

Jay Adams's apartment was on the second floor, reached by a staircase that started out as faux marble in the lobby and became peeling linoleum at the landing between the first two stories. It was a long first flight; buildings like this one had been designed with high vaulted ceilings back in the days before over-imaginative real estate salesmen had coined the term "cathedral" for them. I followed the clacking sounds of a typewriter to the apartment at the end of the hall and rang the bell. The typing didn't stop until I had rung a second time.

The man who opened the door seemed to redefine obese. He couldn't have been more than five foot six, but he probably weighed in at more than three hundred twenty pounds, although people in that condition rarely go near a scale, preferring instead to ignore the fact that they are a heart attack waiting to happen. Perspiration made his face shiny and collected in little puddles in the rolls of fat on his neck. He was wearing a flowing yellow caftan, with leather sandals peeking out from beneath the hem. I

18

suppose the idea was to minimize his girth, but the outfit only succeeded in drawing attention to it.

"Yes?" he said, frowning over the half-glasses that rested low on the bridge of his fleshy nose.

I handed him one of my business cards. "Hello, Mr. Adams. My name is Milan Jacovich."

The frown deepened, and then recognition, along with something wary and almost frightened, clicked on behind the piggy little blue eyes. He backed away from the door a step or two. "If you're one of the advertisers looking for your money back, you've wasted your time coming here. I was just an employee. I didn't know Shane was going to run out on his commitments."

"I'm not here about my own money," I said. "I'm here about someone else's. I've been hired to find Gregory Shane, and since you worked so closely with him, I thought perhaps you could help me."

"Private investigator?" He squinted down at the card. "Oh." He nodded, then said petulantly, "I don't know where Shane is, the son of a bitch."

"May I come in? Just for a minute?"

"Well—I'm in the middle of writing. . . . All right, just for a minute."

He stood aside and I squeezed by him into the apartment. It was incredibly cluttered. Papers, reference books, magazines, and rubber-banded file folders ready to burst open like overstuffed sausage casings littered almost every available surface. In one corner was a student desk, which held a Smith Corona portable and a ream of inexpensive white typing paper. At the desk was a sturdy wooden chair with wraparound arms. Three bed pillows were squashed nearly flat on its seat. An opened can of Pepsi peeped through the debris on the coffee table.

Adams waddled past me and swept aside a stack of magazines so I could sit on one end of an old sofa upholstered in a faded rose pattern. He laboriously lowered himself into the chair by the desk, making a frightful noise in the back of his throat as he relieved his rather spindly legs of their burden.

19

"I really resent the intrusion, I don't mind telling you, Mr. Jacovich."

I corrected his pronunciation of my name. "The 'J' is pronounced like a 'Y.' Jacovich."

"Well, whatever," he said. "I've had about a hundred people in my face since Greg disappeared, from the city police to the Chagrin River Valley police to all the advertisers I spoke with to the other employees on the magazine wanting to get paid. And I'm damn sick of it. This whole thing is playing hell with my work—*and* my reputation. I mean, I'm quite a well-known editor. I have important friends in the publishing business in every major city in America, and I don't need this albatross around my neck."

I made a note about the Chagrin River Valley Police Department. It seemed I was going to be talking to my old friend, Chief Ethan Kemp. "When's the last time you saw Gregory Shane?"

"About two months ago. He and his lawyer came busting in here rattling sabers, for all the good it did them."

I took out my notebook. "Why would Greg Shane come here with an attorney?"

"Look, Mr. Jacovich, you're not dealing with some damn fool here. I know I'm a fat old queen that people laugh at, but I've been around the block a few times—I have a master's degree in journalism from Northwestern—and nobody makes a monkey out of me!"

"Perhaps if you started from the beginning. . . ?"

He took off his glasses and put them on the desk atop the ream of typing paper. There were two purple ridges where the frames had bitten into his wide, fleshy nose. "If any of this gets out, I'm going to have you crucified."

"I'll be the soul of discretion," I assured him.

"All right, then," he said reluctantly. "Just after the holidays last winter Gregory Shane called me. He said he and his wife were starting up a new magazine and were looking for an editor in chief, and that I had been recommended to them."

"Did he tell you where he'd gotten your name?"

"Yes," Adams said. He took some Kleenex from the pop-up box on the desk and mopped the sweat from his face and neck. It took him two tissues. "He had somehow become associated with a man named Dan Mulkey, who used to be a record executive here in town with High-O Records. Their offices are downtown. They do half-assed recordings of up-and-coming young rock groups and distribute the albums locally. I don't know what happened with Mulkey and High-O, but he left them around Thanksgiving time, and he was on the beach. Shane made him an offer to be the production manager for the new magazine."

"And how did Mulkey know you?"

"I had done a story on High-O for *Cleveland Magazine* about two years ago and had interviewed Mulkey then. Did you happen to see it?"

I shook my head, and he seemed genuinely shocked that I hadn't read his article, as though it were the Book of Genesis or *Gone With the Wind*. He managed to contain his disappointment and rushed bravely on. "In terms of people in the record business like Phil Spector and Berry Gordy, Dan Mulkey was strictly Pony League, but he made a decent living here in Cleveland, for a man with minimum talent."

"So Mulkey recommended you, and Shane offered you the job as editor?"

"Editor in *chief*," Adams corrected me. "And the promise that I'd make any and all decisions concerning the editorial content of the magazine. He said he didn't have a lot of start-up money, but that if I'd go along with them for minimum salary until the first issue hit the stands, he'd give me a percentage of the magazine as well as a salary. A big percentage."

"How much?"

"A third," he said. "He and Nettie—that's his wife—would own the other two thirds. Well, the idea of the magazine sounded good to me, even though I knew they were considerably undercapitalized. I liked the idea of being in on the beginning of something, and I also liked the idea of owning part of my own magazine and having total editorial control. So I went to work."

21

"Exactly what was the thrust of the magazine supposed to be? What was your target audience?"

He took a box of extra-long cigarettes from his pocket and put one in his mouth. The cigarette paper was gold-colored. He struck a wooden match and lit the cigarette, extending his pinky so as not to get it singed. "Sometimes in order to justify the making of art, Mr. Jacovich, some commercial considerations have to be weighed. This magazine was aimed at the blue-collar workers of Cleveland and environs, the white-sock crowd, the ethnics. You know, the Poles and the Bohunks and the—oh, dear. I *do* beg your pardon. I didn't mean—"

It seemed *North Coast Magazine* gave different strokes to different suckers. "No offense taken," I said, which was not the first lie I've ever told in my life. "I *am* Slavic and my job might be considered blue-collar by some. But the only white socks I own I wear when I play tennis. And for your information, I have a master's degree of my own."

"The term was not used in any pejorative sense."

"I even know what pejorative means, Mr. Adams. Now, about the magazine. . . ?"

"Well," he whined, happy to have squirmed off the hook, "the idea was to do a couple of feature stories each month, like celebrity profiles and a sports column. For instance, for the premiere issue we did a profile of Vivian Truscott, the Channel 12 News anchorwoman."

"That's a pretty big name," I said. "I hear she's very ambitious."

"I don't know," he said, "but someone talked her into giving the interview, and I wrote the story. It was a good one, too. This was supposed to be a class operation, Mr. Jacovich. There was to be a short-short story each month written by one of the area's top writers. For the first one we had Edna Warriner. She's been writing romance novels and gothics for years, and we were lucky to get her, but she happens to be a dear, dear friend of mine of long standing. There was to be a restaurant guide, but again, the restaurant reviews were to focus on those establishments purchasing ads. I was to have written those, and the theater reviews. The rest of the book was going to be articles written either by or about the small business owners we approached in the community who were foresighted and promotion-minded enough to take out an ad with us. If they wanted to write their own copy, fine. If not, one of the staff would come out and interview them for a story."

This didn't sound like responsible journalism to me, but then what did I know about publishing a magazine? "How many staff members did you have?"

"At that point I *was* the staff," he said. "Of course, Greg promised that when the first issue came out and we were getting something back he'd hire me a couple of assistants. But it never was anything more than Shane, Nettie, and Dan Mulkey. For all the good *he* did."

"Who did what, Mr. Adams?"

"Mulkey drew up lists of businesses for Nettie to call. She'd make the phone contact—she was very good at that—and then Greg would drop whatever he was doing and rush out to pick up the money before the client had a change of heart or had time to check the magazine out. Then, if it was necessary, they'd send me to the client with a tape recorder to do an interview. It made those little shopkeepers feel awfully important. They couldn't know that the Shanes were living from hand to mouth most of the time. A check usually bought them dinner the next night."

I said, "When exactly did you sever connections with the Shanes?"

He looked uneasy. "It was sometime in April. I hadn't been paid a full salary since day one, and I was damn sick of it. But I held on, because I believed in the project with all my heart. I mean, I had other offers every day for editorships, but I kept turning them down as long as I could."

"And you left to take one of those offers?"

He looked a bit sickly and a flush spread across his chubby cheeks. He fanned his face with his hand. "Uh, no. I'm working freelance right now."

I jotted that down.

"But I stayed loyal—until Mr. Hot Shot Leonard Pursglove arrived on the scene."

"Who's Leonard Pursglove?"

"He's a freelance writer here in town. He did a lot of local ad-copy stuff, and he claims to be a gourmet cook. Anyway he was out of work and broke on his ass, and Greg met him somehow or other and hired him to be the resident restaurant critic and to freelance some other stuff, because he thought he'd lend some class to the magazine. Hmph!"

I'd never heard anyone actually say "Hmph!" before. I hope never to have to again.

"He had no *right* to hire anyone without checking with me first," Adams said petulantly. "I was the editor in *chief!*"

"But Shane was the publisher, wasn't he?"

He glared at me. "That doesn't matter. I was the editor in chief."

I certainly didn't want to get into a debate with him, so I merely nodded gravely.

"But no," Adams went on, "Greg and Leonard got to be buddies right away. Birds of a feather, if you ask me. Greg wanted Leonard to go out and do the interviews, because he thought Leonard was a better image for the magazine than I was." I must have looked quizzical because he explained, "Leonard Pursglove is a very good-looking man, very distinguished, a smooth talker and an even smoother operator. Well, it ticked me off mightily that Greg was giving Leonard money for his work when he still owed me for mine. And that damn Leonard played Greg like a fish on a line. He wanted my job from the very beginning. Well, finally I let him have it. And as things turned out, I'm glad I did."

"You quit?"

"I told Greg it was either Leonard or me." He looked a bit wistful. "That's always chancy, but I swear to you I thought Greg and Nettie would have more loyalty to me." His eyes grew teary, although I was unsure whether it was caused by emotion or the intense heat. "Loyalty is as outmoded a concept these days as knighthood; it was stupidity on my part to ever have thought otherwise."

"So what did you do then?"

"Well, I had hired my own art director, a wonderful, talented young man named Oliver Casagrande, and we had put the boards together for the first issue."

"Help me out, Mr. Adams," I said. "What do you mean by boards?"

"We had the articles and the ads all typeset and the pictures all done in the proper sizes, and we pasted them up on these art boards—here, I'll show you."

He heaved himself out of his chair and went to a cabinet behind the desk, where he rummaged around a bit and came up with a bedraggled piece of cardboard on which was printed a grid of squares in blue. Then he got his glasses from the ream of typing paper on the desk and put them on. "This is a board. You paste up the material on here and give it to the printer to take a picture of. When you put it all together you have a magazine."

"I see," I said.

"So anyway, Oliver and I worked for two weeks, day and night, to get the first issue ready. And I told Greg that I'd give him the boards when he paid me the money he owed me. He refused; he said the magazine belonged to him and I had no rights at all. So I refused to give him the boards. That's why he came back with an attorney. Oh, yes, he could afford to pay an attorney." He sat down again, making a strangled grunt with the effort.

"So in effect, Mr. Adams, you were kind of holding the magazine for ransom."

Wounded, he said, "That's a shitty way of putting it."

"What was the attorney's name, do you remember?"

"Zito. Joseph Zito. I have his card somewhere . . ." He started to rise again.

"That's all right," I said. I didn't think I could bear watching him get in and out of that chair one more time. "And what happened when Shane and Zito came here?"

"Oh, they threatened me with all sorts of things, but I wouldn't give in. I was angry and I was hurt and I felt used. I told both of them that if they paid me twenty-two hundred dollars, which according to my calculations was what I had been promised, and paid Oliver as well, they could have their damn magazine back and to hell with them. But the fact was that Greg didn't have that much, because he had been living and paying his rent with the revenue he'd collected from the advertisers."

I said, "Twenty-two hundred doesn't sound like very much money for a person of your experience, Mr. Adams."

He looked embarrassed again and tried to focus his eyes on something several feet above my head. Judging from the rest of his apartment, it must have been a spiderweb. "As I say, I was working for practically nothing to see the thing get started. The ungrateful son of a bitch!"

I was afraid he was going to cry. "So you were no longer with the magazine at all when Greg and Nettie Shane disappeared some time in June?" I asked.

"No. It was smart-ass Pursglove's baby by then. I'm telling you, Mr. Jacovich, I've never been so humiliated in my whole life. I mean, I'm pretty well known in this town, and the idea of getting fired in favor of a nobody pissant like Leonard Pursglove . . ."

"I thought you said you quit."

"I did," he said quickly, "but the effect was the same. There I was, and then all of a sudden there *he* was. My reputation is going to take *years* to repair. Years." He looked mournful, as though he didn't have enough years to take care of it. Probably the strain on his heart from carrying around all that weight was going to make a prophet out of him.

"You wouldn't happen to have a list of the advertisers, would you?"

He pushed his glasses up on his nose. "I don't want to get involved in this. I have nothing to do with it anymore."

"There's been a crime here, Mr. Adams. We can get a court order and subpoena that list, but I'd rather do it the easy way."

He sighed, put-upon. "Very well," he said. The effort it

cost him to get out of the chair again, go to the file cabinet, and bend over and search through a lower drawer was so taxing, it made me look away. He finally came up with another manila folder.

"I'll make copies and get this back to you," I said.

"I hope so."

"Do you have any idea where Greg Shane might have gone?"

"No, but I wish I did."

"Why?"

"Because," he said, "he's a lousy crook and he's publicly humiliated me. If I knew where he was, I'd kill him."

3

When I left Jay Adams I went to the nearest pay phone and called Mary at her office at Channel 12. She's head of the sales department and has her own secretary, a woman who resolutely refuses to recognize my name even though I call at least three times a week. She always asks me what company I'm with and if Mary will know what the call is in regard to, and I had discovered months before that it did no good to get nasty with her, so I played her silly game and finally got connected.

"I was just thinking about you," Mary said when she came on the line.

"That's good," I said.

"You can't have a night like we did last night without it

absolutely affecting your whole day. People have been asking me all morning what I'm smiling about."

"Did you tell them?"

"Of course not," she said. "And it's making them crazy."

I said, "Mary, you know Vivian Truscott, don't you?"

"The first lady of Cleveland television? Sure. We're not exactly buddies—she's too important to associate with us peons who work in the sales office—but I know her. I see her around the studio almost every day. Why?"

"I was going to ask you to tell me about her, but I think you just did."

"Oh, Vivian's all right," she said. "Clawing your way to the top in a major market like this takes a pretty tough-minded lady. And Vivian's not planning on being here for long. Next stop, New York or L.A., and after that, the network. I think she sees herself as the next Diane Sawyer or Barbara Walters, and she's not about to waste time talking to anyone who can't be of direct assistance in getting her there. She says hello when she's spoken to, but I don't think we ever had a conversation."

"Could you have one with her for me tomorrow? I'd like a few minutes of her time."

Mary said, "You mean this is a business call?"

"I would have called you anyway."

"Sure. Well, it's easier to get a papal audience than an interview with Vivian."

"Tell her that it has to do with *North Coast Magazine*."

"You think that'll help?"

"It couldn't hurt," I said.

"I'll do what I can, Milan. But only because you're so good in bed."

I smiled into the phone. "I knew that would come in handy some day," I said.

Edna Warriner lived in genteel respectability off Green Road in Shaker Heights, in a boxy white house with black trim, fronted by a gently sloping lawn that had seen better days. The grass was trimmed to a proper length, but there were sere brown spots on it that bespoke a lack of professional care, and the box hedges that rose up along the edges of the house, all but covering the front windows, had bare sunburned patches as well. It looked as though a high school kid from the neighborhood cut the grass whereas all the other houses on the street benefited from the ministrations of professional gardeners and landscapers.

When I had called her for an appointment that morning, I'd had to repeat my name and my story several times. I wasn't sure if she was slightly hard of hearing or slightly dotty, and after the phone conversation I had doubts about my visit yielding anything positive. But the appointment had been made, and it was more or less in the neighborhood, so I decided to go through with it. Before talking to Jay Adams I had never heard of Edna Warriner, but a quick trip to the library told me she was the author of some twenty-three books, most of which had titles like *The Turret Window* and *The Black Pirate's Woman*. Since my reading tastes run more to mystery writers like Bill Pronzini and Ross Thomas, and to John Updike and Pat Conroy, I could only guess that Ms. Warriner's work was romantic and quasi-historical, or had to do with dreamy young girls who inherited mysterious old castles on the Yorkshire moors.

The woman who opened the door for me was in her early fifties, with a severe haircut and thick glasses. She had the pinched, mean-spirited look of those who go through life judging everyone else to be just the tiniest bit inferior to themselves. She wore a straight blue skirt and a white blouse buttoned up as high as the buttons could go; her legs resembled fence posts in their utilitarian support hose.

"You must be Mr. Jacovich," she said. "Ms. Warriner told me you were expected. I'm Helene Menafee, her secretary. I hope you won't keep Ms. Warriner too long. She's not a young woman, and she tires easily. Please come in." This was delivered in a kind of singsong, as though she'd been rehearsing it for several hours so as not to make any mistakes.

"Thank you," I said, and followed her inside. The house

was as dark as it could get, considering there was a blazing sun outside. The blinds and curtains were drawn in almost every room, and the air conditioner was on high, making the interior of the house seem like twilight in Finland. Helene Menafee led me through a living room full of uncomfortable-looking antiques into a large alcove with only a small, high window to relieve the wall-to-wall bookshelves that lined it. Many of the books bore the name of the householder on their spines.

Edna Warriner herself was seated at a small writing desk piled high with yellow legal pads, many of which were covered with a spidery scrawl, in passionate purple ink. She was in her late sixties, with close-cropped white hair and a network of wrinkles on her leathery cheeks. A few curly white hairs sprouted from her chin. It seemed a stiff breeze might blow her away, but her eyes were alert and bright, twinkly blue. I had the feeling they missed little. Her head movements reminded me of a bird's.

"Come in, young man," she said, waving at a straight-backed chair with a seat upholstered in an ecru needlepoint design. I sat down, realizing too late that it was the only other chair in the room and that Helene Menafee had remained standing in the archway between the alcove and the living room. "I'm Edna Warriner."

"It's nice to meet you," I said. "I appreciate your taking the time to see me."

"Time is what I have the least of," she said, "so we'll have to be brief, won't we?"

I took the hint. "As I told you on the phone, I'm a private investigator. I'm trying to ascertain the whereabouts of Gregory Shane, the publisher of *North Coast Magazine*."

"Well, my goodness, what makes you think I'd know?" she said, and then before I could answer she glanced up at her secretary. "Don't just stand there, Helene, go on about your business."

Ms. Menafee nodded, humiliated, and withdrew, and Ms. Warriner turned her piercing blue gaze directly on me.

"I'm trying to get some background," I said. "I'm told that you submitted a story to their magazine for the premiere issue."

"You're told correctly, then," she said, "although I'm not sure 'submitted' is the word I would use. I was told they would print whatever I sent them. It was a short-short, actually, called 'Freebooter's Girl.' One of my old ones, and not one of my best, I'm sorry to say. But for the money they offered—well!"

"Would it be rude of me to ask how much money?"

She laughed without mirth. "It would indeed," she said, "but I'll tell you anyway. Ten dollars. A bit of an insult to someone of my reputation. At first I told them to go peddle their papers, even though I've known Jay Adams for many years. But Helene, my secretary, insisted that it would be a good idea, so I finally gave in."

"What was your impression of Mr. Shane?"

She cupped her hand behind her ear. "Pardon me?"

I repeated my question, turning up the volume.

"I never met the man, although when I gave Mr. Adams the story I got a very nice handwritten thank-you note from him. I understand he's done a vanishing act."

I smiled at her slang. "That's where I come in," I said.

"Well, I hope you find him," she said. "I'm a well-established writer, and he can't do anything to me one way or the other. But there are a lot of people who trusted him and believed in him who got hurt, including poor Jay Adams, and apparently a lot of gullible people who placed ads in the magazine. I suppose I was a bit gullible myself—or Helene was." She smiled and continued, "In any case, I hope they hang the son of a bitch."

I laughed, and after a moment she joined me.

"I wasn't always a little old lady, you know. I can cuss with the best of them."

"I'll bet you can."

"Bet big," she said. I love feisty old ladies.

"If Mr. Shane makes an attempt to get in touch with you, I wonder if you could give me a call." I handed her one of my business cards. She examined it carefully and ran her fingertip over the face of it to make sure the printing was raised. It wouldn't do to have ordinary printed business cards, I was sure.

"I will," she said. "But I can't imagine why he'd call me. As I say, I've never met the man, or talked to him on the telephone. Just Jay Adams and a Mr. Mulkey."

"How do you know Dan Mulkey?"

"I don't know him, Mr. Jacovich. I only met him once. He dropped by here to pick up the story and to deliver my check."

I stood, and she looked up at me. I felt as tall and as wide as Paul Bunyan in the stuffy little alcove with this tiny old woman and her frail-looking furniture. "I'd hazard a guess that you've never read one of my books," she said.

"I'm ashamed to say so."

She waved that away with a sound suspiciously like a Bronx cheer. "No need," she said. "I write for ladies. Bodice-rippers, they call them in the publishing business."

"Pardon me?"

" 'His strong hands ripped open the bodice of her gown . . .' It's pap, I admit, but I take my readers out of themselves, out of their day-to-day washing and cooking and grocery shopping. I provide some romance and adventure in their lives. From the looks of you, young man, you have no need for either. To some people, a fortunate few, all of life is an adventure. And as for romance . . . well, you have a certain smug and self-satisfied look that tells me you're doing all right in that department, too."

I grinned, a little embarrassed. "I guess that's what makes you such a good writer," I said.

She smiled ruefully, her lips drawing back from long yellow teeth. "Oh, I'm pretty good at peeling folks down to the original layer. Sometimes too much so. You find out things you don't particularly want to know. It's a curse and a blessing, both."

"Well in any case," I said, "thank you for taking the time to see me."

She craned her neck to look around my bulk and croaked, "Helene!" and almost at once Ms. Menafee appeared. She had obviously been waiting just outside the alcove, out of sight but within earshot. "Show the gentleman out."

"Yes, Ms. Warriner." Ms. Menafee stood aside so I could preceed her out of the alcove and back into the living room.

When we reached the vestibule by the front door, she said, "I hope you won't be bothering Ms. Warriner with this nonsense again. She's not well, and not very strong."

"I'll try not to," I said, although Edna Warriner seemed about as strong as an ox, at least mentally. "Ms. Menafee, have you ever met Gregory Shane?"

"I don't believe so," she said.

"How about Jay Adams?"

"Of course. He and Ms. Warriner are old friends. He has been to the house several times over the years."

"Ms. Warriner tells me that giving *North Coast* her story was your idea."

"It wasn't my *idea*, Mr. Jacovich. They proposed it and I thought it would be a good thing to do."

"Why is that, Ms. Menafee?"

"Well," she said, "anything that gets Ms. Warriner's name before the public is a good thing."

"She's pretty well established, though, isn't she?"

She shrugged and crossed her arms tightly beneath her breasts. "It isn't as if she wrote a new story for them. It was one that was just hanging around."

"I see. May I ask you how long you've worked for Ms. Warriner?"

"Twenty-three years. Twenty-four in January."

I gave one of my business cards to her too. "If you hear from Mr. Shane again I'd be grateful if you'd let me know. If I need to speak to you other than during business hours, is there a number where you can be reached?"

She met my gaze with her own, unblinking and challenging. "I live here," she said, and opened the door. Going from the numbing chill of the air conditioning into the heat of an August afternoon, I wondered why all of us didn't have pneumonia.

The address Hippsley-Tate had given me for Leonard Purs-glove was downtown, just a few blocks from City Hall, in a section of old industrial buildings whose faces had been lifted and whose lofts had been converted into overpriced living space for the upwardly mobile. From the street I could see the new picture windows that had been installed to replace the old sweatshop affairs, and inside to the track lighting that crisscrossed the ceiling. Personally, I think the downtown area of any large city is a lousy place to live, but sometimes what is fashionable takes precedence over comfort. From the names on the doorbells outside the big metal door, it seemed Pursglove and another tenant, J. Rose, were the only occupants of the building. I rang Pursglove's buzzer and moved my mouth close to the intercom box, ready to identify myself, but nobody wanted to know who I was or what I wanted. After ringing a second time and waiting, I rang J. Rose's bell too, for the hell of it, but he or she didn't seem to be at home either. I gave it up after a while, feeling silly standing there in a doorway in the middle of downtown. Clambering in and out of the car all day was hard, hot work. My next stop was only eight blocks away, but this time I had to park in an underground cavern that charged six dollars for the first hour and two dollars every half hour thereafter.

Arriving at the law offices of Carnahan and Zito without an appointment, I figured I'd be lucky if Joseph Zito saw me at all. When I told his secretary my name and business, she buzzed him on the phone, and he came out of his office to talk to me in the reception room. I guessed this was his way of letting me know it wasn't to be a lengthy interview. Zito was youngish, shortish, thinnish, and as officious as hell. His hair was combed forward and to the side to disguise the fact that he didn't have very much of it; should he meet a strong wind head on, the whole world would know about his male pattern baldness. He looked and acted like a lawyer. And after he corroborated Jay Adams's story, he informed me that Greg Shane had given him a bum check to pay for his services.

"He seemed so damn sincere," Zito said, "that I fell for his line. By the time the check bounced, he and his wife had disappeared."

"Tell me a little about his wife, Mr. Zito. Had you met her?"

"Oh, yes, once," he said. "She looks like the kind of middle-aged barmaid you might find in a neighborhood gin mill, with a voice like a champion hog caller. I think she drinks a little bit."

"You could tell that from one meeting?"

He shrugged. "I don't know. Something in the eyes—or more correctly, something that should have been there and wasn't. And the puffiness of her face, the skin tone—that kind of thing. You know the type."

"I do indeed, Mr. Zito. And when the check was returned, you naturally called him up?"

"To discover a disconnected number, yes. I'll have the bastard's ass if I ever catch up with him," Zito said. "You just don't stiff your attorney!"

"Why not?"

He regarded me as if I'd made a shameful suggestion. In his canon, I suppose I had. "It's not done, Mr. Jacovich."

I told him I'd have to remember that. Certain people are, in their own minds, supposed to be immune to the slings and arrows that plague the rest of us, and cry foul when they discover they aren't. But Zito had a legitimate grievance; Greg Shane had certainly spent lots of time spreading sunshine and goodwill wherever he went.

I ransomed my car from the subterranean garage and headed for home. About half a block behind me a blue Toyota Celica pulled out from the curb and leisurely followed me down Prospect Avenue toward University Circle. From what I could see in the rearview mirror the driver was male with reddish hair and was smoking a cigarette and letting the smoke blow out the open window. He didn't seem to be making much effort to disguise the fact that he was tailing me, staying comfortably three cars behind me until I reached my apartment. When I turned into the driveway of my building he cruised by slowly, then headed on up Cedar Hill until I lost sight of him. He was too far away for me to catch his license number.

Maybe he was a lawyer that someone had stiffed.

4

I decided to grab something to eat at Vuk's Tavern on St. Clair Avenue, one of my hangouts from the early days, an honest neighborhood bar that made no pretense of being anything else. Dinner at Vuk's usually consisted of a klobasa sandwich, potato chips, and a kosher pickle. No Yuppie Chow was allowed at Vuk's. I'd finished eating and was enjoying my third icy bottle of Stroh's, watching the Minnesota Twins make the Indians look like Little League. It was one of those nights when Carter went three for four with a triple and Cory Snyder hit two home runs and the Indians were still losing by four at the end of the seventh inning. Gopher balls were flying out of the stadium like blackbirds from a freshly opened pie, the pitching on both sides was hapless, and everyone in Vuk's had pretty much lost interest in the outcome and had settled into some serious beer drinking and bitching about their wives and their bosses.

Vuk, the genial boniface-bartender-bouncer of the tavern that bears his name, was standing in front of me, smoking my cigarettes, talking about the way the old neighborhood was changing. Time was that everyone within a two-mile radius of the corner of St. Clair and East Fifty-fifth was of Yugoslavian descent, mostly Slovenian and Serbian, and the community was fairly tightknit, insular, and comfortable. But in the past few years the entire city had awakened and stretched; ethnic neighborhoods had either been infiltrated or had shifted altogether, and the face of Slavic Town had quietly changed. Now there is a Jewish bakery over on Fifty-fourth Street and the guys who own the filling stations are Arabic or Iranian. The baby boomers from the west side have discovered Slavic Town and are on their way to replacing their normal diets of duck liver pizza and arugula and radicchio with *cevapcici* and *gibanica* as they make nightly forays to St. Clair Avenue in their late-model Beemers. Vuk— Louis Vukovich to his mother, but Vuk to the rest of the world—was fairly stoic about the whole thing, but that was his style. He had accepted it, the same way he'd accepted the American League's designated hitter rule and the advent of panty hose, but it made him feel better to talk about it. And talk was one of Vuk's strong suits. Since I got divorced and moved out of the neighborhood I don't hang out in there as much as I used to, but every once in a while I like to go back, lift a few beers, connect with the guys I went to school with, get a smattering of Slovenian conversation, and listen to one of Vuk's polemics on the state of things. My master's degree really hasn't changed what I am all that much, and an occasional evening of beer, smokes, and televised sports at Vuk's helps me remember my roots.

I was sitting at the bar when I sensed a presence behind me. I could hear his breathing even over the noise of the conversation and the bitching and the droning of the play-by-play guy on TV, and I saw the look on Vuk's face, one he reserves for strangers or outlanders who have the temerity to wander into his tavern to see if they can pick up a woman, place a bet, or get into a game of horse. Vuk's hands were out of sight under the bar, where I knew he keeps his peacemaker, a Reggie Jackson model thirty-eight-ounce baseball bat with the handle sawed off. Vuk was four for four with that bat. When I turned to look at the guy behind me I didn't wonder that Vuk was giving him the fish eye.

He was medium-size, if you happened to be talking about Cape buffalos, about six foot six and pushing two eighty, and not much of it was fat either. His reddish sideburns came down level with the bottoms of his rather pendulous earlobes, and his cinnamon brown eyes peered out of a round face that looked as though a six-year-old had fashioned it out of pinkish Play-Doh. His mustache drooped at the ends and was the same ginger color as his thinning hair. The loud breathing came through a nose that had long ago been broken and that hadn't been set properly. His skin had the kind of pallor that comes from a lot of years out of the sun—like in the penitentiary out of the sun. He was wearing the type of lowbrow outfit that unkind newspaper columnists have dubbed the "Full Cleveland"—a polyester leisure suit, this one in bilious lime green, over an open beige sports shirt with a vaguely Western design on the points of the collar. A white belt bisected his paunch and a pair of matching shiny white shoes with a few black scuff marks on the toes completed the ensemble. I couldn't be sure, but I thought it was the guy in the Toyota who had trailed me home from Joseph Zito's office.

He was some piece of work.

"Are you Milan Jacovich?" he said. He pronounced it correctly, as though the first letter were a Y.

"Hello," I said.

He had a nice smile, open and friendly. "My name is Buddy Bustamente."

I shook his outstretched paw; my hand felt as though someone had slammed a car door on it.

"Nice to meet you," I said. "New in the neighborhood?"

"More or less," he said.

"How do you like your Celica? Give you much trouble?"

He grinned, caught with his fist in the cookie jar, but not embarrassed about it. "It runs okay," he said easily, "but there isn't a hell of a lot of leg room. Those Japs are all five foot five. I should be driving a full-size car like yours."

I nodded at him. Things were at least out in the open. "You want a beer?"

"I don't mind," he said.

I signaled to Vuk to bring us two more, which he did reluctantly, as though being asked to serve a hairy transvestite or a seven-foot Watusi warrior in full regalia with a bone through his nose. He continued to eye my visitor with a suspicion bordering on acute paranoia as he slammed the two bottles onto the bar. Vuk is a man of many prejudices, and he's not shy about expressing them.

We toasted and drank. I eschewed a glass, as was the custom at Vuk's, but Buddy poured his beer into the frosty mug Vuk always provided. "Hits the spot," he said, exhaling noisily. "Nothing like a cold beer on a hot night to make things okay."

"So what's the deal, Buddy?"

"Deal?"

"I think you know what I mean. You're following me."

"Oh. Well, I'm kind of a friend of Victor Gaimari."

Victor Gaimari was no friend of mine.

He wasn't exactly an enemy, either—at least, not any more. We'd been through the adversary stage some time back, when he had threatened my family and I'd punched him in the nose and then he had sent three of his soldiers to smack me around. Victor could do things like that, because he and his mentor, feisty old Giancarlo D'Allessandro, more or less ran the rackets in the Cleveland area, and they had plenty of people on their payroll with nothing between their ears except muscle and Alberto VO5. He had even called me up afterward to apologize and ask me how I was feeling, and it's hard to stay really angry at someone so solicitous and caring about your welfare, even when you forgave him through swollen lips and a black eye. So we had more or less put our beefs aside and decided to coexist peacefully.

41

But Victor Gaimari was no friend of mine.

"The last time Victor Gaimari sent anyone to see me," I said, "I ached for a month."

"Oh, no," Buddy said, "nothing like that. Mr. Gaimari was just wondering if you could drop by his office this evening to talk to him." He nodded up at the TV set. "If you want to stay and watch the end of the game, there's no hurry."

I didn't care about the game. Kirby Puckett had doubled and Hrbek homered him across and the Tribe was biting the dust once again. Buddy said, "They got to get some decent pitching. The Indians, their pitching is shit."

"Cleveland hasn't had pitching since Bob Feller and Early Wynn," I pointed out. "Is this an invitation from Gaimari, Buddy, or a command performance?"

"Mr. Gaimari told me to bring you," he said. "I just work here."

"And what if I don't want to get brung?"

He shrugged and smiled almost apologetically. "Then it's gonna be you and me."

I swung around on the barstool to face him. Slowly. He was not the kind of guy at whom anyone made too-quick moves. "Buddy," I said, "the jacket I'm wearing cost me about a hundred and forty dollars, and if we tangle it's going to get wrecked. To make it worth my while I'm going to have to have a hundred and forty bucks' worth of fun."

His eyes went flat all of a sudden, devoid of expression, the way they'd be in a not very good painting, and unless you were watching for it you wouldn't have noticed how he quietly shifted his weight to the balls of his feet. "You might not have all that much fun."

"One way to find out."

He gave me a disarming smile, all except for the eyes. "I wouldn't like for that to happen, and I don't think you would either."

"You're not that much bigger than I am," I said. "You might lose."

"I might," he said, as if the thought had never occurred to

him, "but either way both of us are gonna get hurt, and that seems kind of silly, doesn't it?"

"You're right," I admitted. "We don't want to be silly. Can I finish my beer?"

"Sounds like a plan to me."

We watched the ball game without much interest. During one of the commercials, occasioned by another Indians pitching change, I said, "I haven't seen you around. Been in town long?"

"About two months," he answered, an early frost of foam hanging on his mustache. "I'm from Buffalo."

So Gaimari had imported some Buffalo muscle. It didn't mean much. Maybe Buffalo had gotten too hot for Buddy Busta-mente, maybe there was something going down that made Gaimari want to build up his troop strength. If that were the case, I hoped it had nothing to do with what he wanted to talk to me about. Those guys were known to play hardball.

As for the other group that played hardball in my town, the Indians got a run back in the ninth, but then Brook Jacoby popped up with a man on second and it was all over. The boys at Vuk's mumbled their postmortems as they dispersed, heading home to their wives or their mothers or their furnished bachelor pads.

"Ready?" I said.

"Whenever you say."

We took his Celica, heading downtown toward Terminal Tower, illuminated by floodlights, dominating the Cleveland skyline. That's where Victor Gaimari had his office, and although he worked at it and was quite a successful stockbroker, the real headquarters, where all the action happened, was in Little Italy, just beyond University Heights.

When we got to Superior Avenue and Ninth, I said, "Where did you do your time?"

I might have been asking where he went to high school; he didn't bat an eye. "Attica. Thirty-seven months and two days. Felonious assault. I been out about four months now."

"Must feel good."

"Don't even ask. Mr. D'Allessandro and Mr. Gaimari have

43

been really nice to me. Mr. D'Allessandro is related to my mother some way I haven't been able to figure out. His father's cousin was connected to my mother's uncle by marriage or some damn thing. Anyway, they told me there'd be a place for me here as soon as I got out. I've been driving for Mr. Gaimari. They're nice people."

"Salt of the earth," I said.

"Mr. Gaimari is really fond of you. He talks about you a lot. I guess you and he were involved in some stuff before."

"Not always happily."

"Well, I'm looking forward to working with you," he said, as if he were a junior accountant and I an auditor. Sometimes I think life was a lot easier before the mob got civilized, when they broke knees and fashioned cement overshoes. At least you always knew where you stood with them. Back in the days of Capone, the Purple Gang, and Murder Incorporated, no wise guy ever told you they were looking forward to working with you.

"You ought to know, Buddy, that I used to be a cop."

"I heard. It's okay—you're not one no more."

He parked in a lot across the street from Terminal Tower and we crossed Public Square and elevatored up to the seventh floor. I had been in Gaimari's office before, and that time I'd left its tenant on the carpet with a bloody nose, but that's another story. Of course, that time he hadn't had Buddy Bustamente riding shotgun. If anyone's nose was going to bleed tonight, you could get odds it would be mine.

I'd last seen Victor Gaimari during the winter. Tonight he was standing behind his desk, wearing a summer-weight tan suit with an elegantly patterned paisley tie and a beige silk shirt, looking as collar-ad handsome as ever, and sporting a suntan he had probably acquired in a tanning salon. His dark mustache was carefully groomed, and his big brown eyes were bright and eager. It was rare that anyone ever saw Victor Gaimari when he wasn't smiling, and when I came in he widened that smile in welcome.

"Milan, it's great to see you again," he said in that peculiar high-pitched, almost effeminate voice of his. I shook his hand. I couldn't exactly say it was great to see *him* again, but it wasn't terrible either. If you were able to ignore a lot of things you knew about him and concentrate on the social amenities, Victor wasn't really such a bad egg.

"Victor, they have this new invention now. It's called the telephone. Easy to use. It's a much simpler way of getting in touch with people than sending someone to follow them around town and drag them out of bars. I highly recommend it."

He laughed. "The phone is so impersonal. I'd rather talk face to face, especially when it's an old friend like you. How about something to drink, Milan? I have iced tea, Diet Pepsi, beer, or the hard stuff."

I sat down on the pebbled leather sofa beneath an oil painting of the Cleveland skyline, which prominently included the building we were in. "Nothing, Victor, thanks." I really wanted a beer, but I'd had several already, and it was best to keep a clear head when dealing with these guys.

He said, "I'll have a beer, Buddy," and Buddy went into the next room to get one. He brought back an Old Peculier and a frosted glass. I wasn't surprised; Victor Gaimari was hardly the Stroh's or Budweiser type. His suit was probably a week's salary for most people.

"You know, Milan," he said as Buddy expertly poured the beer so that it was topped off by exactly an inch of foam, "I really like you. We ought to see more of each other. Socially."

"You and I don't exactly run in the same circles."

"Now, we both know that's a crock of shit, but I'll accept it for the time being. I'd like for us to be friends. I'm hoping we can work together."

I fired up a cigarette, my thirty-fourth of the day. I was up to two packs a day now and not happy about it. "We've talked about that before, Victor, and I told you then: I'd prefer not getting involved with you people."

He toasted me with his beer. "You're already involved, whether you know it or not."

"How so?"

"I'm told you're looking into the *North Coast Magazine* situation."

"Who told you?"

"It's not important."

"I think it is."

He shrugged. "You're doing some work for the Lake Shore Hotel."

I didn't say anything. This was Gaimari's party.

"We have an interest there."

"What interest is that? Or don't tell me, let me guess. You own the damn place, right? I should have figured. Nothing that big could happen in this town without you guys putting your fingerprints all over it."

He smiled around his pilsner glass. "As a matter of fact, we set up a whole new company to finance the hotel—sixty-five percent of it, anyway. It's called Lakerie Development. One word, Lakerie."

"Cute," I said. "And at the moment Lakerie is out forty-two thousand dollars."

"That's a lot of money, Milan."

"Depends on your point of view, I suppose."

"I don't much like getting skinned."

"No one does, Victor. Me, I'm a sucker, a born mark. Con artists can smell me coming at fifty paces. I even have a twenty-dollar bottle of miracle hair restorer somewhere under my bathroom basin, and you can see how much good it did me. But you wise guys are supposed to be too smart for that."

Victor Gaimari's dazzling smile almost failed him. "Wise guys. Milan, lighten up. We aren't always. Wise, I mean. Actually, the deal was cut by the hotel's manager without our knowledge. He feels rather badly about it, as you know."

"How bad? A slab at the bottom of the lake bad?"

Victor shook his head. "You spent too many years on the police force, hanging around with the wrong element. We don't do things like that anymore. We're legitimate businessmen."

"Sure. So what do you want from me, Victor? You must

46

know that Hippsley-Tate already hired me to find Shane and get the money back."

"I frankly have a little trouble trusting Mr. Hippsley-Tate," he said. "I want to make sure that money comes back to where it belongs."

"Victor, this smells like a Lake Erie whitefish that washed up on the shore last Tuesday. We've had this conversation once before, and if you remember, it ended up unhappily—for both of us. I don't do this kind of thing."

"What kind of thing?"

"I'm not going to hunt some poor bastard down so you can turn him into Genoa sausages in one of your meat-packing plants on the river."

"There you go again," he said, all at once a wounded Reagan shaking his head at the injustice of it all. "Making us sound like a bunch of gangsters."

"Can you ever forgive me?"

"Look, I absolutely guarantee Shane's safety. We'll take every step of this legally. When we find him, if we don't recover our money, we'll prosecute. Through the courts. I can promise you no harm will come to him, and Milan, you know I keep my promises. I wouldn't be in business ten minutes if I didn't."

"I've already taken on a client. I'll deliver Shane's whereabouts to him, and that's it. I'm not going to report to you, I'm not going to call you up. I don't work for you."

Gaimari preened his mustache and looked at Buddy, who was holding up the wall near the door. "How about this, then? Let Buddy come along with you while you look. Maybe he can be some help. A back-up. Then anything I need to know, he'll tell me, and you won't have to do anything that violates your code of ethics."

"That's out, Victor. I work alone. You know that."

"I won't get in the way," Buddy said. "I won't even talk unless someone asks me something."

"It's out of the question," I said. "Nothing personal, but I can't operate that way. It'd cramp my style."

Victor Gaimari sat down, taking great care to give the crease in his trousers a little tug so the knees wouldn't get baggy. He rested his elbow on the desk and hooked the buffed nail of his index finger over his front tooth. I guess that was his thinking pose.

"Milan, there are two ways to do this," he said. "What I've proposed is the easy way; the other way is that Buddy is going to be on your tail every minute. No matter where you go, no matter what you're doing, he'll be all over you like a cheap suit until you find Greg Shane. He won't bother you, but he won't make any effort to stay out of sight. He'll be like your shadow. Do you want that? Won't *that* cramp your style? Wouldn't it be easier for the two of you just to work together? I mean, you don't want him camped outside the door when you spend the evening with Ms. Soderberg, do you?"

My muscles tensed and I leaned forward on the sofa, ready to take on Gaimari, Buddy, and the whole Italian army. When anyone threatens the people I love, I tend to lose control. But Victor held up a warning hand, his dark eyes glittering.

"Don't hit me again, Milan. I want to be your friend, but don't ever hit me again, because next time it won't just be a beating." Victor's manner of speaking, even when making a death threat, was so cheerful and pleasant and open, it was dangerously easy to forget that in the mob hierarchy of northern Ohio he was second only to old Giancarlo D'Allessandro himself. The concept of mafioso-as-Big-Ten-alumnus is one we're all going to have to get used to. They are a new breed now—at least on the surface. But scratch that smooth veneer and they're the same kind of punks that used to terrorize Chicago and Detroit with machine guns in violin cases.

I ran my hand through my hair. I do that when I'm frustrated—and every time I do I'm dismayed that there's a bit less hair there. I got up and went over to the window to watch the late traffic on the expressway. It was moving nicely now that the evening rush was over. The air conditioner blew cold against my stomach, and I turned so that the stream of air hit me in the small of the back.

"What if I resign from the case altogether?"

"You could do that," Victor said. "But I know Mr. Hippsley-Tate is paying you a lot of money. And you talk about ethics and loyalty to your client. Is it loyal, is it fair to just quit on him for no reason?"

I said, "I love your idea of no reason."

"I'll watch, Milan," Buddy said. "I won't give you any trouble at all." And he darted a glance at Gaimari to make sure he hadn't spoken out of turn.

"Buddy's right," Gaimari said generously. "You're still running this investigation. You call the shots. He's just a quiet observer. And you bank a nice paycheck in the process."

I sighed. "Victor, you've got my nuts in a wringer."

He laughed. "It makes you easier to do business with. When this problem first came up, it was Mr. D'Allessandro's idea to contact you. He didn't order it, but he let it be known to Hippsley-Tate, through a few different people, that you were the best PI in town. He was very impressed with you that one time he met you. He said you were a classy guy."

"For a Slovenian, huh?"

Victor had an almost girlish laugh. "No, really. There's no point tiptoeing around. The last time we saw one another it was an awkward situation, and we handled it rather badly. Both of us. But I'm glad there are no hard feelings, glad we can talk together like civilized people. Matter of fact, Mr. D'Allessandro wanted to extend an invitation to you and Ms. Soderberg to come down to the restaurant some evening and have dinner as his guest." He smirked. "If you give me a ring ahead of time, perhaps I could join you. I'll try to scare up a date somewhere."

"Victor, it's bad enough having your man up my ass all day. It doesn't mean you and I are going to go halves on a condo."

He looked genuinely sad. "Is an unforgiving nature a Yugoslavian trait, Milan, or is it just you?"

"I don't like being squeezed."

"No one is squeezing you. You have your priorities and we

have ours, that's all. When they dovetail like this it seems pretty foolish not to help one another out."

I shoved my hands into my pockets, angry with myself for letting him manipulate me. But I didn't know what else to do. "Buddy, I start at nine in the morning," I said. "If you're coming along, be at my place a few minutes beforehand."

He nodded.

Victor said, "Milan, Mr. D'Allessandro appreciates your help on this. Sincerely."

"I haven't done anything yet."

"No, but you will. I have every confidence."

I started for the door, seething inside. I had been out-maneuvered, and I didn't like it much.

"I'll drive you back, Milan," Buddy Bustamente said. And then he gave me a winning Norman Rockwell–kid grin. "I'll meet you at your place in the morning. It'll be fun."

5

I never just drop in on Mary. We don't have that kind of relationship, not yet. But after my meeting with Victor Gaimari I was too wired to go home to sleep, and I felt the need to be with someone sympathetic who wasn't going to make any demands on me. I called Mary and asked if I could come over. Even though it was ten o'clock at night, she said yes without hesitation, and when I got there a freshly popped bowl of buttered popcorn was waiting for me, along with an ice-cold Stroh's. I'm sure Mary Soderberg never kept Stroh's beer in her refrigerator until I came into her life.

I slipped off my shoes and we sort of snuggled on the sofa together and watched Vivian Truscott do the eleven o'clock news, and after that I don't know what was on because I was going through all sorts of Sturm und Drang in my head and cursing the day I'd ever run afoul of Gaimari and his bunch in the first place.

Mary said, "Penny." I guess I'd been pretty quiet for a while.

"Sorry."

"You must have been thinking pretty deep thoughts."

"One of the really neat things about thinking is that you don't have to tell."

She laughed. "I always know when you're on an interesting case, Milan, because you drift in and out on me."

"It's not all that interesting. My client got ripped off and he wants me to track down the perpetrator."

"Alleged perpetrator, you mean. Sometimes you talk like the eleven o'clock news."

"Not like the news on your station," I said. "I'm not that show biz."

"Happy news brings happy ratings," she chanted as if it were the personal mantra of everyone at Channel 12. "And by the way, I've arranged for Vivian Truscott to talk to you tomorrow afternoon."

"Thanks, Mary," I said.

She shifted around on the sofa, tucking her legs under her. I hadn't given her much time to pretty herself up, and she was wearing a pair of faded jeans with a hole in the knee and a Cleveland Browns T-shirt about three sizes too big for her. "Can you tell me about this rip-off, or is it strictly confidential?"

"Well, I wouldn't put it in the papers, but I guess I can tell you," I said, giving her a little kiss. I filled her in about the *North Coast Magazine* scam and how it related to Gaimari and his friends.

She shook her head. "Guys like that make it tough for legitimate people like us to sell advertising. And they make it doubly tough on anyone trying to start up an honest magazine. Where do you think this Greg Shane ran off to?"

"I don't know. If it were me I'd be in Costa Rica someplace. I sure as hell wouldn't like the owners of the Lake Shore Hotel mad at me."

Mary said, "Maybe he didn't know who the owners were. I mean, it's possible he had no idea he was stepping on such dangerous toes."

"You know, you could be right," I said.

"I wonder if he's ever done this before?"

"Shane?"

She nodded, nibbling an unpopped old maid from the bottom of the popcorn bowl. "Maybe he's tried this same con game in other cities. It's not a bad racket. I wish I'd thought of it."

"The trouble with it is, it's dime store stuff. I mean, most of the advertisers got nicked for two hundred bucks or so—that's what they tried to get out of me. It would take an awful lot of suckers to make an operation like that really worthwhile. If they were cold-calling every small business in town, their phone bill alone had to be the national debt."

"That's true," she said. "But if he got enough small-potatoes suckers, it would have made it a lot easier to hit a big mark like the hotel."

"Huh?"

Her blue eyes sparkled. "Look," she said, leaning forward and putting a hand on my arm, making me tingle all over as I did whenever she touched me. "If he could go in to a big outfit like that to hit them up for an expensive ad, he'd have a better shot at it if he could show them a two-foot-long list of advertisers who had already committed. They wouldn't have to know all the ads were for two hundred dollars or whatever he could beg. It'd be damn impressive. And I'll bet that's what he was looking for, a big score like that."

I didn't say anything.

"It makes sense, though, doesn't it, Milan?"

"I guess."

She leaned back against the cushions of the couch, a self-satisfied smirk on her face. "How's that for detective work?"

"Why do I suddenly feel like Nick Charles?"

"Who's he?"

"In *The Thin Man*."

53

She reached over and patted my stomach. "Not to worry," she said.

I left Mary's apartment in Shaker Heights shortly after seven. We had set an early alarm because we both like to make love by first light, and then she was up and showering and doing all those mysterious things women do to make themselves beautiful when they get out of bed in the morning, although Mary was never more beautiful than just after we'd made love, snuggled against my shoulder with her skin smooth and warm against mine. I made coffee and toasted a few bagels while she put on her makeup, and after a few more kisses that tasted of cream cheese, we went our separate ways, she to Channel 12 downtown and me to my apartment, which also serves as my office. It was a little bit cooler at the top of Cedar Hill than it had been in Shaker, but not much.

I climbed the stairs to the second floor and stopped. Buddy Bustamente was lounging in front of my door, chewing a wad of gum and reading the sports section of the *Plain Dealer* he'd collected from my welcome mat. He was wearing a variation of the outfit I'd first seen him in, only this one was powder blue polyester with a navy shirt. The white belt and shoes remained the same.

"Morning, Milan," he said easily, as if this were our normal pattern for starting the day. He grinned. "Big night, huh? Or did you just go out for an early breakfast?"

I had forgotten about Buddy and our arrangement. Finding him there was a surprise. Like discovering you had crab lice.

"I'm all set to go to work," he told me. His enthusiasm reminded me of a high school yell leader, and I had the feeling it was going to wear pretty thin. I unlocked the door and he followed me inside.

"I really don't need you here, Buddy."

"Well, let me drive you, then."

"I like to drive myself, if that's okay with you and Mr. Gaimari."

"Isn't there something I can do to help?"

He was so damn earnest I started feeling like a rat. "Can you make coffee?"

He brightened. "Sure thing." He bustled out into the kitchen and I heard him clanking around looking for the coffee can, dumping yesterday's grounds out of my Mr. Coffee, running the water. I shook my head and aimed myself at the shower.

Twenty minutes later I came out of the bedroom dressed for the day. Buddy was at my kitchen table. He had toasted six pieces of bread, which he'd slathered with grape jelly and arranged on a plate in front of him. There was a place set for me, too, with a cup, saucer, spoon and napkin, and he had brought out the sugar bowl and a carton of milk.

"I take it black," I said. "No sugar."

"Okay, Milan, I'll remember." He got up, put the milk back in the refrigerator, poured me a fresh cup of coffee, and then sat back down opposite me. The morning paper was in the center of the table between us. "Gonna be another hot one, it says."

I sipped the coffee. It was pretty good. He made it rather strong, the way I like it but rarely make it for myself. "Buddy, you're not going to come by and fix breakfast for me every morning, are you?"

"I will if you want me to," he said.

"I don't want you to. I don't need a wife. And I don't need a chauffeur or a valet or a handyman, either. I work by myself. I prefer it that way. That's why I quit the police force. I keep my own hours and work my own schedule. And it's generally better to talk to people alone; they're not as intimidated."

He shrugged helplessly. "I'm just trying to do my job, Milan."

"And I'm trying to do mine."

He said, "Well, maybe we can help each other out."

I wasn't very comfortable about Buddy's appearing at my door like an abandoned infant. He seemed so damn eager and naive, it was hard to trust him. For a guy who'd spent time in the lockup, he seemed curiously childlike.

I decided I'd worry about Buddy Bustamente some other time. Right now my first priority was to call my friend at the Cleveland *Plain Dealer*, Ed Stahl. We had been pals ever since my rookie year on the police force, and Ed could always be counted upon for lunch, good tickets to baseball games, and information. As one of the mainstays of the paper's dayside staff, Ed was privy to almost everything that went on in Cleveland, political, social, financial, and sexual. I marveled at the amount of hard knowledge he always had at his fingertips, and at his willingness to share it with no strings attached. Friends like Ed Stahl are not easy to find, and I am often saddened that our busy lives rarely leave enough time for nurturing that friendship.

"Milan Jacovich," Ed said, his voice a whiskey rumble on the phone. "I thought you'd left town—or been run out. How the hell are you?"

"Keeping busy, Ed," I said, feeling guilty for not having called him in more than a month.

"There's a couple of Indians tickets here with our names on 'em. The Royals are in town next week."

"Sounds good to me," I told him, "but right now I'm up to here."

His voice changed ever so slightly. "And you're calling me because you need some poop."

"Isn't that what you peddle?"

"Yeah, but we call it by a less polite name down here. What's going on?"

When I told Ed I was looking into matters pertaining to Greg Shane and *North Coast Magazine*, he simply snorted derisively. "That imaginary rag scammed more suckers than Yellow Kid Weil," he said. "It caused quite a flurry around here a few months ago, but we didn't do a story on it because most of the people who got skinned were too embarrassed about it to want their names in the paper. They'd rather just keep quiet and eat their losses. Not sure I blame them any."

"I suppose not."

"Well, the chronology of it is, Greg Shane blew into town about a year ago, from the West Coast, as I recall. The word was that he'd been in Vegas and then L.A., and he got some fairly heavy hitters very annoyed with him back there and had to move on to someplace where he wasn't likely to be shot on sight. I don't think he was using the name Gregory Shane then, but I'm not clear on that point. His wife, I understand, is a former knockout, now gone to seed and vodka tonics, and rumor hath it that about ten or eleven years back she used to mart her ass for chips in the Las Vegas casinos, before Shane made an honest woman out of her."

"Ed, you're the only man I know who would even consider using 'mart' as a verb, especially with 'ass' as its object."

"That's why they pay me the big bucks. Anyway, the Shanes rented an old run-down house in Ohio City and started their own little bucket shop in the garage, selling advertising for this magazine. Nettie Shane used to tell her prospects that *North Coast* was going to revolutionize the publishing business here in town. As I heard it, she was dynamite on the telephone getting people to say yes, and then her husband would pay a visit to the mark and collect the money, and half the time he'd get them to upgrade to a bigger and more expensive ad. It's an old and dishonorable journalistic tradition, the paid editorial, but the way they went on about it, you'd think they'd invented it or something. Mostly they hit small businesses—beauty parlors, dancing schools, chiropractors, dog groomers, caterers, automotive repairs. And as close as I can figure out they nicked everyone for the same thing: around two hundred dollars, more or less, which is not a big score in anyone's book. However, there were a couple of companies, including the new hotel out on the lake, that went in for more—much more. . . . Ah, wait a minute, Milan, this is beginning to fall together."

I heard him strike a match and suck on his ever present pipe for a while to get it going.

"Word reached me that D'Allessandro and his people are not a little miffed at the strange disappearance of Mr. and Mrs. Shane and are going to leave no turn unstoned to find him. I wouldn't be surprised if your old pal Victor Gaimari got you involved in this."

I glanced at Buddy, who was staring at me with naked and undisguised interest. "I have no comment on that, Ed."

"Off the record, Milan."

"Even so."

He sighed. "You private tickets with your code of Bushido. Okay, I'll do all the talking. God, I feel so used."

"Ed, you know if there's a story here it's yours first."

"Yeah, yeah, for old times' sake," he said, and from the sound of his puffs I was sure his entire corner of the city room was becoming engulfed in blue smoke. "Anyway, for a while there was a guy named Dan Mulkey working with them. Used to be in the music business."

"I know all about him," I said. "But I don't know exactly what he was doing for them." I glanced over at Buddy, who was reading the sports section of the *Plain Dealer* again and moving his lips.

"Mulkey was out of work when Shane picked him up, but a guy like that has to have some pretty big-buck connections. He was raising money, venture capital, to keep the magazine running until it became self-supporting. Or that was the story. He also knew most of our town's celebrities—all four of them—and that was part of his job, too, sucking around the rich and over-paid for interviews and endorsements."

"What happened that he left?"

"You'll have to ask him, Milan. He didn't confide in me."

"And where do I find him?"

"In the phone book, I suppose. If he's not listed, call me back and I'll see what I can do."

Dan Mulkey was indeed listed in the book, about a block from the Lakewood Park Cemetery in Rocky River. There was no answer when I called. Then I rang up my friend downtown at the Hall of Records, Renee, a nice blue-haired grandma who had taken the news of my divorce as if it had been the announcement of a new strain of Black Plague come to ravage Ohio and had been trying to fix me up with her divorced niece ever since. I asked about her toddler grandkid and was treated to a few of the unbearably cute things he'd been saying lately, and when I could stem the torrent of grandmotherly pride for a minute, I talked her into looking up the legal owner of the house that was Greg Shane's last known address in Ohio City. It turned out to be a Mrs. Alan Greenberg, who lived a few blocks away. I thanked Renee and jotted down a note to myself to drop by the hall with a toy for Junior. Fortunately, Mrs. Greenberg was in the book. I got her on the line; she sounded like an angry little terrier of a woman.

"Those bastards just moved out without a good-bye or a kiss my ass," she told me. "They owed about two weeks' rent, and when I couldn't get any satisfaction from them I went to the courts to get an eviction order. But before I could serve it, they were gone. Left the place like a stable too. I had to hire a colored woman to go in and scrub it down."

"So you don't know where they are, then, Mrs. Greenberg?"

"Oh, don't I wish. It will cost me about a hundred dollars or so to get the place clean and livable before I can rent it out again. I don't understand how people can be such pigs."

"How much was the house renting for?"

"Seven eighty, plus utilities," she told me. "And it was a steal at that price. But he cried poormouth to me, that Shane. Said he was trying to start up a business and had cash-flow problems at the beginning, and asked couldn't I help a nice Jewish boy like him out a little. He promised that once his magazine hit the stands he was going to do a lot of remodeling and repairing and fixing-up at his own expense, and I, like a damn fool, believed him. Well, never again, I can tell you. The rent is going up to nine fifty now, and I don't care what kind of sad stories anyone tells me. Screw me once, shame on you—screw me twice, shame on *me*. I'm not a charitable institution. My husband and I bought that house for rental income, and now he's gone it's doubly important to keep it occupied with people who aren't going to be deadbeats and losers. I've got to live too, y' know."

I wondered if "gone" meant that her husband had passed away or quietly slipped out of her life. I could have ventured a guess. I expressed my sympathies and thanked her for talking to me, giving her my number in the unlikely event she had any news of the Shanes. Wherever they had disappeared to, they had been careful not to leave a trail of bread crumbs behind them.

6

Cleveland is to be commended for its urban renewal of the past ten years. But when they started building up the inner city, the poor people who lived there were squeezed eastward, pushing the middle class into formerly upper-class Shaker Heights, and causing the rich folks to move even further eastward into the new suburbs of Beachwood and Pepper Pike. The *very* rich wandered into the Chagrin River Valley, where last year's Cadillac was simply a second car. Gates Mills and Hunting Valley became impressive addresses, and the city of Chagrin Falls, whose two claims to fame seem to be the picturesque waterfall that gives the town its name and the boyhood home of television comedian Tim Conway, was a major tourist stop. One of the businesses on *North Coast Magazine*'s sucker list was The Mentor Academy, a private school for the kiddies of the rich, and it was located in the Valley, which might possibly have accounted for the Chagrin Valley Police Department's interest in Jay Adams. So it was to the Chagrin River Valley that Buddy and I headed. I insisted we take my car, as it was roomier and had a more reliable air conditioner.

From past experience I knew better than to go riding into Chagrin Valley without first paying a duty call on the local constabulary, which consisted mainly of the Valley chief of police, one Ethan Kemp. A genial young giant who affected cowboy garb and a John Wayne squint, Kemp was one of the brightest cops I'd run into in a long while, but he was pretty territorial when it came to private detectives messing around in his bailiwick, and he was one guy whose bad side was definitely not the place to be on. It would cost me about half an hour of small talk, but it would be well worth it.

My new partner was less than enchanted when he heard where we were going. "I don't like police stations," he said. "They give me the creeps." And as though to illustrate, he gnawed the skin on the inside of his thumb.

"It's kind of a courtesy call," I explained.

"I never heard of no courtesy in police stations, Milan. I'm not walking into no police station for no reason. I have some bad memories of police stations."

"You can wait for me in a restaurant, then," I said. "I won't be very long."

He relaxed against the upholstery and gave me a little half smile. "Anything you say, Milan."

I was frankly relieved at not having to explain Buddy to Ethan Kemp. I dropped him off at a quaint little coffee shop in Chagrin Falls furnished in colonial decor with early American waitresses to match, assuring him that if he ordered pancakes he'd be treated to maple syrup produced about fifteen miles away in the town of Burton. He was a bit uneasy at the thought of disobeying Gaimari's directive to stick with me, but the icicles that formed in his heart at the threat of exposure to anyone with a badge overcame his loyalty. Besides, he was hungry again. Six

62

pieces of toast was just a light snack to a growing boy like Buddy.

The Chagrin Valley P.D. headquarters was about four miles from the town of Chagrin Falls, an undistinguished cinder-block-and-glass building nestled between two hills, surrounded by box elder and oak trees and backed up against the banks of the river that gives the valley its name and character. Ethan Kemp had toiled for the narcotics, vice, and homicide squads of Indianapolis before moving one state east and donning a chief's hat, and although Indianapolis is not exactly the crime capital of the world, the bucolic atmosphere of Chagrin Valley must have seemed like a little slice of paradise by comparison.

"Well, Milan," he said when I walked into his office, "I haven't seen you in half a year. Come on in and grab yourself some coffee." He uncoiled his six feet five inches like a giant king cobra, rising to engulf my hand in his. The heels of the cowboy boots he always wore added three more inches to his height, and I felt as if I were talking to someone of another, more evolved species. Any time Ethan Kemp decided to give up law enforcement, I'm sure there would be a career for him playing policemen on television.

"How've you been, Ethan?" I asked when we were seated.

"You know how it is, Milan. Keeping the snotty rich kids from driving ninety miles an hour on River Road. A dirty job, but somebody's got to do it. What brings you this far east? I get the feeling this isn't just a social visit."

"As a matter of fact," I said truthfully, "I've been thinking about calling you to have a sandwich or a drink or something for quite some time, but you know how it is when you get busy. But no, I'm not just passing through."

"Has somebody in my valley been naughty?"

"I don't know," I said. "That's what I was hoping you could tell me. Some time back you contacted a freelance editor in Cleveland by the name of Jay Adams. About *North Coast Magazine*."

63

He squinted for a moment and then nodded his head. "I remember him. A little fat guy with a limp wrist."

"That's the one," I said. "I'm doing some work looking into that magazine myself, and I thought we could exchange notes."

He grinned. "Good. What've you got?"

"Not a damn thing. I guess you know that the publisher went south with a lot of advertising money and there are a lot of angry citizens looking for him."

"Now, they operated from outside of my jurisdiction," Ethan said, "but one of the people he stung has a business in this valley, and he came to me for help."

"That would be The Mentor Academy?"

"That's exactly right," he said. It was his favorite expression. "Mr. Alex Malleson. He filed a complaint against the publisher. What's his name again?"

"Gregory Shane."

"Yeah. Sounds phony to me, doesn't it to you?"

"The word is that he used other names in other places."

He leaned forward in his chair. "Oh?"

"Like Las Vegas and Los Angeles."

"Ah, he was one of the boys, then?" He pushed his nose comically to one side with a finger.

"At one time. Apparently he ran afoul of them somehow and had to get out pretty quickly. I don't know the details, though." I lit a cigarette and flipped the match into his already crowded ashtray. "Tell me about The Mentor Academy."

Ethan tilted his Stetson down over his eyes and leaned back in his chair. "A private school for young ladies and gentlemen," he said. "Costs your right lung to get in, and even if you can afford it they won't accept your kid unless his pedigree goes back to the Founding Fathers. Things of that nature just make me sick."

"I know what you mean," I said. "The type of place that keeps your kids from ever rubbing elbows with real people."

"Alex Malleson is just the guy to run a shop like that. Got a steel rod shoved all the way up. Talks with a phony limey

64

accent, too. But he's great at stroking the parents and getting every last nickel he can out of them."

"I was thinking about driving over there to see him."

"Better get you some new clothes, then. They got an off-the-rack detector at the door. You try to go through there without a tailor-made suit, alarms and whistles go off."

"So it's all right with you if I poke around?"

Ethan Kemp put the size thirteen cowboy boots up on the desk. "The last time you poked around out here somebody shot at you."

"This will surprise you, Ethan, but I remember."

"Sure, go on out and see Malleson. But don't hassle him so bad he starts complaining to me. And keep your head down, will you? I don't feel like blotting you up off the sidewalk."

"I'll make every effort to see that you don't get your boots all bloody," I said.

"And gimme a ring some time," he said. "The wife and I can have you out to dinner."

When I left the police station I doubled back into the town of Chagrin Falls, where I found Buddy wandering the streets, peering into the windows of the expensive shops and galleries as though viewing a fanciful diorama in Tomorrowland. Chagrin Falls bears scant resemblance to the Italian section of Buffalo. He was eating a cone he'd bought at the ice cream shop just in front of the falls, and some of it—rocky road, from the look of it— had dribbled onto the pale blue lapel of his leisure suit. I made him finish it before getting into the car. I miss having my kids with me all the time, but one of the advantages of being a non-custodial parent is not getting ice cream stains on your car interior, and if Milan Jr. and Stephen weren't going to mess up my upholstery, I'd be damned if I'd put up with it from a Buffalo hoodlum. Buddy polished off the half eaten cone by shoving it into his mouth all at once. Then he daintily wiped his lips with a napkin and tossed it into the gutter.

"We didn't get much ice cream in Attica," he explained. He

bunched his lapel between his fingers and licked at the stain, which didn't help at all.

When we arrived at The Mentor Academy I tried to talk him into staying in the car, but this time he was adamant. There would be no policemen in a private school that was closed for the summer, and he wanted to do his job as he saw it. I decided not to argue, but as we made our way into the stuffy but oh so tasteful building that housed the administrative offices, I found myself mortified. Buddy's appearance was tacky enough at the best of times, and now the problem was compounded by the ice cream on his suit; I felt a bit ashamed at my own snobbery, of which I'd been unaware until that moment.

To my practiced eye, Alex Malleson was a glittering phony, Central Casting's idea of what the director of an exclusive private academy for young ladies and gentlemen should look like. He managed to keep up the Oxford accent about ninety percent of the time, which wasn't quite good enough unless you were there with your checkbook in your hand, hoping to be dazzled, wanting to be reassured that this was absolutely the *only* place your little lady or gentleman could learn both reading and mathematics, along with the rudiments of gracious capitalistic living, without being contaminated by unacceptable types like Jews and Catholics and blacks. But to his credit Malleson never actually *said* he was from England; perhaps he spoke like the host of *Masterpiece Theater* because he couldn't help it.

We sat in his study, which was furnished to look as much like a British headmaster's as possible. In fact, the whole place much more resembled an English country home than it did a school, the architecture of the house being Tudor style and the grounds well manicured and covered with grass that was a lush dark green and all of a length. I had the feeling it wouldn't dare turn brown or sprout crabgrass, no matter what the circumstances. Being midsummer, there weren't any kids about, but I doubted if they would have been running around playing tag or ball or hide-and-go-seek anyway; they probably would have all been walking around checking morning stock prices in *The Wall*

Street Journal and nodding sagely because they'd dumped AT&T at just the right time.

Alex Malleson was a few years older than I and had the kind of patrician, aquiline nose that looked like he never blew it. I had the distinct impression he wanted me to go away. He sat behind his huge antique desk, his nails manicured and buffed, wearing a lightweight gray suit that had never seen a wrinkle, an ash gray tie, and impeccable white linen, but he seemed uncomfortable somehow, as if this were my home turf instead of his. He had balked about the interview when we arrived at the top of the horseshoe driveway, and it was only my promise that I would stay no more than ten minutes that made him relent and talk to me at all. He kept staring at Buddy; it was obvious very few people visited The Mentor Academy wearing polyester. The ice cream stains were just icing on an already unpleasant cake.

"I've said all I had to say to Chief Kemp," Malleson told me nervously. He had a way of stroking his chin that made me think he might once have worn a beard. "I'm afraid there's no way I can help you, Mr. Jacovich." He spoke my Eastern European name as though it were an abomination on the tongue.

"Would you happen to have a copy of the agreement you signed with *North Coast Magazine?*"

"No," he said. Too quickly, I thought.

"I'd think you'd keep your receipt."

He didn't say anything.

"Did Mr. Shane come out here personally to pick the money up?"

"Yes," he said. "He was in a jogging suit. I was absolutely appalled. It was during the school year, too, and all the children saw him. An uncouth man. I should have known, I suppose, but I was trying to be civic-minded and help a new business get off the ground."

"What did Greg Shane say when he spoke to you?"

Malleson looked around the room as if searching for an escape hatch. "Just that he felt his new magazine would be a good

67

medium for The Mentor Academy's advertising. What else could he have said?"

"Did he talk to you about the circulation?"

He looked blank.

I said, "He must have said something about how many copies were going to be in circulation."

"I don't believe he did." He made a point of looking at his watch. It was a Patek Philippe. I ignored the hint.

"How many students do you have here, Mr. Malleson? In a given year."

"Oh, perhaps fifty-five or so, give or take a few."

"And from where do you draw most of your students?"

"Why, from the area," he said. "The people who live here in the Valley and the surrounding communities. This is a day school, Mr. Jacovich; we don't have boarding facilities."

"Do you solicit business?"

He looked down his thin nose at me like a matador sighting down the killing sword. "Certainly not. This is a private facility with a fine reputation. We don't go out and hustle customers. As a matter of fact, we have a sizable waiting list."

"You mean you couldn't handle very many more than fifty-five students?"

He shook his head. "We don't have the room, and we don't have the staff. We pride ourselves on the individualized attention we give each pupil. Look, our fall term begins in a few weeks. I'm sure you must appreciate that there is much to do here, so if there is nothing else. . . ?"

"Just a few things."

"You said ten minutes, Mr. Jacovich."

"Give me twelve. You are the director of this school, Mr. Malleson?"

"That's correct."

"For how long?"

"I'm sorry?"

"How long have you been at Mentor?"

"Oh. This is my fourth year coming up."

"I assume you've been at other schools before this one?"

68

"Certainly."

God, I hate it when people answer a question with "Certainly." It makes me feel as if I'd asked something stupid, and I didn't think that question was stupid at all. I said, "Are you from the Cleveland area?"

"No, I'm not," he said, as if the very idea was too absurd to discuss.

"Where were you before you came here?"

His eyes darted around the room. "California." If I wanted to wait, I supposed he'd elaborate and tell me where in California sometime within the next seventy-two hours. I didn't want to wait.

"All private schools like this? For the rich?"

There was a mustache of sweat droplets across Malleson's upper lip, and he had far too much breeding to wipe it away. "You have something against rich people?"

Buddy uncrossed his legs and crossed them the other way, and the fabric of his pants made a whispering sound. Malleson glanced at him nervously.

I smiled. "Only that I'm not one of them, I suppose."

He gave me a hard and haughty stare. "I don't see anything dishonorable about someone wealthy spending their money on a first-class education for their children. Do you have any children?"

I nodded. "Two boys, thirteen and nine. But I'm afraid The Mentor Academy is a little out of my price range."

"Pity," he said dryly. "We *are* exclusive, here. Our clients demand it, and they're willing to pay for it."

"Are you also the owner?"

His stare wavered a bit. "No. No, there is a board of directors, all of whom have investment in the school."

"In essence, then, you are an employee?"

He narrowed his eyes at me as if I'd passed wind. A stiff little nod was as far as he'd go by way of corroboration.

"But you make all the decisions?"

"Of course. I'm the director."

69

"Uh-huh. And it was your decision to take out an ad in *North Coast Magazine?*"

"I'm afraid I have to plead—" His smile was sickly. "Yes, it was my decision."

"And you haven't heard from Gregory Shane since then?"

"No." He shook his head and said it again, "No. He picked up my money, and then Leonard Pursglove came out a few days later to do an interview with me, and that's the last I heard of them. And good riddance, too, if you ask me."

I left him my business card, asking him to call me if for some reason Shane were to contact him. As I drove back down the sweeping driveway to River Road, I was glad to get out of the place. The Mentor Academy and its director made me feel like a sharecropper visiting the manor house, and I'd thought I'd gone beyond feelings like that.

"Asshole," Buddy said as we pulled out onto the road, wrapping it up very succinctly.

For once I agreed with him. Malleson had given me some things to think about, though. As for instance, why he hadn't kept a receipt or a copy of a services contract with Gregory Shane. And more curious, why a school with a space problem, whose lengthy waiting list was made up of anxious millionaires, needed to advertise, especially in a magazine that also ran the ads of chiropractors and body shops.

7

We headed back downtown from Chagrin Valley. I didn't want to be late for my audience with Vivian Truscott. *Audience* is the operative word here, because from what Mary had said I felt as though I were meeting a head of state, a pope, or a reigning monarch instead of the co-anchorperson of a television news program in Cleveland, Ohio. The more dealings I have with self-important, overpaid people, the happier I am that I chose the path in life that I did. I'll never have a million dollars or my own television show, but at least I have myself, and that, to me, is more important. I suppose it's nice to have headwaiters fuss over you and strangers on the street doff their caps, but when you start believing your own public relations, it seems to me that you are doomed to an existence of self-delusion. Somewhere along the line, most mature adults ought to be able to open their eyes and say, "You're nothing but a pack of cards!"

Channel 12 is in a blighted neighborhood tucked between the eastern fringe of downtown and the gentrified cultural climes of University Heights, an area that can no longer remember its better days. The recent renaissance of Playhouse Square and the financial district and the Flats had not quite reached this far on Euclid Avenue, and visiting Channel 12's studios and executive offices was an experience I didn't like to undertake unarmed. I would have worried about Mary leaving work after dark if the employee parking lot hadn't been equipped with a complicated security system and an armed watchman twenty-four hours a day. Not being one of the chosen supplied with a plastic card that opened the gate, I had to park in a public lot a block away and walk. It was early afternoon, hot and muggy on the street, in stark contrast to the icy air inside the studios.

"Are you just going to talk to this broad, Milan?" Buddy wanted to know.

"What else would I do with her, Buddy?"

"Jesus, it's boring for me, just sitting there."

"I'll try to make it interesting."

I wasn't looking forward to presenting Buddy to a self-styled media celebrity. Taking him in to The Mentor Academy had been bad enough; I had no idea how I would explain his presence to Vivian Truscott, who apparently didn't take kindly to strangers anyway.

Vivian Truscott had a large office—sitting room on the third floor, where she was relaxing prior to going before the cameras for her five o'clock news broadcast. She was the type of woman often described as a cool blond, but I found her more cold than cool. I'd seen her hundreds of times on television, of course, but in the flesh there was a steely strength in her that didn't come across on the tube. There was a regality in her bearing, but whether it was inborn or a latter-day affectation I couldn't really tell. In any case, her attitude toward me was one part public relations, one part noblesse oblige. She treated Buddy as if he were a Seeing Eye dog, which is to say that she acknowledged the introduction with a small nod and then proceeded to ignore him.

"It's nice to meet you, Milan," she said, extending a long slender hand for me to shake or kiss. I opted for a shake. "Mary's told me so much about you." I knew, of course, that that was a lie; Mary had said Vivian Truscott hardly knew of her existence.

"I'll try not to take up too much of your time," I said. "I understand you gave an interview to Jay Adams of *North Coast Magazine* a few months ago."

"Who?"

"Jay Adams."

She shook her head as if a gnat was buzzing around her eyes. "I don't know that name. Dan Mulkey called me first and told me they wanted me for their premiere issue cover story. When I agreed, a man named Pursglove came and talked to me, and he wrote the story."

I frowned. Adams had led me to believe the La Truscott interview had been his coup. "From what I know about you— which isn't much more than most people here in town who see you on TV—you normally don't give interviews."

"That's right," she said with a toss of her head. "I don't. I prefer to let my work on camera speak for itself."

"How did you happen to let yourself be talked into it this time?"

"Well," she said with a shrug of her attractive shoulders, "it was a new venture trying to get off the ground, and Mr. Mulkey was very persuasive about how much Cleveland needed such a magazine. Besides"—and she gave an embarrassed little smile—"they promised me my picture would be on the cover." There was a little bit of uncertainty cracking her cool facade. "There's surely nothing wrong with that, is there?"

"Not at all," I said. "You must be disappointed that it didn't work out."

"Win a few, lose a few. It would have been nice, but I don't really need it."

"Had you known Mulkey or Shane or Pursglove before? I

hear Pursglove is a pretty well-known freelance writer around town."

"I never heard of Shane or Pursglove until Dan Mulkey contacted me. I had met Mulkey about a year before that, when we did a story for the five o'clock news on a rock group that his company had just recorded." She glanced away from me. "I'm not sure I understand what it is you want to know, Milan," she said. "Maybe you could be a little more specific?"

"Specifically," I said, "Greg Shane has disappeared, and I'm trying to find him."

She wet her lips. "It was some sort of con game, then? I thought so. I mean, when I never heard from them after the interview, and then when the magazine didn't come out when it was supposed to."

"Did you try contacting them?"

"No. Why should I? My part of it was done."

"You weren't curious?"

"Not enough to do anything about it. I write all my own copy for the newscast, and that keeps me pretty busy."

"I really love your show," Buddy gushed, as surprising as a gastric indiscretion in church. Vivian looked blankly at him for a moment as if he'd spoken in Urdu, then turned back to me.

"And I have a husband to take care of, too, you know."

"Oh, I didn't know."

"I don't advertise the fact of my marriage."

"Why is that?"

"Well, it's not a secret. It's just that I think a public figure's image is more interesting when people don't know that much about her personal life, don't you?"

"I don't know," I said. "I never worry about images. You do the news very well, and that's all I care about."

She fluttered her eyelashes. She was being the public Vivian, the warm and folksy Vivian, the one she trotted out for local political dinners and ribbon cuttings. "Thank you, sir."

"So you're saying, Ms. Truscott—"

"Vivian, please. After all, you're a friend of, um . . . Mary's."

"Vivian, then. You're saying that the only contact you had with *North Coast Magazine* was your first conversation with Dan Mulkey and your interview with Leonard Pursglove?"

"That's right," she said, nodding vigorously. "They sold me a bill of goods, and I'm feeling a bit stupid about it. I'll be a hell of a lot more careful in the future, I can tell you."

"Careful?"

She smiled knowingly. "Who I say yes to," she said lightly. "You know, Milan, when you're as visible as a news anchor, especially in a middle-size market like this one, people are always after you for something or other. Appear at a benefit here, speak at a luncheon there, show up at a party, do interviews, give endorsements. This charity, that civic project, some other 'worthy cause.'" She spoke the two words as if they described some sort of shameful sexual aberration. "In Las Vegas, for instance, where I got my start, there are always bigger celebrities for people to go after for that sort of thing, but here in Cleveland we're kind of lacking in star power, if you don't count the jocks. Of course, the station management would love it if I spent my whole life doing personal appearances. They think it would help their ratings. But if you say yes to one, you have to say yes to all of them. That's why I've been so reluctant to do anything like this in the past. But Mulkey just about begged me. I mean, this was the magazine's start-up issue, and they needed someone with a strong Cleveland identification for the feature story. And Dan Mulkey led me to believe that Mr. Shane had sunk his life savings into the magazine, that this was his big chance." She gave a self-deprecating little laugh. "So I let him talk me into it."

"Tell me a little about the interview, if you will," I said. "Was it here, or at their office?"

"It was over lunch at Danny's in the Flats," she said. "Mr. Pursglove said the least the magazine could do was buy lunch." She smiled ruefully. "As things turned out, that's all I got out of it."

"What was the slant on the piece?"

"I'm sorry?"

"What was the angle? What was the theme of the story going to be?"

"Oh, the usual celebrity interview—although God knows I don't think of myself as a celebrity. I'm just a working journalist, that's all. They wanted to know my history. My education, my background, when and how I came to Cleveland, how I feel about Cleveland. The usual sort of thing."

"How *do* you feel about Cleveland?"

"It's a great city," she said. "The people are warm and wonderful, the city's cultural opportunities are really surprising, and it's a beautiful place as well." She rolled her eyes. "Of course, there are those winters!" I had the feeling this speech was canned, that she trotted it out whenever some civic booster or local pol or Jaycee lady asked her how she liked our little town. Not that there was anything wrong with her assessment. Cleveland *is* a great city. When the people who live here start believing it and stop heeding the knocks in the press and the bad jokes on television, things are going to be all right.

"Do you mean," I asked her, "if you got an offer from a network-owned station or from the network itself, you'd turn it down to stay here?"

She looked at me oddly. "*This* is beginning to sound like an interview. No, of course I wouldn't turn it down. Would you turn down half a million dollars a year just for the pleasure of living in Cleveland?"

"I don't know," I told her. "I guess it would depend on what I'd have to do to earn the half a million dollars."

Her face somehow changed then, closed up, as if some of the bones under her jaws and mouth had suddenly collapsed. She said, "Well, Milan, I've certainly enjoyed meeting you, but I really do have to start getting ready for the show. Five o'clock comes early around here. So if there's nothing else. . . ?"

"Vivian, thanks. It was nice meeting you too. Now when I watch the news I'll feel more personally connected to it."

"What a charming thought," Vivian Truscott said.

High-O Records had their corporate headquarters about four blocks from City Hall, just off Lakeside Avenue, in a building that looked for all the world like a converted industrial laundry. Buddy and I climbed the stairs to the second floor, where we were confronted with a locked door and a glassed-in reception cubicle, in which sat a young girl with jet black bangs in a geometric cut and enough eye makeup to qualify her for the lead in a bus-and-truck tour of *Antony and Cleopatra*. She was reading a paperback Jackie Collins novel that looked battered and worn enough to have passed through the hands of everyone else in the office before it got to her. She looked up as Buddy and I approached, and I told her we were with the Bedford Credit Corporation and wanted some information on one of their former employees, Dan Mulkey, and asked if it would be possible to speak to someone in the personnel department. It took a few seconds for her to absorb all the information and then she picked up the telephone, mumbled something into the mouthpiece, and hung up and reached under her desk. A buzzer sounded, and I correctly guessed that was my signal to open the security door and go on in.

"Down the hallway, turn left and it's the first door on the right," she said. I wasn't sure whether she was giving us directions to the personnel department or the men's room.

We dutifully went down the long hallway and took the first left turn. I knocked on the open door of the first office on the right. In it, sitting behind a battered metal desk, was a man in his late twenties whose shoulder-length wavy brown hair would have been the envy of any Cleveland State coed. He looked bulimic, with a face the color of library paste. His baggy Wrangler jeans were frayed at the cuffs and a faded half-sleeve T-shirt announced Michael Jackson's Victory Tour of several years ago.

"Come on in," he said.

We entered the office, which smelled of stale marijuana smoke, and took the chairs he waved us into.

"Hello," I said. "I'm Michael Hart, with Bedford Credit in Bedford. This is my associate, Mr. Rizzo." Buddy looked stunned, but didn't contradict me. I suppose I should have told him he was going to be Mr. Rizzo, but I frankly only thought of it at that very moment. "Are you the personnel director?"

"No, man," he said, "I'm the executive vice president of this joint. Tom Bratt." He put out a languid hand for me to shake. "What's up?"

"We're running a credit check on one of your former employees here. Daniel Mulkey?"

"Right, that's what Traci said. Is Dan in like some kind of trouble?"

I thought that was a curious question, one I'd have to address a bit later in our interview. "Not at all. As I said, this is a routine credit check." I took out my notebook and a pen. "He did work here?"

"Sure did."

"For how long?"

"I don't know, man. Three years or so."

"And he left when?"

Bratt shrugged his disinterest. "End of last year. November, I guess."

"What was his position here?"

"He was a producer."

"What was his reason for leaving?"

Bratt hesitated. I wasn't sure if it was because he wanted to think out his answer carefully or if he was too stoned to understand the question. Then he said, "Look, man, I don't want to like dump on anybody, you know?"

"Then his termination wasn't voluntary?"

"Talk English, man. You mean was he fired?"

I nodded.

"Yeah, you might say that."

I frowned, trying to look troubled. "Why?"

"This is personal shit, man."

"Mr. Bratt," I said, "whatever you tell me will be held in the strictest confidence. But it won't reflect as badly on Mr. Mulkey's credit worthiness as your not answering at all."

"Yeah," he sighed. It took him about a minute to think it over. "You know what we do here, don't you?" he said finally.

"You make records," Buddy said. I incinerated him with a look, and he grinned a shame-face at me for having forgotten his promise.

"Right," Tom Bratt said. "How it works is, a local group, say one that's playing around in the clubs here, wants to get recorded. Not a demo, but an honest to God album. They like pay us to make it for them, and then we see that it's placed in all the stores around here. We've got a pretty fair distribution system. I can't honestly say any group has broken out nationally because of us, but they get their money's worth."

"Okay," I said.

"Dan Mulkey was our house producer. He like picked the songs, supervised the mix—you cats dig what a mix is?"

I told him I dug before Buddy had a chance to say that he didn't dig.

"He helped design the album cover, did the liner notes, handled press releases. Like the whole nine yards. We came to find out he was like misrepresenting to these groups, you know? I mean he was like taking kickbacks. Told them that's the only way they'd get good distribution, you know?"

I made dutiful notes.

"So when I found out about it, Dan was history. I mean, it makes the whole company look like shit, you know?"

"I know," I said. "And this was last November?"

He nodded.

"Do you know what he did when he left here? Where he went?"

"No, man. It's like with a chick, you know? When it's over, it's over."

"Where is Dan Mulkey now, Mr. Bratt? Is he still living out in Rocky River?"

"I don't know and I could care less," he said.

"When I first came in, you asked if Mulkey were in trouble. What made you say that?"

He took a swig out of a cracked mug on his desk. It looked like water, but who knew? "Danny was always hustling," he said. "He liked to work angles. He was a lot more interested in his own number than in the company, and that's a dangerous kind of guy to have hanging around. I mean, like I don't wish him any bad shit, but I don't particularly wish him any good shit, either."

I rose. "I guess that tells me what I need to know."

"Hey, man," Bratt said, "I hope I didn't cause him any trouble."

"Not at all, Mr. Bratt," I said.

Buddy added, "And like, thanks."

We went back through the corridor the way we'd come, back past Traci in her little glass cubicle, who tore herself away from Jackie Collins long enough to buzz us out through the door, regarding us as though we were either extraterrestrials or narcs. In Traci's world, I wasn't sure which was worse.

8

After we left High-O I drove back over to Leonard Pursglove's place, but he evidently was still out somewhere, and J. Rose hadn't returned yet either. It was getting to be dinnertime, and I was downtown anyway, so I dropped Buddy off at Terminal Tower, figuring however he got back to my place to pick up his Celica was someone else's problem. He didn't seem bothered by the inconvenience and waved good-bye with the cheery reminder that he'd see me in the morning. I drove the few blocks to the Flats, parked in an outdoor lot with the nose of my Chevy wagon sticking out over the river, and went into DiPoo's to get something to eat.

Unlike many of the other currently fashionable restaurants in the Flats that make their headquarters in converted warehouses, cater to young stockbrokers and corporate attorneys, and charge outrageous prices for almost microscopic portions of new cuisine, DiPoo's on the River was a no-nonsense steak-and-broiled-fish house that drew its youngish clientele from the ranks of secretaries, middle management drones, insurance underwriters, and a host of civil service employees from the Frank J. Lausche State Office Building just up the hill on Superior Avenue. Inside, DiPoo's was vaguely nautical in design, with a rather incongruous pair of elk antlers mounted over one of the booths and, for some strange reason, real brass musical instruments hanging on the walls. In the corner was a dance floor the size of a stall in the men's room and a glass-enclosed DJ station, deserted at this early hour, painted in eyesore Day-Glo colors. The sound system was playing the Beatles' White Album.

I elbowed my way between two three-piece suits at the bar who were bitching about their female boss and ordered a Stroh's. Then I let the hostess know I wanted to have dinner. She was dressed in a floor-length gown with a tropical floral print, and she didn't look old enough to be there. She led me to a table by the window where I could look out at barge traffic on the murky river, and after I gave the spike-haired waitress my dinner order I took out my notebook and reviewed what I had so far.

Richardson Hippsley-Tate had been skinned for forty-two thousand dollars by a couple of guys who owned a magazine that didn't exist. He wanted me to recover his money, but what he didn't tell me was that the northern Ohio mob, led by Victor Gaimari and his mentor, Giancarlo D'Allessandro, owned a large hunk of the Lake Shore Hotel, which might have accounted for an elegantly dressed general manager who said things like "anyways" and "like I said" and "forty-two grand."

The publisher of the magazine, Greg Shane, had some vague mob connections on the West Coast and was married to a former hooker with a drinking problem. His local associates included an ex–record producer who took kickbacks, a grossly overweight gay editor, and a slick freelance writer. His big-name author was an elderly lesbian who wrote turgid romance novels, and the lead story in his nonexistent magazine was to have been about a local TV news anchorwoman who usually never gave interviews and who didn't know what I meant when I asked her about a story's "slant." And one of his advertisers was a tony private school that didn't need any new customers, especially from the white-sock crowd. It was all very interesting, but it didn't add up to much that I could figure in terms of finding Greg Shane and recovering the hotel's money.

I glanced at my watch. It was just past six, which meant that it was three hours earlier on the West Coast. And there were a few things on the West Coast I needed to know about. I got up and went to the pay phone and got the number I wanted from Los Angeles directory assistance.

A few years before, I had attended a convention in Las Vegas for security companies and had made the acquaintance of a Los Angeles PI named Saxon. He was a movie actor whenever anyone would hire him, and he had the ego to go with it, but he was a pretty engaging guy for all that, and we had spent much of our spare time between seminars and meetings drinking together and seeing the Las Vegas sights, including the two-legged blond variety, in which Saxon had shown inordinate interest. If he pursued his second career as relentlessly as he did leggy show-girls, he'd be a damn good investigator. Since that time we'd exchanged a few Christmas cards and short notes, but not much more.

I was lucky enough to catch him in his office. I guess things were slow for him in the acting business, since he wasn't off somewhere on location doing a picture. It was the first time I'd talked to him in more than a year, and we chatted for a while about the usual trivia: how are the kids from him, have you done any movies lately from me. Then I told him I could use some help from him out on the West Coast.

"Sure, Milan, what do you need?" he said. "Not much goes on here in the summertime, and I'm tired of working on my tan."

I filled him in on the Lake Shore Hotel situation.

"Sounds sticky."

"It may be. What I need is as much information as you can get for me on Greg Shane and his wife Nettie. I know they were on the West Coast for a while and that they have connections with the boys in Vegas, but frankly I'm not even sure they used those names when they were out there."

I heard him muttering, obviously making notes. "That might be tough but not impossible," he said.

"I'd also like you to check on two other people for me."

"Okay, shoot."

"First of all, a TV newslady named Vivian Truscott, from Las Vegas. She's our five o'clock anchor out here."

"Don't tell me," Saxon said. "Tall, blond, imposing-looking, and all the warmth of the iceberg that did in the *Titanic*."

I was surprised. "You know her?"

"No," he admitted, "it was a shot in the dark. But every anchorwoman I've ever seen looks like that, unless she's black and looks like Jayne Kennedy. You mean I'm right?"

"In every detail."

He chuckled. "I ought to be a detective. Who else?"

"Alex Malleson," I said. "He runs a very exclusive private school in a suburb I can't even afford to visit. He supposedly did the same thing in California a few years ago."

"Los Angeles?"

"I'm not sure. He just said California."

"This is a big state, Milan."

"I know."

"But usually if someone's from up north he'll say so—San Francisco, or northern California. If he just says California he probably means down south here. I'll check it out if I can."

"Great," I said. "And while you're at it, dig up something for me on one Richardson Hippsley-Tate."

He laughed. "You're kidding. Nobody is named Richardson Hippsley-Tate."

"It's not the kind of a name a guy makes up. He's the manager of the hotel, and he says he used to run a high-class little joint in Manhattan Beach. That's in L.A., isn't it?"

"Kind of," Saxon said, "it's south of here, not too far from the airport. You have the name of the hotel?"

"No, but he said they had antiques in all the rooms, if that's any help."

"It narrows it down," he said. "Is that it?"

"For now."

"I suppose you're in a tearing hurry about this?"

"The longer I wait the colder the trail gets."

"I know the feeling. Okay, I'll get right on it."

"You've got my number; give me a ring when you find anything out. And send me a bill."

"That," Saxon said, "you can be sure of."

I went back to my window table and watched the river amble by while I wolfed down a green salad with the house ranch dressing, a somewhat overcooked filet mignon, and a baked potato with butter and sour cream. I had asked them to hold the chives but they didn't, and I spent a few annoying minutes picking them out of the sour cream. I had two more Stroh's and a few cups of coffee, and after the obligatory visit to the facilities I bailed my car out of the lot for three dollars. It was all on the expense account.

I drove up the hill out of the Flats, swung around the block back onto Superior Avenue, and headed across the Detroit-Superior Bridge, which turns into Detroit Avenue once it reaches the river's west bank. The setting summer sun was right in my face, about the same size and color as a basketball. I pulled down the sun visor inside my car, but the sun was too low for it to do any good, so I flipped it up again and squinted into the bright orange glare. Since I couldn't find Greg and Nettie Shane, it seemed to me that Dan Mulkey's name had cropped up in enough conversations to warrant a trip out to Rocky River to see him, and I was so relieved to be spared the company of my Buddy the oversize shadow that I was actually looking forward to the trip.

Like many large urban centers in America, Cleveland is a city divided. Just as Chicagoans who live on the North Side rarely venture beyond the Loop to the South Side, so did few Clevelanders from the east side ever sojourn westward. For all practical purposes there are two Clevelands, one on either side of the Cuyahoga. Both have their poverty pockets, their old rich and new rich, their largely black or middle-European blue-collar class, and a great many taverns, furniture stores, and plumbing supply houses, but each bank of the river has a flavor and a character all its own. I'd never dare to say it out loud in the old neighborhood, but I rather like the west side. Its average resident is a bit younger than those on the east side, its shops more upscale, and its lakefront more beautiful and more residential. But having been born and raised in Slavic Town on East Fifty-third Street, it's never occurred to me to live across the river. If you're an east sider who goes to live on the west side, you might as well do it whole hog and move to Cincinnati, there to develop a taste for chili and root for the hated Bengals.

Rocky River could be classified, I suppose, as somewhere between the upper and the middle class. The homes had a market price in the vicinity of a hundred thousand dollars and up—mostly up—and were newer than many other west side neighborhood houses, well cared for, and for the most part efficient and compact, built solidly on small lots with skimpy front lawns and back yards just big enough for a picnic table and a barbecue kettle in the warm weather. During the snow season no one ever goes out into the back yard anyway, so I suppose to Rocky Riverites the postage-stamp lots are outweighed by living in a relatively crime free area among neighbors they don't know, but whose incomes and skin color and cultural interests mirror their own.

The address I had for Dan Mulkey turned out to be a pleasant two-story gray frame house with white trim and a roof that peaked on one side, giving the house a lopsided but architecturally interesting look. Across a narrow cobbled walkway was a two-car detached garage. Between house and garage I glimpsed the typical cell-size back yard, which ended in an abrupt bluff dropping almost straight down about a hundred feet to a stand of dense woods, with the expressway beyond. I parked my car in the drive and made my way up the winding walk to the front door. I noticed a big stack of mail stuffed into the small mailbox on the porch, including a copy of *Billboard*, the magazine of the recording industry, and *Variety*, the show business weekly. There was also a letter from a magazine publishing house with a picture of Ed McMahon on the front. Showing through the little window it said, "How would you like us to present a check for ten million dollars to D. MULKEY on national television? Not hard to take, eh, D. MULKEY????" Either D. Mulkey was very popular or he hadn't picked up his mail in several days. I guessed the latter, since on the porch floor beneath the mailbox, right next to the raffia mat that said WELCOME, were two copies of the *Plain Dealer*, haphazardly thrown. I pushed the button next to the door; the sound of the doorbell was shrill, like an old-fashioned telephone, and gave me a bit of a start. It didn't matter, because no one answered its summons even after I rang a second time. Through the front window I could see a light on in the rear of the house, probably the kitchen, but that didn't mean much. Most people leave at least one light burning when they aren't home. I don't know why. A single light doesn't fool burglars a bit; often it attracts them.

I went to the garage and peered in the window. It was set high in the wall, but I'm set rather high myself and had little trouble getting a look inside. There was a late-model Honda Accord in one of the spaces, and a Kawasaki motorcycle in the other. Wherever Mulkey might have been, someone else had probably taken him there. I walked around the side of the house to the back yard, where I ascertained that it was indeed the kitchen light that had been left burning. The storm door to the glassed-in porch was open, so I went up the steps and past the Kenmore washer and dryer to the back door. I knocked loudly and it swung open a few inches at the impact. It hadn't been latched. I stepped into the kitchen and said, "Hello?" but I didn't really expect any response, because in some strange way the house had a deserted feel to it, a sort of desolate emptiness, like the landscape in a Mad Max movie, despite the fact that there was a light on, furniture, some mild clutter, signs of habitation. I remembered the vill sweeps I'd been part of in Vietnam, an American squad or fire team swooping down on a little cluster of hootches and outbuildings where the bedding was still warm, the rice pot was still on the fire, the sweet smell of tobacco still hung in the dampness, and the air itself quivered with recent activity, but there was no movement or sign of life anywhere. Mulkey's house felt like that. It made me nervous.

In for a penny already, I closed the door behind me and looked around the kitchen. *The Plain Dealer* was open to the movie page on the counter, which served as an eating area. The date was from three days ago. An almost empty bottle of Heineken stood beside it. There was a pot of pinto beans on the stove, cooked but cold and starting to smell a little rank. The glass carafe from a Braun coffee maker stood full of water in the sink, and next to it was a dish bearing the remains of a serving of Cheerios. There were several forks and spoons in the sink as well.

I went out into the dining room. The walls were painted dove gray, and even the warm orange sunlight coming in the window did nothing to dispel the depressing effect the color had on me. There was a long table made of black-lacquered teak and six matching chairs upholstered in bright red vinyl. On the table were two red ceramic candle holders. The only other furniture in the room was a large credenza, atop which stood an abstract crystal whatnot, about two feet tall and rather phallic in appearance. On the wall was an expensively framed Leroy Neiman print showing an Olympic Games race. Despite the weather the room felt cold, like a decorative showroom display in a model home, not a place in which one could eat good food, drink good wine, and share companionship with one's fellows.

I knew I could be arrested and have my license yanked if I were caught wandering around in Mulkey's home, and neither my status as an ex-cop nor my long-standing friendship with Marko Meglich would help me, but my curiosity was getting the better of me and I decided to explore the rest of the house. The living room was done in a bloodless modern style as well, almost all black and white, accented by an occasional electric blue throw pillow. A stack of magazines, most having to do with the music and recording industries, served as the only clutter on a low lacquered Chinese table in front of the sofa. There was a black upright piano in one corner, and next to it a complicated setup of electronic keyboards and synthesizers. The stereo system that covered almost an entire wall at the far end of the room must have cost upwards of five thousand dollars. The only warm colors breaking the monotony of black and white and high tech came from several framed gold records hanging on the walls. I looked at their labels, but I had never heard of any of the songs or recording artists. There were no indications that the gold awards had been sanctioned by the National Association of Recording Artists, or by anyone else. For all I know, if you want a gold record hanging in your living room you simply go out and buy one.

The entryway by the front door was virtually empty. A framed poster of Billy Idol in concert, with his lips grimacing to reveal his teeth and his arm flung skyward to show his underarm hair, hung on the wall halfway up the stairs, which were carpeted in a kind of champagne white. On the second floor was a bathroom, cluttered the way a bachelor's bathroom usually is, with shaving paraphernalia, shampoo, a hairbrush, and three different kinds of mouthwash in red, green, and yellow on the countertop. It had a lived-in look. Mulkey was going to have to replace the roll of toilet paper before too long, and I noticed he preferred his with the new sheets coming from underneath. I'm an over-the-top man myself. The shower dripped a little; not much, but enough to be annoying if one were trying to sleep in the adjoining room.

The bedroom itself contained a king-size bed that had been made up rather carelessly, and a dresser, atop which were a variety of papers, bills and letters, many packets of matches from some of the in restaurants downtown and from Shooters in the Flats, and a jumble of loose change, not quite three dollars' worth. There was also an inexpensive cassette player, open but with no tape inside. The sliding doors of the closet were partially open, revealing a mostly casual wardrobe: several pairs of jeans, sports shirts with designer labels, cashmere jackets, leisure slacks in a riot of plaids and bright solids, and a variety of loafers and athletic shoes in different colors. On the shelf above was a white fedora, which would probably go well with a summer jacket, open shirt, and ascot. It certainly wasn't my style, but judging from the rest of the clothing, it must have been Mulkey's. Next to the hat were several stacks of audio cassette tapes in their plastic boxes. None of them seemed to be commercially produced and packaged versions of hit rock albums. They all had been identified with scrawls in felt-tipped pen, and bore number and letter codes rather than titles. I figured most of them were Dan Mulkey's own personal tapes, and I wondered why they weren't kept somewhere down in the living room with the rest of the audio equipment. I didn't touch anything.

The only other room upstairs was a dormer-roofed guest bedroom with a queen-size bed and at least fifteen pillows, a cheap dresser, and an old-fashioned window seat covered in a flowered fabric. The room was neat but dusty, as though it hadn't been used in a long time. The interior of Dan Mulkey's house had netted me a fat zero in terms of useful information, but I'd learned something about the personality of the man who lived there.

I went back downstairs and out the way I had come, annoyed with myself for risking entry in the first place and for having wasted the evening with a trip to the west side. As I walked down the two stone steps to the back yard I noticed the redwood picnic table. There was a paper plate on it nestled in a wicker holder, a knife and fork, and several paper napkins secured against the summer breezes by a large jar of fancy Dijon mustard. I went to look at the hibachi close by, which bore the remnants of two hamburger patties, burned to a crisp, and beneath them the cold ashes of a charcoal fire. Under the hibachi was a can of charcoal starter and a half empty bag of mesquite briquets; grilling food over a mesquite fire was one of the latest trends among the baby boom set. On the ground near one of the legs of the hibachi was a long-handled spatula on which the grease had coagulated. It looked as though someone had abandoned their barbecue rather quickly.

I looked around the yard. The grass was patchy and uneven, leaving several bare spots to the mercy of the weeds, and it grew an inch or so higher along the base of the hedge that had been planted at the rim of the bluff, indicating either a careless gardener or one who didn't own a lawn edger. Facing west into the burning afternoon sun as it did, the back lawn probably never had much chance at survival anyway, and the care it had been given seemed cursory at best. I noticed a double set of tracks that had broken the grass down: two long grooves in the ground, which was wet from a rainstorm a few days before, ending at a slight gap in the otherwise symmetrical line of bushes. I thought about it for a minute and then followed the double gouges in the grass to the hedge.

The small branches of the hedge were snapped and broken at the gap, and several of the silver-green leaves had fallen off and carpeted the ground at the roots of the bush. I knelt down, noticing a brownish stain on some of the lower leaves. I had seen stains like that before. I hadn't liked them any better then.

I moved a few feet along the hedge and created a gap of my own, wrestling my way through the brambly bushes and trying to keep my eyes out of the way of the branches as they snapped back in my face, until I could see down into the stand of woods at the foot of the bluff. The trees were at their most lush, a midsummer emerald green, glowing in the slight cooling-off time before the orange-hued sun went all the way down. In the twilight it was hard to see through the leaves, but there was something down there that wasn't growing, wasn't even moving, something not green or brown. It was turquoise blue on top and white on the bottom, and dim light or no, it was evident that it was the body of someone wearing white duck trousers and a turquoise T-shirt.

9

Marko Meglich finished the last of his coffee, threw the foam cup into his wastebasket, and made a grimace of disgust. "Foam coffee cups," he said. "Worst damn invention since throwaway razors. Cardboard's bad enough, it makes your coffee taste funny. But foam! You know what that stuff's made of?"

I admitted I didn't.

"It's all synthetic. Chemicals. I always feel like I'm ingesting little particles along with my coffee and that some day I'm going to wake up with radioactive ulcers, or hemorrhoids that glow in the dark or something." He shook his head. "I ought to have my own coffee mug in here. With my name on it. Or my badge number. I'm a lieutenant, for God's sake, I'm entitled. I paid my dues."

"Lieutenants shouldn't drink foam," I agreed gravely. "Anybody with the rank of detective first or above shouldn't have to ingest foam particles."

"You laugh," Marko said, "but I worry about it."

"It's too late at night to be drinking coffee anyway," I told him, glancing at my watch. It was just past midnight, more than five hours after I'd found Dan Mulkey's body in the woods behind his house and called the police. I had figured to spend most of the night at headquarters; now, after having been debriefed by a homicide detective from Rocky River and again by Marko Meglich, to whom I had told the whole *North Coast Magazine* story, the evening seemed to be winding down and I was counting myself fortunate.

"You're right, Milan," he said. "It's this damn job. Dead people. You spend half your working life with dead people, it makes you drink a lot of coffee, just to keep you sane." He leaned back in his leather executive's chair. He was wearing a dark blue vest that matched his pants, a white shirt that looked as though he'd just unwrapped it five minutes ago, and a silver-blue tie; his suit coat was hung up neatly on a wooden hanger behind the door. His gun and holster I assumed were in the desk drawer, so as not to wrinkle his clothes. "It's just a damn good thing you went out to Mulkey's place," he said. "Otherwise he might have stayed in those woods for a month."

"Glad to help our boys in blue any time," I said.

"You do have a knack for turning up dead bodies. I wonder why that is?"

"Some guys attract money, and some attract beautiful women. I guess I'm just lucky."

"Well, we'll get the autopsy report on Mulkey first thing in the morning, but it seems someone blew a big hole in the back of his head. You don't have to go to med school to figure that out."

I nodded. "Who? And why?"

"The question of the day—or night. Someone from his days in the music business, maybe. Someone who didn't like rock and roll."

"A classical music lover. But I've got a feeling it has something to do with *North Coast Magazine.*"

"One of your famous feelings. Want to help me out a little and tell me why you think so?"

"I can't, Marko," I said. "But there are things about that magazine and the people involved with it that don't add up."

"Such as?"

I took out my notebook. "We have an elegant hotel manager who talks like a hood. We have an editor who's expressed a desire to kill Gregory Shane. We have the most exclusive private school in northern Ohio, with a waiting list a mile long they can't accommodate, advertising in a blue-collar magazine. And we have a TV anchorwoman who didn't know what I meant when I asked her about the slant on a story. It's like a bunch of actors together on one stage, but they're each doing a different play."

"How does any of that relate to Mulkey?" Marko said.

"I don't know. I don't know if it does or not. But my job is looking for Greg Shane, and I'm going to keep doing that. Maybe when I find him it'll explain a lot of things."

"You think Shane killed Mulkey?"

"I don't even know if Shane is still alive," I said. "He seems to have done the vanishing trick of the year."

"Maybe whoever killed Mulkey dusted Shane too."

I started to laugh. "Marko, you're making all sorts of assumptions here. Let's not try to force the pieces to fit. You've got everything I've got, and you've got those tapes from Mulkey's closet. It doesn't necessarily figure that someone who got nicked for a couple of bucks by a small-time con artist is going to murder the con artist's associate, or murder the con artist. It's just . . . curious, that's all."

"When you find Shane, I want to know about it, Milan. This is not screwing around anymore. It's a murder case."

"As soon as I get the okay from my client."

"Don't you think it's about time you told me who you're working for?"

I shook my head. "You know better than to ask."

"We're talking homicide here."

"I know," I said. "But there's no reason to think there's a connection between said homicide and my client."

"You just said you thought there was!"

"I know I did. But there's no real proof, and until there is I have the right—the obligation—to keep my client's name out of it."

"I'd like to keep everyone's name out of it, Milan. I'm not releasing this story to the press just yet, and I'd rather you didn't either."

"I never talk to the press."

"Oh, bullshit. You and Ed Stahl are best friends—I know that from when you were walking a beat."

"That doesn't mean I rattle his cage every time I get wind of half a piece of a story."

"Well, see, that's the thing. I mean, I don't want to go public with this Mulkey business until we know what we're dealing with here."

I shook my last cigarette out of the pack and lit it with his Dunhill lighter. "You mean you don't want any publicity until you've made an arrest."

Meglich shook his head sadly. "Why didn't you stay with the department, Milan? You and I understand each other. We could be making history now, Cleveland history. What a team! Two guys from the old neighborhood. They'd be calling us Batman and Robin in the newspaper every time we made a collar, or Butch and Sundance."

"Or Laurel and Hardy. Thanks for the coffee, Marko. If I start pissing liquid uranium, you'll be the first to know."

"It's not funny!" he protested. "Everything either causes cancer or heart disease or makes your hair fall out! The whole world is going synthetic on us."

"Not me," I assured him.

We waffled around for another fifteen minutes or so until I began looking at my watch and yawning loudly, and Marko decided I had been as much use to the homicide bureau as I was going to be for a while. Then he said, "You need some sleep,

Milan, and so do I. But keep me up to date on this business, will you? If you find a connection between what you're doing and what I'm doing, I want to know about it."

"That's a promise, Marko," I said.

I drove home through quiet muggy streets. The headlights of one car showed in my rearview mirror; other than that the city was all but deserted. Cleveland never has been a late night town; most people call it a day before the eleven o'clock news so they can be fresh to go down to work the next morning. Clevelanders always "go down to work," no matter where their place of business might be. And when they visit their families they always "go over their grandmother's." Even on Saturday night they turn in early so as not to miss church. A nice, homey kind of town that was in danger of getting too big for its britches.

As I started up Cedar Hill I flipped the radio on. We do have an all-night jazz station, which is some consolation to the handful of insomniacs here, and the later at night it gets the wilder the bebop they play. I was enjoying it; it seemed to blast out all the surmisals about the Dan Mulkey murder that were bouncing around in my head. It turned out to have been a mistake, because I was so intent on the Buddy Rich sides they were playing I didn't notice the car behind me speeding up until it was next to me in the left lane, and then what got my attention wasn't even the noise, but the muzzle flash as the driver fired a shot at me that shattered the window beside my left ear. I felt the wind disturbance from the bullet as it sizzled past my face and embedded itself in the headliner on the right side of the car.

Reflexively I averted my face and jerked the wheel to the right to get away from my assailant. My car bounced up over the curb and swept across the sidewalk to ram into the stone wall that curved up the hill. My head snapped back and then forward on my spine, and the steering column crunched into my chest, a firm chastisement for not wearing my seat belt. The breath rushed out of my lungs like a sat-upon whoopee cushion, and I sucked in air with the desperation of a drowning man who suddenly bobs to the surface. By the time I'd reclaimed my senses, the shooter's car had roared up Cedar Hill and was out of sight before I could tell what make or color it was. The impact with the wall had smashed my front grille and my radiator, and steaming water and all-weather coolant was gushing from underneath the car and making wet, oily rainbows on the pavement in the light of the arc lamps.

I felt my ribs carefully. They were sore as hell but none seemed to be broken, a development I was only slightly less thankful for than for the faulty aim of whoever had shot at me. With great effort I slid out from under the wheel and leaned against the crumpled fender, panting. Fear had taken my breath away.

I'd thought I had seen the last of the inside of police headquarters for that night, but obviously I'd been wrong.

It had been a pretty harrowing evening by the time I finally arrived home, my head throbbing, my neck stiff, and my chest aching with every breath. I had a lot on my mind. That tends to happen when people try to kill me. Solving murders was the police department's job; mine was to find a missing bunco artist. But now the two had seemingly fused. I was no longer sure whether Greg and Nettie Shane had taken off by their own volition or were tucked away in some leafy glade, the way Dan Mulkey had been. If they were still alive, my finding them might be what kept them that way. It might also, however, wind up getting me dead, and that made it personal. Either way I had the gut feeling that time was of the essence.

It was close enough to first thing in the morning to make the idea of sleep impractical, so I just brewed myself a pot of very strong coffee laced with cinnamon and drank it down within an hour. I showered and shaved, made myself some raisin toast and another potful. The big change in my morning ritual was that I went out to collect the newspaper from my doormat with a loaded .357 Magnum in my hand. I usually keep it in the top drawer of my desk, just so I can reach it handily. I felt like a jerk standing there in my bathrobe with a weapon powerful enough to blow a hole through a brick wall, but there was no sense in being reckless. Someone had taken a shot at me already, and I wasn't about to stick my head out the door without being prepared for the worst. The worst didn't come: my hallway was as peaceful as it always is at seven o'clock in the morning.

I read last night's baseball scores. The Tribe had dropped another one to the Twins, this time in the ninth inning, courtesy of a wild pitch, a stolen base, and a home run by Gary Gaetti. It wasn't quite as earth-shattering as Dan Mulkey's killing and the attempt on my life, but it was a momentary gloomy distraction before getting into the serious work of the day.

The next distraction of the morning arrived when Buddy Bustamente rang my doorbell.

He seemed to have an inexhaustible supply of those polyester leisure suits. This one was the color of baby shit, and he'd paired it with a kelly green shirt. I wasn't sure if his sartorial style reflected his own taste or if he figured that since he now lived in Cleveland he should dress like he thought the natives do. Mary has often gently chided me for my plaid jackets, too wide ties, and lace-up clodhopper shoes, but next to Buddy I was the Duke of Edinburgh.

"Buddy," I said, "I was beginning to worry you weren't coming."

Blissfully unaware of the irony, he walked past me into the apartment and headed directly for the kitchen, where he proceeded to help himself to a cup of coffee and three pieces of toast. "I know, Milan, and I'm sorry. I was at Mr. Gaimari's house. Hell of a thing what happened to Dan Mulkey last night, wasn't it? And to you, too. You've got to be more careful. Are you okay?"

"Yeah, I'm fine except for a couple of bruised ribs and a nervous system that will never be the same." I looked right at him. "Where'd you hear about Dan Mulkey?"

"Mr. Gaimari told me."

"Mr. Gaimari seems to be pretty well informed about what goes on down at police headquarters. Who's his ears down there?"

"Gee, you've got me, Milan. I'm just the hired help."

"Buddy," I said, "I don't want to do this anymore. Someone tried to kill me last night and I'm going to find out who it is."

"Well, the important thing is, you're okay."

"Yeah, thanks. And as charming a companion as you might be, I work much better alone."

He put half a slice of toast in his mouth and said around it, "I'm just following orders, Milan."

"So was Josef Mengele."

"Who?"

"Never mind," I said. "You want some more toast?"

"I've had breakfast already, thanks. Maybe some fruit, though."

"I don't have any fruit."

"Oh. That's okay. Where are we going today?"

The last thing in the world I wanted was to try and do a difficult and now dangerous job with a clown like Buddy Bustamente hanging over my shoulder. If the truth were known, I also wasn't too anxious to be out in public with him while he was dressed that way, and since I'd never seen him dressed any other way, I had little faith in asking him to go home and change. But Victor Gaimari was, after all, paying for my time, if indirectly, and paying quite well. I'd turned down money from clients before when they wanted me to do something I didn't want to do, but usually those turndowns had been for moral or ethical reasons. There was nothing unethical about letting Buddy Bustamente trot around behind me while I worked, it was simply a very unappealing prospect.

I had gotten pretty deep into the *North Coast Magazine* situation already, though, and now that it had become personal with me, there was no way I'd pull out without seeing it through to its conclusion. I wanted to find Gregory Shane, and I wanted my curiosity assuaged about Hippsley-Tate and Alex Malleson and Vivian Truscott, and the only way I was going to do that was to stay on the case, Buddy and his Full Cleveland look notwithstanding. I felt like a butterfly impaled on a pin.

The good news was that if whoever shot at me made another try, I couldn't think of a guy I'd rather have along to ride shotgun. There was a toughness inside Buddy, a callused place he'd built up through a lot of hard times. He was working on his second cup of coffee and reading my newspaper, avidly absorbing the story of the Indians' most recent drubbing as though it were Holy Writ. He would occasionally glance up at me with a little boy naiveté that was strangely touching. I couldn't think of anything else to do so I glared at him, which for some reason made his face light up in a rather appealing way for a guy who was built like an oil tanker. He folded the newspaper, as though coffee break was over. "Ready to go, Milan?"

Since my car was pretty much out of commission for a while—sitting in the police impound lot, where it had been towed, with a smashed radiator and a ruptured front end—we took his Celica. I had to admit that for once Buddy's presence had come in handy. He sat there in the driver's seat beside me, a supernumerary suddenly imposed on me as a leading player against my will and my wishes, chattering happily about nothing in particular, which is why I am having trouble remembering it now. It seems to me he was comparing the finer points of Buffalo to those of Cleveland as he gazed out the window. I know he asked me if it was all right to smoke in the car and assured me that if I objected there would be no problem. Other than that, I tried to pretend he wasn't there, which was no mean feat, considering he was the size of two men.

The Merlys Mercer School of Dance was located a few blocks to the south of University Circle in something that was called the Circle Mall Shopping Center, and it was there I had scheduled my first stop of the morning. It was one of the businesses that had ponied up precious advertising dollars to *North Coast Magazine*, and I planned to spend most of my day visiting those businesses, hoping that the persons in charge could shed some light on the whereabouts of Greg Shane. With Dan Mulkey's death, the need to locate Shane seemed imperative—to save him or to stop him, I didn't know which. And somehow knowing didn't seem important.

When we pulled into the parking lot of the minimall, one of

hundreds which seem to be popping up all over town like a plague of locusts, Buddy started to get out of the car. I had a sudden vivid picture of him inside the dancing school and stopped him. "I'd rather you didn't come in," I said.

"Mr. Gaimari said I was supposed to stick close to you, Milan."

"Mr. Gaimari isn't here."

"What if you need a backup?"

I said, "It's a dancing school for little girls, Buddy. What do you think they're going to do, kick my brains out with their tap shoes? Why don't you wait in the car?"

"It's in the eighties," he said, not without some justification. "I'll boil to death."

I looked around. There were several stores ringing the semi-circular parking lot. I said, "There's a bookstore, Buddy. I'm sure it'll be air-conditioned. Why don't you go in and browse?"

He looked at me as if I'd suggested he expose himself in Public Square. "A bookstore?"

"Ask if they have anything by Will and Ariel Durant."

I left him mumbling unhappily and went into the Merlys Mercer School of Dance. There were eight women, none over thirty, most in sweat pants and a few in curlers, sitting in the reception room reading back issues of *Dance Magazine* or *Reader's Digest*. They glanced up at me with a certain degree of suspicion; I looked as if I belonged there only slightly more than Buddy. From the next room I heard a piano, badly in need of tuning. The song was the old Shirley Temple showstopper, "Animal Crackers." The sounds of metallic taps accompanied the music, not always in rhythm.

I said to no one in particular, "I'm looking for Merlys Mercer."

One of the women looked up at me, an interloper, and said, "She's teaching a tap class right now. She'll be finished in about ten minutes."

I thanked her and sat down on one of the deep cushioned couches covered in cracked vinyl. The music stopped and a reedy, high-pitched woman's voice said something I couldn't quite make out, but it held the unmistakable cadence and tone of a teacher admonishing a student, and then the piano started up again, and the tapping with it. I picked up a dance magazine from one of the tables in the waiting room and read a long article about someone I'd never heard of named Alwin Nikolais. When I finished that I read another, shorter article about Mikhail Baryshnikov. At least I knew who he was. I hadn't quite finished my reading when the music stopped again and the woman's voice said something. A thunder of taps came closer, the door to the dance studio flew open, and eight little girls in leotards and tap shoes came blasting out, heading for their respective mothers, full of news about how the lesson had gone. On a well-built young woman, tights and leotards are sexy; on a seven-year-old's flat bottom they're baggy and somehow touching, accentuating the delicacy and vulnerability of little girls. Since both my kids were of the male persuasion, I didn't have much firsthand knowledge of the care and feeding of girl children from babyhood upward—tap and ballet lessons and leotards, tea sets and dolls and Mary Janes for Sunday. I found myself wondering if perhaps the softening effect of a little girl in the house might have made a difference between Lila and me. Probably not, I decided.

I walked through the hubbub in the reception room, Gulliver among the Lilliputians, and into the studio. It was a large room, with floor-to-ceiling mirrors on three sides and a wooden barre running all the way around the room about thigh high—my thigh, not a seven-year-old's. It looked pretty much the way you'd imagine a dance studio in a middle-class neighborhood might look, a little tacky and a little tired. A middle-aged woman with three chins, whose dark red hair showed vivid purple highlights straight out of a bottle purchased in a discount drugstore, was sitting at an old upright piano, gathering up stacks of dog-eared sheet music that had probably gone through a thousand tap lessons. She was wearing black stretch slacks that were just a tad too tight for her ample rump, a white blouse, and a black vest. I figured her for third runner-up in an Ernest Borgnine look-alike contest. Her glasses had rhinestone frames in a vaguely Oriental fashion, with wings that swept up at her temples. On the opposite side of the room was a younger woman with hair so blond it was almost white. She wore leotards and tights similar to those of the little girls, and although she was well into her thirties the effect of the dance clothes was the same as on her young pupils, her figure being only marginally more womanly. She was draping a towel around the back of her neck. It was still early in the morning but she looked exhausted, in the way someone who is sick of her life is exhausted, as though she'd been teaching tap classes nonstop since the dawn of civilization, with only five-minute breaks in between.

"Ms. Mercer?"

She looked up, her greenish-blue eyes all at once startled and afraid. I lumbered across the rehearsal room toward her, my peripheral vision catching my own reflection in the mirrors on all sides of me. I felt like a rhinoceros navigating that long expanse of bare floor. "My name is Milan Jacovich. I wonder if I could have a few minutes of your time?"

She glanced nervously up at the clock on the only nonmirrored wall. "Do you have a child you want to register?"

"No," I said. "This is about another matter."

"Uh, I have another class in fifteen minutes."

"It won't take long," I said. I handed her one of my business cards, and she peered at it closely in the manner of one who needed glasses but was too vain to wear them.

"Security?"

"I'm a private detective."

The woman at the piano squared her linebacker's shoulders. "You want me to stay, Merlys?" Maybe she was a bouncer who doubled on keyboards.

Merlys Mercer looked at her, then at me, then at her again. "Give me a few minutes, all right, Mae?"

Mae sniffed, not exactly offended but a little bent out of shape, gathered up her sheet music, and stalked out into the reception room, where the mothers were toweling off their daughters and bundling them out of the dancing school to their cars. The door closed behind her. It wasn't exactly a slam, but it managed to convey her displeasure.

Merlys Mercer allowed herself a heavy sigh and went over and sat down on one of the metallic folding chairs against the wall, indicating I should do the same. She stretched her legs out in front of her to take all the weight off them and slid down into the chair on her coccyx. "Is anything wrong?" she said.

"Not at all. I just have a few questions I'd like to ask you."

She had very sallow skin with purplish pouches under her eyes, which for some reason made her look as if she belonged in the twenties. I saw that the pale blond hair was her natural color. She wasn't pretty at all, nor was she homely. She was simply one of those nondescript women who goes through life never getting any attention one way or the other, which was the saddest kind of all.

I explained to her quickly why I was there, what had happened with Gregory Shane, and how there was not going to be any *North Coast Magazine* with a story about her. I didn't say anything about Dan Mulkey. When I was through she shook her head in resignation, as though this were one more cross she'd have to add to the already impressive collection she lugged around with her.

"I was a fool," she said, and there was more bitterness in her tone than the situation seemed to warrant. "Mr. Shane was such a good salesman I couldn't say no, but I had a funny feeling about it after I gave him the money."

"What kind of feeling?"

"Like I was being robbed," she said.

I didn't say anything, but I raised my eyebrows a little, which seemed to encourage her to go on.

"I don't really do that much advertising. I make up fliers sometimes that we put on car windshields, and there are some stores and shops here in the neighborhood that let me put up little posters, but I've never advertised in a magazine or a paper or anything. I mean, this is a neighborhood business. If you don't live within four miles of here, you're going to take your kid to some other dance studio anyway. So for me to advertise in a book that's going to be read all over the city is a waste of money."

"Why'd you do it, then?"

She twisted a few strands of her pale hair around her fingers. I had the feeling it was something she did a lot, which could account for her hair being so lank and lacking in body. "Actually, they spoke to my mother first and convinced her. And then she talked me into it."

"Did they promise you an article in the magazine in addition to the ad?"

She nodded. "And the editor—Mr. Pursglove? He came out to interview me a few days later."

"Leonard Pursglove?"

"I believe so, yes. I told him that I was having second thoughts, but he said that the ad had already gone to the typesetters and it was too late to change my mind. And then we talked for a while—he had a tape recorder—and he said thank you and went away, and that's the last I ever saw of anyone from that magazine—or of my two hundred dollars." She looked almost ready to cry.

"I work hard here, Mr. Jacovich," she went on. "I mean, it's just me. I don't have any other teachers, I don't have an accountant or an attorney, I don't have a husband to support me during my slow times." There was such naked sadness to that admission I wanted to look away. "And there are lots of slow times. Tap dancing is a lost art these days, like juggling, or acrobatics. I have to pay the rent on this place, I give Mae ten dollars an hour to play for me, I teach every single class myself—I even clean the studio up at night, including the bathroom. You ever see a bathroom after a hundred little girls have used it? Two hundred dollars is a lot of money to me. And now I'm not even going to have any story or any ad to show for it." She gave her hair an extra little twist. "There never was any magazine, was there?"

"I'm sorry," I said. "Greg Shane was a con man, and *North Coast Magazine* was just a small-time sting."

"Oh, God," she said very softly. She stood up and walked

around for a few minutes, each step accompanied by the metallic taps of her shoes hitting the bare floor. It was like an old radio program, with all the sound effects exaggerated. Her voice was weary. "I don't know why I stay here. Maybe I'll just close up the studio and get a regular job somewhere."

I said, "How'd you get into this business anyway, Ms. Mercer?"

"Oh, the usual way," she said. "My mother wanted to make a dancer out of me. She's a born-again Christian now, plays the organ over at the Foursquare Gospel Church every Sunday and serves on their board of directors, and she thinks that show business is pretty frivolous. But she'd been a dancer in her younger days, or tried to be. She never really got anywhere, and I suppose she's always been frustrated about that. You know, or maybe you don't, dance teachers are always dancers that never made it themselves. So she taught me, she pushed me. When I was fourteen I was a regular on a television show here locally. Do you remember *Stars of Cleveland on Parade?*"

I would have given anything if I'd remembered, but I didn't, and I wasn't going to lie about it. I shook my head.

"That's all right," she said, "nobody does. It was on one of the local stations on Saturday mornings when most kids were watching cartoons and most grown-ups were watching sports. It was on for about two years. No, not quite two years. Anyway, it was kind of a showcase for local people who had some sort of talent. Kids, mostly, but sometimes a couple of grown-ups who sang or danced or played the piano or the trumpet." She laughed at a memory that wasn't particularly funny. "There was a little black boy, couldn't have been more than seven years old, who played the trumpet. He only knew two songs, 'South Rampart Street Parade' and 'Saints Go Marching In.' He'd play one song one week and the other the next. His mother and father used to dress up in their churchgoing clothes and come down to the studio to watch him. They were just so proud! I don't know what happened to him, or if he ever got anywhere with his music. One girl was a baton twirler—she did the same routine every week to a different record. Another boy, about eighteen, wanted to be a comedian. He'd do routines he'd heard professional comics do on television. He was awful, but people laughed. I guess they were laughing at him, not with him, but it didn't matter. And there were a bunch of other people from around here who were on once or twice and then never again. It wasn't a very good show, I guess. But several local businesses sponsored the darn thing. *We* never got any money—we were all thrilled to death just to be on TV. The producer was a pretty good salesman himself, and he talked a lot of people into paying money to keep the show on the air. He went into the music business after that, I understand, and did pretty well with it."

"The music business?" I asked, leaning forward. I guess it was something in my voice that made her stop tip-tapping around and turn to look at me. "Do you remember his name?"

"The man who gave me my 'big break?' How could I forget?" Something in her face got hard and cold, and my initial impression of her as a poor thing evaporated like a drop of alcohol in Death Valley, and I knew even before she answered that she was going to say "Dan Mulkey."

I went into the bookstore to collect Buddy Bustamente. He was engrossed in reading a Peanuts cartoon book.

"Everything okay, Milan?" he said.

"Everything's fine, Buddy."

"They got a lot of books in here."

"It's a bookstore."

"You read a lot of books, Milan?"

"Some."

We started out to the car. He said, "I asked them for that book you told me, but when I looked at it I didn't think I'd like it."

"What book?"

"By those Durantes." He pronounced it the way Jimmy used to. I was glad he was bending down to put the key in the lock on his side of the car so he couldn't see me struggling to suppress my laughter. I didn't know which was the more appealing image—Buddy Bustamente reading *The Story of Civilization* or Will and Ariel Durant singing "Inka Dinka Doo."

"Where we going now?" Buddy said. He was bound and determined to be perky, and it grated on me like fingernails on a blackboard. I didn't know if I could take it all day long.

"West side," I said. "Auto repair shop."

"Could we stop and get a doughnut somewhere?" Buddy said, "I'm getting a little hungry. We don't have to stay there, I'll eat it in the car."

We stopped and got a dozen doughnuts to go, and two large coffees. They came in cardboard containers, which didn't seem to me to be any improvement at all over foam. Buddy devoured five of the doughnuts before we ever got over the bridge.

"Can I come in with you this time, Milan? I won't say anything. I like to watch how you operate. I mean, that's the way you learn, right?"

The trouble with Buddy Bustamente was that I never knew when he was serious or if he was kidding the pants off me. I was to learn that he almost never joked. He was a true naïf. His ingenuousness was not cultivated at all, but natural. I looked over at him. Remnants of doughnut glaze stuck to the corners of his mouth. His eagerness to "help" me was almost puppyish in its intensity, and I was afraid that it might lead to his making a serious mistake. I said, "Buddy, you just stay in the car this time. I'll call you if I need you."

I wouldn't exactly say that he sulked; sulking was too ridiculous a concept when applied to a man that size. But he did get strangely silent, and his lower lip was a bit more extended than normal, and he avoided looking at me during the rest of the drive out to Parma. I got the idea his feelings were hurt.

Parma Automotive was located in that community, a few blocks away from the St. Stanislaus Novitiate, and its owner was listed as one Earl Faggerty, a name which probably had forced young Earl to get very tough very quickly in school just in order to survive. The shop didn't seem terribly busy for eleven thirty in the morning, but then business was bad all over, and I didn't think too much of it. I parked in front of one of the service bays, got out of the car, and said to Buddy, "I'll just be a minute." He didn't answer me.

There was a Nissan Sentra on the rack in the only occupied service bay, and I could see the bottom half of a blue-clad mechanic under it, bleeding the old oil from the crank case. "Hello," I called.

The man came out from under the car. He had the kind of face that made me wish he'd stayed under there. Around six feet tall and thin in a hard, hickory way, he was pockmarked from his hairline to where his neck disappeared into the blue work shirt, which had *Earl* stitched onto a white patch just above the left pocket. His nose had been broken more than once, and in such a way that it now dribbled down his face like a melted ice cream cone. His eyes were a watery blue, baleful like a basset hound's, and his hair might have been blond beneath the dirt and grease. He looked to be in his middle thirties. He didn't say hello back, and the suspicion bristled out of him when he saw me. Maybe I didn't look like the kind of guy whose car needed work.

"Earl Faggerty?" I said.

He nodded.

"My name's Milan Jacovich." I handed him one of my business cards. He took it, looked at it without interest, and gave it back to me. Since he'd left a black, oily thumbprint on its face, I doubted I'd hand it out again.

"So?"

"I understand you took an ad out in a magazine called *North Coast* a few months ago."

"That's my business," he said in a nasal whine. I could hear the twang of southern Ohio in the few words. People who associate Ohio with the big cities like Cleveland and Cincinnati fail to realize how largely rural the rest of the state is.

"I'm trying to locate the publisher, Greg Shane."

"I don' know where he is," he said flatly.

"When was the last time you heard from him?"

He shook his head almost angrily. "Look, I'm busy here."

"It won't take but a minute."

"That's too long," he said. "I don' wanna talk to you." He went back around the Nissan Sentra.

I followed him. "I'm not selling anything, Mr. Faggerty, I'm just trying to get some information."

He looked at me dully. "I got three more cars to get out before closing. I ain't got the time to talk to nobody."

"Could you just tell me how much money you gave *North Coast?*"

"Don' recall." He turned his back on me. He was standing near a long tool shelf that ran the length of the back wall of the shop, from which he took a pack of Camels. He lit one and inhaled. The white cigarette paper was grubby where his fingers touched it.

"Who contacted you first?" I said. "Was it Greg Shane or somebody else?"

He didn't answer.

"Did someone come out here to do an interview with you for a story in the magazine?"

He had only taken two puffs of the cigarette, but he dropped it on the floor and squashed it out with the toe of his grimy work shoe. "I don' wanna talk about it!" he said. "Don' you fuckin' understand English?" His rheumy eyes blazed anger. "Now pound sand!"

"Hey, take it easy," I said.

He came back around the Sentra. He had picked up a lug wrench from the tool shelf and was holding it in his right hand, down against the side of his leg, but I could see his knuckles were white from squeezing it. He walked toward me slowly, slapping it against his thigh, angling for position so he could get a good swing. "I'll take it easy," he growled. "I've eaten about as much shit as I'm gonna from you fuckers. Enough is enough! Now you amble your ass outta here or you're gonna be suckin' floor!"

I couldn't tell if he was more anxious for me to leave or to open up my skull. Lug wrench or no, I thought I could take him, but I could see no reason for making a big deal out of it. I certainly didn't understand why he was reacting so violently, and I

110

would have liked to discuss it with him, but he'd made it clear he wasn't in a talking mood.

"All right, Earl, I'm going," I said, backing up a few steps, my hands in front of me, hoping to make a dignified retreat. But my luck wasn't running that way these days. From behind me I heard a familiar voice.

"Trouble, Milan?"

I glanced to my right as Buddy Bustamente moved past me. I managed to croak out, "Buddy—" but that's about all I had time for.

Earl Faggerty apparently hadn't been impressed by my superior size and weight, but Buddy, who had three inches and seventy pounds on me, was a bit more intimidating. At least, Faggerty had to stop and think for about a quarter of a second. Then whatever was eating at his innards got the better of his judgment, and he reared back like a fastball pitcher and swung the lug wrench at Buddy's skull. I moved forward, but as it turned out, there was no need.

Buddy's left hand was a blur as it flashed up and caught Faggerty's wrist when the wrench was about three inches from his head, seizing and immobilizing it. Faggerty got white around the mouth and grimaced in pain. They stood there straining against one another, hardly moving, a living statue of gladiators in combat. After a few seconds the wrench dropped out of Faggerty's grasp. Buddy held on to his wrist just long enough for Faggerty's fingers to start turning blue, and then, without even using his other hand, he threw the smaller man against the tool shelf. A bunch of tools and nuts and bolts clattered to the floor, to be quickly followed by Earl Faggerty himself, who sat there looking up, wide-eyed, at the looming giant who had just tossed him away like an old Kleenex.

"Go ahead," Faggerty croaked, but his cracking voice belied the challenge. "Do your damnedest. Beat on me, break my arms, kill me if you wanna, but not another fucking nickel!"

I think Buddy wanted to continue the discussion, but I almost barked his name, my voice echoing in the nearly empty garage. He backed off reluctantly, as though feeling deprived at not being allowed to continue, and stood there flexing his fingers, his arms hanging a few inches from his sides. It seemed as if his entire body was quivering.

I said, "I think you have the wrong idea here, Mr. Faggerty."

Faggerty rubbed his sore wrist. "Come ahead," he said belligerently, "but I'll take at least one a you fuckers with me!" Brave words indeed for a guy outweighed and outnumbered, sitting on the floor in a jumble of automotive parts, but they were spoken in a vibrato of fear. It always amazes me how that particular emotion will completely destroy someone's common sense.

"Nobody wants to hurt you," I said.

"Then git you outta my place! Go on, git!" His voice broke with the strain. I figured in another minute or two he'd be hysterical.

"Come on, Buddy," I said.

"Let me fuck with this guy, Milan."

"Buddy . . ."

Buddy took a deep breath, his massive shoulders rising and falling. "You lucked out this time, asshole," he said to the fallen Faggerty. He sounded disappointed, like a kid who'd been promised ice cream and then denied it.

I waited for a moment to make sure the fireworks were over before I walked out of the service bay to the car. Buddy backed out cautiously, not wanting a thrown lug wrench to crease the back of his skull, but there wasn't too much to worry about, because Earl Faggerty stayed where he was on the floor, paralyzed with pain and shock. We got into the car and drove away.

When we had gone about four blocks Buddy turned to me, beaming. "See, Milan?" he said. "Aren't you glad I was around? For backup?"

I was of two minds about that. I think I could have gotten out of Parma Automotive by myself without any violence, which would have been preferable. But it was somewhat comforting to know that Buddy could handle himself so well in a crisis. As fast

112

as he was with his hands, I wondered if he'd ever fought professionally. With his size to go with his quickness, he would have been awesome across a boxing ring. Heavyweight class.

What I wondered about even more was what Faggerty had been talking about when he had sworn, "Not another fucking nickel!" I decided to find out.

10

There is a little Greek restaurant in Ohio City, just across the bridge from downtown, where I had eaten a few times before, once with Ed Stahl for lunch and one time for dinner with Mary. It was called Kukla, not in honor of the television puppet of the forties but, like the puppet, from the Greek word meaning "doll." Buddy and I decided to have lunch there after our encounter with Earl Faggerty, for several reasons: the food was excellent, it was on our way back to the east side, and Kukla was on the list of advertisers that had been skinned when Greg Shane and *North Coast Magazine* had pulled their vanishing act.

We had finished a tangy avgolemono soup and delicious dolmades, grape leaves stuffed with spinach and ground lamb, and Buddy had ordered and consumed two pieces of baklava. We were working on two cups of thick, strong Greek coffee when he asked if I knew where the men's room was.

"I got to take a dump real bad," he said.

"Thank you for sharing that with me," I said, pushing my own baklava away, and directed him to the rest rooms in the back. When he'd gone I asked the Adonis-handsome waiter if I could speak to the owner. Have you ever noticed that all Greek waiters are as handsome as movie stars? And have you ever wondered why Greek movie stars like Michael Constantine and Telly Savalas are not handsome at all?

Peter Kazakis, the owner of Kukla, was closer to Kojak than he was to Adonis, a little fireplug of a man with not much hair and flashing brown eyes. If anyone could have figured out some way to bottle and sell Kazakis's energy they would have made millions. He sat at our table and ordered some Greek coffee for himself.

"Son of a bitch!" was his reaction to the news that Shane's magazine was stillborn. "Two hundred fifty dollars in the toilet! An' I was trying to do that son of a bitch a favor. Son of a bitch!"

"How do you mean, a favor?"

He paused to shout something in Greek at the passing busboy, then turned back to me. "I don't need to advertise," he explained. "Nights, weekends, you can't get in the place. This is the best Greek food in town—in the state, you know?"

"I'd have to agree with that," I said. "Lunch was great."

He beamed. "Sure," he said. "Greek people, you know, they got the . . ." He searched for the right word. "The *knack*. They got the knack for cooking. You ever meet a Greek wasn't a great cook? So I didn't need the advertising. The guy, he say he's starting a new business, I do him a favor."

"Did they offer to do a story on the restaurant, too?"

"They say they gonna 'review' the restaurant," he said. "I don't need no damn review! Everybody knows Kukla's the best. You come in some night, try the lamb."

"Did they do a review?"

"I don't know; little fat sissy guy come out here, ask me a

115

lot of questions, turn on a whatchamacallit, recorder. I tell him how I used to be a ship's cook on a freighter. I come ashore in California, work in a Greek restaurant in San Pedro, then fifteen years ago I come here and open Kukla. They take my money and then waste my time!" He stirred his coffee with a thick finger. "An' the little fat guy, he gets a free dinner out of me, too. Avgolemono soup, Greek salad, souvlaki, spanakopita, roast lamb, a bottle of retsina, and two kinds dessert. I like a man enjoys his food, but this guy, he ate everything but the napkins. Free! Son of a bitch!"

As if on cue, Buddy returned to the table to hear the end of the discussion of voracious appetites, a subject on which he was a qualified expert.

"And they haven't contacted you since?" I asked Kazakis.

"Whattayou think, they gonna call up and say, 'Hey, Kazakis! We gonna take your money and run away now?'"

"I guess not."

"Sure not," Kazakis said. "There's crooks all over. Some come and stick a gun in your face and take, some do it different. All over, the crooks." He looked across the room and loosed a barrage of Greek invective at one of the waiters, who bobbed his head and ran into the kitchen. The waiter might have been a crook too.

I gave Peter Kazakis one of my business cards. "Will you call me in case you happen to hear from them?"

"I ain't gonna hear from them. They probably in South America by now. But if I do, I punch their face for them." Then he brightened. "Hey, you like the food, eh?"

"Very much."

"So you come again, you tell your friends. Best Greek restaurant in the whole Ohio," he said. He rose with a small good-bye wave, yelling at one or another of his employees before he was completely upright.

"So what, Milan?" Buddy said. "You get anything out of that?"

"Just a good lunch. The information we could've gotten over the phone."

"That *was* good. I'm thinking about having another piece of that—what do you call it?"

"Baklava. Forget it, Buddy, it's bad for your complexion. Besides, we've got places to go and things to do."

One of those things was just over the bridge on Ninth Street in a gleaming steel and glass skyscraper that hadn't been there ten years ago. His name was Judd Cowper, and he was a psychiatric social worker, or so it said on the *North Coast* sucker list Jay Adams had given me.

Cowper's office was on the tenth floor and there was an unattended waiting room stocked with current copies of *Psychology Today* and *Forbes* and *Esquire*. A plastic plaque with engraved white letters informed us that a session was in progress and to please have a seat. I looked at my watch; it was 1:35. If Cowper held to the tradition of the fifty-minute hour I had a fifteen-minute wait. Of course, I wouldn't be bored because I had Buddy to talk to.

We'd had a spirited discussion down in the underground garage, and he had pointed out to me that had he not been present when Earl Faggerty got testy I might now be wearing my hair parted in the middle, and he also reminded me of how quiet he had been while I was talking to Mr. Kazakis. The argument I offered—that a psychiatric social worker was unlikely to take a lug wrench to me—did little good, so I allowed Buddy to accompany me upstairs to Cowper's office, although I made it clear he would have to stay in the reception area during the actual questioning. He didn't feel too good about that. *Forbes* and *Psychology Today* were no more to his liking than *The Story of Civilization.*

My calculations had been pretty good. At 1:46 a pretty thirty-something matron came out of the inner office, dressed in a tailored summer outfit and looking almost as though she'd just come from lunch at Danny's with the girls. But she had a wadded-up tissue in her hand; she'd been crying. She didn't look at me at all, but one could hardly be unaware of Buddy, his size and his yellow-brown polyester and his unfashionable mustache and sideburns, and she stared openly at him, no doubt wondering what problems such a person might be bringing to Judd Cowper's couch.

Before the office door could close I stood, crossed the waiting area in two strides, and said loudly, "Dr. Cowper?" The man inside opened the door all the way and looked at me. He was in his forties, javelin slim with salt-and-pepper hair and a fake-tan glow. His tailoring said Fifth Avenue.

"Yes?" he said with the kind of caution usually reserved for an unexpected visit from the Jehovah's Witnesses. His eyes moved quickly from me to Buddy and then to the retreating back of his last patient as she moved out into the hallway.

I told him my name and why I had come, and he didn't look any happier than he had when he'd thought I was going to hand him a copy of *The Watchtower*.

"I have a client coming in ten minutes," he said.

"I won't take any longer than that," I told him as I walked past him into his consulting room uninvited. Maybe I was learning something from Buddy Bustamente after all.

The inner office looked like a yuppie living room. The furnishings were ultramodern without being stark, but there was little feeling of warmth to the off-white sofa, the light blue armchair, the glass-topped desk, and the various diplomas hanging on the ecru-painted walls in black art deco frames. I thought that the troubled people who came to Cowper with challenges they could no longer face might have enjoyed a setting that looked and felt a little more homey. I glanced at the diplomas. The bachelor's degree was from Southern Methodist and the master's was from Duke. Both were made out to Emerson Judd Cowper.

I sat down in the deep cushioned armchair and felt as if I'd been swallowed by a whale. Cowper was still at the door, trying to decide whether or not to throw me out. Another quick look at my companion in the waiting room disabused him of the notion, and he quietly shut us in the office, going around to sit behind the desk.

"I really have nothing to say to you," he said.

"I just have a few questions, Doctor."

118

"I'm not a doctor," he said, "I'm a psychiatric social worker. That's an M.A., not a Ph.D."

His supercilious manner made me long to tell him I had an M.A. of my own, but I didn't think it would serve any purpose. "Actually it would be to your benefit to talk to me," I said. "If I locate Mr. Shane, we might be able to get your money back for you."

"It's not a question of money. I don't like private detectives coming in here and interrupting my office routine."

I raised my eyebrows at him. "Does that happen often?"

"Once is too often," he said, looking at his watch. "And I happen to know that legally I don't have to talk to you if I don't choose to."

He was right about that. Police detectives have a great advantage over private operatives: when *they* question someone they have the entire weight of the U.S. Constitution behind them, and the moral imperative of every law-abiding citizen to do his duty to make our streets safe and our cities a better place to live. Failing that, the cop with a badge always has the threat of stirring things up downtown so that the recalcitrant witness can expect a visit from the building inspector or the department of sanitation or, at the very least, the motor vehicle people. A private investigator such as myself has no such instruments of persuasion, so he has to kill the subject with kindness instead.

"I don't want you to do anything you don't want to do, Mr. Cowper," I said. "There are a lot of other people who were cheated by Gregory Shane, and I'm sure they'd be more than happy to cooperate with our inquiry. I just thought an educated man such as yourself, trained to recognize patterns and variations in human behavior, would be a lot more helpful to me than a plumber or a shopkeeper. That's why I came to you first."

He drew himself up a little straighter at that, and a smile flickered at the corners of his mouth. Bingo, I thought. You never go far wrong when you appeal to someone's ego.

"Well," he said, and cleared his throat. Then he thought carefully about what he was going to say next. "Well, I would

119

like to help. I mean, if you'd made an *appointment* . . ." He consulted his watch again. It was a bright yellow-gold Rolex, and from the look of it Cowper could tell the day, date, month, year, relative humidity, wind velocity, elevation, not to mention the time in Bangladesh, Dubai, or Sierra Leone at a single glance. "Well, just a few questions, perhaps."

"Who first contacted you about the magazine?" I said.

"Well"—he seemed to cherish the word only slightly less than Ronald Reagan—"It was Mr. Mulkey—no, Mrs. Shane, I think, who called me on the phone. I said no the first time. The next day Dan Mulkey called me, and we talked for a while and I finally gave in. Then Mr. Pursglove came here to pick up the money that afternoon."

"The money?" I said. "You paid cash?"

"Why, yes, I—I was going to the bank anyway that afternoon, and I thought—is that important?"

"No, sir," I said respectfully. "Please go on. Did anyone come to interview you for a story?"

"Mr. Pursglove," he said. "He came the next week and we had a nice chat for about half an hour."

"No patients that day?"

"Uh, as a matter of fact, it was late afternoon, after my last client. They're clients, not patients. As I told you—"

"You're not a doctor, yes. And did any of them contact you after that?"

"No, they didn't, to my recollection," Cowper said.

"What kind of interview did Pursglove conduct with you?"

"Oh, the usual thing. He asked me my background, where I was born, where I'd practiced before, how long I'd been in Cleveland, the kinds of cases I handle."

"Where did you practice before, Mr. Cowper?"

He frowned at me. "I don't see where that would be germane to tracking down Mr. Shane."

"Sorry," I said, "just curious." I handed him a card. "Perhaps you'd be kind enough to call me if you think of anything that is germane."

"I hardly think that's a likelihood," he said. The question

about his background had brought back his superiority complex with a vengeance. He tossed my card into a drawer. "And now if you'll excuse me, I have a client waiting."

He walked with me to the door and opened it for me. As I went out into the waiting room I saw Buddy in earnest conversation with another young woman, dressed even more expensively than the last one. She was listening to him intently as he sorted out the problems of her life.

"Listen, honey," he was saying, "a pretty girl like you don't need to hang around with a married man. Get yourself a nice young guy wants to settle down and have babies and make a life for yourself. You're young, you're good-lookin', you got your whole life ahead of you—"

"Buddy!" I said, aghast. He looked up at me with almost a newborn's innocence.

I glanced apologetically at Judd Cowper, who was looking at me like I had set off a stink bomb in his waiting room. "Come in, Miss Lake," he invited his client frostily. The woman gathered up her purse and smiled an uncertain good-bye at Buddy, walking past Cowper into the consultation room the way she might have tiptoed past her father on the way to the woodshed.

When the door closed, Buddy said, "Poor kid. She's been seeing this real louse, keeps telling her he's gonna get a divorce, but every time she asks him when, he tells her it's not the right time. What a loser! So I told her—"

"Buddy," I said, making an effort to keep my voice down. "I wasn't gone five minutes. How in the hell did you find out all about that girl's personal problems?"

"I figure she's gotta be comin' to a shrink for a reason," he said, "so I asked her why, and she told me. Damn shame, a pretty kid like that. So I was tryin' to help her." I opened the outer door and went out into the hall and he trotted along beside me. "Hey, Milan," he said, "what'd I, do somethin' wrong?"

Back at my place Buddy helped himself to a Stroh's while I checked the calls on my machine. There had been three. One

121

was from Victor Gaimari, one was from Marko Meglich, and one was from my ex-wife, Lila. I called her first.

"I just wanted to remind you," she said in a tone so distant that it broke my heart, "that tomorrow at ten are Milan Jr.'s football tryouts, and I know he'd like you to be there."

I chewed on my bottom lip. "I'll try," I said, "but I don't know—"

"God damn it, Milan," she said mildly, "you're the one that wanted him to play football, not me."

Buddy Bustamente wandered into my den, a beer in each hand. He opened both, put one in front of me, and sat down in the chair on the other side of my desk. The idea that he was eavesdropping on a private conversation didn't occur to him.

Lila went on, "You know damn well that I hate the whole idea! I'll be worried sick every day that he's going to get hurt, that he'll get a back injury or a head injury or something. But no, you said football would be good for him. Now you can't even come down to watch the tryouts!"

"Lila, I'm working on a murder case!"

"The police work on murder cases, Milan. You're not with the police anymore. The least you can do is—"

"Lila, I said I'd try."

There was silence on the other end, the kind of silence that shatters eardrums. I knew Lila's silences from long years of experience. I should have been prepared for what came next, but I wasn't.

"All right, Milan, never mind. I'm sure Joe can get off work to come and watch Milan Jr. try out."

The rug suddenly disappeared from under my feet, and the floor along with it, and I was there in limbo, dangling, a hot rock in my throat where my Adam's apple was supposed to be. Joe. Wimpy Joe Bradac, the class nerd, who'd hung around on the fringes of our crowd in high school, who'd hung around the fringes of the neighborhood during our adulthood, and who had moved into Lila's life within a month of our separation, apparently after a lifetime of wishful thinking in her direction. Joe now ate at my table, slept in my bed, and took my sons to movies and ball games and on weekend outings and was tomorrow planning to watch Milan Jr. go out for the frosh football team. While I ran around finding bodies and poking into the lives of strangers. Good old Joe.

"You can tell Joe—"

"What?" she said dangerously.

Like a dud firecracker, I sputtered and then went out. "Tomorrow at ten at the school. Tell Milan Jr. I'll be there, Lila, okay?"

I didn't do a very good job of not slamming the receiver down in its cradle. I hate being manipulated that way, but it didn't surprise me. When it comes to laying guilt, my ex-wife is the midwestern distributor.

Buddy wordlessly handed me the other beer and smiled sympathetically. I guzzled half of it without even coming up for air. Then I put it down and called Marko.

"Two things," he said. "First of all, how's your time tomorrow?"

"I'm still on the case," I said.

"I thought maybe you'd like to come downtown and listen to some tapes."

"Mulkey's? What's on them?"

"I don't know," he said patiently, "that's the whole point of listening to them. It may be several hours of second-rate rock and roll, for all I know. You game?"

"I'll be there at nine," I said. "And I appreciate the invitation. You don't have to do that, you know."

"For old times," he said, "and because for a dumb jock with muscle between your ears you've got a pretty good mind. Whatever's on the tapes maybe we can bat around. You just might come up with something the old lieutenant misses."

"Fair enough. You said two things."

"Yeah, right. They did the PM on Mulkey."

"Let me guess," I said. "Somebody shot him."

"According to our esteemed medical examiner," he told me, "Dan Mulkey died about twenty-four to twenty-eight hours before you found him, helped along into the great beyond by what seems to be a large slug, possibly a nine-millimeter, fired into the back of his neck at close range. The trajectory was upward, and the exit wound was about an inch above his hairline. From what the forensics guys are able to figure out, he was standing at or near the barbecue thing when he was shot, and then his body was dragged across the backyard, through the bushes, and unceremoniously flung off the bluff like an Aztec virgin being sacrificed to the volcano god."

I laughed. It was grisly, but I laughed.

"They're looking for the slug in the grass now—they'll probably find it, too." He paused, and I heard him take a slurp of something. From a coffee cup, maybe? "How do you read it, Milan?"

"That the perp was somebody he knew well."

"Why?"

"The hibachi was in the middle of the backyard. No one could've tiptoed up so close without Mulkey seeing them."

"So it was someone he'd invited over for a picnic?"

"No," I said. "There was only one plate, one set of utensils, and only two hamburger patties. Whoever it was came over pretty much unannounced, but Mulkey knew them well enough to stand there and cook burgers while they talked. And he didn't expect them to put him in the pond, either, or he wouldn't have turned his back."

"See? You're still a cop at heart, Jacovich," he said. "You got anything for me?"

"Maybe a little," I said, and told him about Earl Faggerty's violent reaction to our visit. I edited a bit; I was not ready to spring Buddy's presence in my life—and in this case—on Marko Meglich.

"What does that say to you?"

"That Faggerty's being squeezed about something. What do you suppose he has to hide? A criminal record?"

"I'll run it through the computer, but it won't prove diddly. Half the guys in this town have sheets. Faggerty's an auto mechanic, not a federal judge. A guy fixes your car good, do you really give a damn whether he's a choirboy?"

"I might if he's an ax murderer out on parole. It's something I'm going to have to think about."

Buddy was looking at me with interest when I hung up. He smiled that smile of his, but it didn't entitle him to any information.

"I have to call your boss," I said.

He nodded. "Okay." He was always so damn agreeable it made me nervous.

I dialed Gaimari's office and had to wade through two different secretaries before I got to him. "I'm very concerned about this Dan Mulkey thing, Milan," he said. "And I'm worried about what happened to you last night, too."

"I'm very concerned as to how you found out, Victor. I don't remember seeing anything about my problem last night in the papers."

"Be that as it may," he said, which meant I wasn't going to get an answer. "Do you suppose that Mulkey getting killed has anything to do with Greg Shane?"

"I'm not clairvoyant," I said.

"But what do you think?"

"I think, Victor, that I'm being paid to trace a skip, not solve a murder. And I'm really not too shot in the ass about making daily reports, especially since you are legally not my client."

"Why do you have to talk so tough all the time, Milan? We ought to be friends. We both want the same thing, don't we?"

The bastard had me there.

After I'd finished talking to his boss, I said to Buddy, "Look, tomorrow morning I'm going down to police headquarters to listen to some tapes. I don't think Lieutenant Meglich is going to want you there, and I wouldn't think you'd be all that happy about sitting around a cop shop, either."

He said, "You got that right, Milan. But I thought you're supposed to see your son at ten tomorrow. Football tryouts?"

"Shit!" I exploded, and slammed the beer can down on my desk. Buddy managed to look artless and helpful at the same time. When I didn't say anything else he tactfully and quietly went into the other room. I slumped in my chair, thinking about my options and my priorities, rumbling like a sleeping grizzly just about ready to wake up and eat a Pontiac. The deciding factor was how annoyed I was at Victor Gaimari. I called Marko back and rescheduled our appointment at headquarters for eleven thirty.

Buddy was washing up the breakfast dishes when I went into the kitchen.

"Stop that!" I said. "You aren't the goddamn maid."

"Idle hands," Buddy sang. "Are we going to do anything more on the case now, Milan?"

"We're going to go and see Jay Adams, I think."

"Who's that?"

"The editor of Shane's magazine, or one of them."

"You think he knows where Shane is?"

"That's what I want to find out."

"I can shake it out of him, Milan."

"I don't operate that way."

"It'd just make things go faster."

"I'm in no hurry," I said, "and don't tell me that Mr. Gaimari is."

Buddy shrugged elaborately and finished drying the morning's coffee mugs. When he had put them away in the cupboard he said, "After we talk to this guy, do you think we could get something to eat?"

Adams's apartment house was situated on a twisting, somewhat hilly street near a three-way corner, so that coming at it from the west as we were it was difficult to see oncoming traffic from the bottom of the hill until it came around the curve and was right in your face. A panel truck came roaring around the curve, brakes protesting loudly, and barreled past us about forty miles an hour faster than was safe on such a small residential street. Buddy had to jerk quickly to the right to avoid being plowed under, our two right wheels going up onto the sidewalk. Fortunately there was an ordinance in Shaker banning overnight parking, so most of the residents had either pulled their cars into

126

their garages or up into their driveways. The Celica's engine coughed like an old man first thing in the morning and died. Buddy was busy loosing a string of curses at the driver of the truck, and my heart was beating double time as well with memories of the night before on Cedar Hill, but when I was able to catch my breath, what really struck me about the incident was that the panel truck had the words PARMA AUTOMOTIVE painted on its side.

It couldn't have been a coincidence. I don't believe in coincidence, for one thing. I've never known one to actually occur. For another thing, Parma is clear on the other side of Cleveland from Adams's neighborhood, and there are an awful lot of more conveniently located east side mechanics who can change the oil on a Nissan Sentra. I had to assume that Earl Faggerty, or someone who was driving his panel truck, had just been to visit Jay Adams.

Buddy fired up the car again, bounced the right wheels off the curb, and continued on up the hill until he spotted a parking space. This time he just slouched down in the seat before we could have any discussion about his coming with me or not. This time, as it turned out, I would have been glad to have him along. Mulkey's murder, the attempt on my life, and the morning's confrontation with Earl Faggerty was making me happy Buddy was there.

Buddy thought otherwise. "That was that damn redneck from Parma in that truck," he said. "I got a bad feeling about this. Maybe my going in there is not such a hot idea, Milan. After all, I've got a record."

"You're right, Buddy. Stay in the car."

I checked to be sure my .38 police special was loaded. I had a permit for it. According to the law, even with a permit you're not supposed to carry a loaded gun; you're supposed to keep the ammo in a separate place. But normally I don't throw down on anyone who isn't armed himself, and I can't really see asking an armed adversary to please wait while I put bullets in my gun. The .38 was in a holster designed for shoulder wear, made of ballistic nylon, which is lightweight and hardly makes more of a bulge under a jacket than does the weapon itself. However, since the evening was warm and I wasn't wearing a jacket, I just took the .38 out of the holster and stuck it in the waistband of my slacks. I was wearing tan cords that I'd bought about eight pounds ago, so they were snug around the middle, and I was confident the .38 wouldn't fall into my pants and down my leg.

I went into the building, up the smelly stairway, and down the second-floor hallway to Adams's door. It was standing open. I put my hand on the butt of the pistol. "Mr. Adams," I said. "Are you in there?" I had the feeling he was, and I wished he wasn't. For his sake. I walked into the foyer and then into the living room.

Jay Adams's Smith Corona typewriter was turned on, making a humming noise. In the roller was a piece of paper which seemed to have part of a novel or a short story typed on it. Like so many writers, Jay Adams was apparently attempting to create the great American whatever. But when I went into the kitchen I knew he was never going to finish it. Writing is tough enough at the best of times; with a bullet hole in your forehead it must be well nigh impossible. The smell of cordite in the room was unmistakable, and the blood that was trickling out of the wound in Jay Adams's temple was still fresh. A bullet in the head does strange bloating things to the face, like a sudden jolt of helium. He was lying on the floor next to the range, his legs sprawled out in front of him and his head resting against the oven door. On the tile wall behind the range was a lot of blood and some other stuff I didn't particularly want to think about. Just to his right was a large metallic spoon that had food on it, and on one of the burners a pot of what smelled like lamb stew was simmering merrily. A full pot was warming on the Mr. Coffee on the counter. If the same person had killed both Mulkey and Adams, he seemed to have a penchant for doing it just before dinner. It didn't seem fair that the condemned men had been cheated out of their last hearty meal.

11

At nine o'clock the next morning, a Saturday, I'd already showered and dressed and had coffee and a couple of English muffins and read the paper, and I was ready to leave the house when the doorbell rang. I didn't have to guess who, only what color today's leisure suit would be. Turned out to be black with a white shirt, maybe formal in honor of the weekend. I knew Buddy Bustamente was supposed to be my constant companion while on the Greg Shane investigation, but I had no idea he would also accompany me to watch my older son's football tryouts.

"Aw, I forgot about that, Milan," he said as he fixed himself a heaping bowl of Grape-nuts, which he drowned in milk and buried under enough sugar to form several little peaks across the top of the cereal. Then he poured himself the remainder of

.the coffee and used what was left in the sugar bowl to sweeten it. I was amazed his teeth didn't fall out before he finished breakfast. Buddy had catholic tastes when it came to food, which is to say he would eat anything that wasn't still moving. When he'd taken four giant spoonsful of cereal he beamed one of those cherubic smiles that indicated he had an idea. "Mind if I come along with you?" he said, his mouth full of Grape-nuts. "I love football."

"Buddy, this is my kid."

"I won't say anything, Milan, I'll just kind of watch." He said wistfully, "I haven't seen kids playing for a long time. In the joint we didn't get to see any kids. Except on TV. Come on, please?"

I sighed. If nothing else, Buddy was giving me a great incentive for finding Greg Shane.

The football field behind the high school was in bad shape, burned brown by the summer sun and full of bare patches where the grass had been destroyed by the ravages of the previous winter. A crowd of nervous thirteen-year-olds milled around uneasily on the field, while anxious relatives huddled in the stands for moral support. I had no trouble locating Milan Jr. in the crowd of youngsters; he was the second tallest, olive-skinned and black-haired and with a tendency toward brooding, like his Serbian mother. His shoulders were already beginning to broaden up from his almost nonexistent waist, and a smudge of fuzz darkened his upper lip. His mouth was set tensely, and he squinted hawklike into the eastern sky. He saw me waving to him and nodded almost imperceptibly. He was at that age where any more demonstrative acknowledgment of a parent's presence was considered unmanly. His quick look at my companion revealed no curiosity or surprise, but a slight cock of his left eyebrow indicated his opinion of Buddy's costume.

"Which one's yours, Milan?" Buddy asked.

"The tall one in the red T-shirt."

"Nice-looking kid."

"Thanks," I said. "He's a good kid, too." We sat down in

the bleachers, and within seconds I felt strong young arms around my neck and a soft face pressing against my ear.

"Dad! Dad!"

I reached back and pulled the wriggling youngster around onto my lap. "Hey, champ," I said.

Stephen was nine years old, seventy-five pounds of laughter and mischief, and the light of my life. Blond, sunny and easygoing, he had inherited the genes of the Slovenes from me. I sorely missed seeing him every day. He squirmed around on my lap until we were face to face and gave me another hard squeeze. He was getting stronger all the time, and the hug played havoc with my bruised ribs, but I didn't care. It felt wonderful. "Milan's trying out for the team," he explained, forgetting that was the reason I was there. "Can we all go out for ice cream after?"

"I'd love to, Stephen, but I've got to go down to police headquarters." His face fell. "Important case."

That helped to salve his disappointment. He looked quizzically at Buddy. "Hi," he said, not relinquishing his stranglehold on me.

"Stephen, this is my . . . friend, Buddy."

"Hey, Stephen," Buddy said, devouring the child's small hand with his huge one. "It's nice to meet you. Your dad's told me a lot about you."

"Are you a policeman?" Stephen asked. He probably didn't notice Buddy's wince.

"Are you here with Mom?" I said.

The boy looked away for just a millisecond. "Nuh-uh," he said, and then he looked over my shoulder, and uncertainty flickered in his sky blue eyes. I turned around to the man standing tentatively behind me.

"Hello, Joe," I said.

"Hiya, Milan." Joe Bradac had his hands jammed into the pockets of a light tan windbreaker worn over a blue work shirt, and his thin shoulders were hunched forward. The sun glinted off his glasses so I couldn't see his eyes. Neither of us was inclined to shake hands. "Lila wasn't sure if you'd be here, so I

131

brought the boys. . . . Look, I can come back when tryouts are over. I mean, you want me to split?"

I did, desperately. "That's okay, Joe. I guess you have the right. Sit down and enjoy yourself."

He hovered for a moment, looking down at my son and me. "I'll just . . . be over there," he said, and walked over to the next set of bleachers and sat down by himself, a forlorn figure in the dewy morning. I knew how he felt. I wasn't sure which one of us didn't belong there.

"Who's that?" Buddy growled.

I was almost afraid to tell him. I didn't want him tearing Joe's head off. Or maybe I did. At any rate, I didn't have to say anything. Stephen took care of the explanations for me, in great detail, and when he'd finished Buddy folded his arms across his chest like the guardian of a seraglio and glowered across the bleachers at Joe, who fortunately was looking elsewhere or he might have died of fright.

Down on the field the coaches had split the aspirants into three groups. Milan Jr. wasn't in the first group, and he came over and sat in the first row of the bleachers beneath us. I could see him wrestling with a decision, and when he finally made it he turned around and looked at me.

"Hi," he said. I appreciated his saying hello, as I knew what it had cost him.

"Hi. All set to go?"

"I dunno." His voice was no longer a little-kid voice like his younger brother's, and yet it wasn't the bass-baritone of adulthood either. It was somewhere in between, and sometimes it cracked and hit a high note or two like in the last eight bars of a Benny Goodman solo, and I'd hear him struggle manfully to bring the adolescent croaking down into the frequency range where someone besides a dog could hear it. From the two words I could sense his anxiety. He wanted to make the freshman team very much.

"You trying out for tight end?"

"Wide receiver," he said.

"All right. Don't forget to limber up before you take off

and do any running," I said, wanting to bite off the end of my
tongue the minute I'd said it. Milan had been an athlete all his
young life, and he knew about limbering up without being told.
My attempt at parenting was a miscalculation. It's no wonder
that sons have such problems relating to their fathers. If my
warning upset him he didn't let on. In fact, he didn't say anything.

"Hey, good luck, Milan," I said lamely, "I'm rooting for
you. I'm always in your corner, kid."

"Yeah," he said, and turned his attention to the doings on
the field.

"Talk to you later," I said. I felt silly. Unnecessary. The
fifth wheel, the bull's tits, the fish's bicycle.

Stephen nuzzled into my neck. "Milan's a dork."

"Hey, knock that stuff off," I said, not too gruffly. The
emptiness in my chest was pushing outward against my lungs
and making it hard to breathe. There's a lot more to marrying
and parenting and divorcing than one might suppose before one
jumps in with both feet and does it. Our divorce had not been
my idea, but Milan Junior had never left off blaming me for it,
probably because when a marriage breaks up one of the prin-
cipals has to move out of the house and in the Jacovich family I
was elected, and the loss of his good feelings was hard for me to
bear at the best of times. I called to talk to the boys almost every
day, took them to a game or a carnival or a movie most Sundays
when I wasn't working. But although Stephen's love and need
for me grew more intense each time he saw me, Milan Junior
seemed to be moving farther away. I told myself it was his age.
He was on the cusp between childhood and adolescence and
needed to reject the values of his parents in order to find his
own. But it didn't make it any easier.

As far as I could tell, he acquitted himself well in the
tryouts. He dashed a respectable forty; he caught every pass that
was thrown to him, and he executed the pass patterns just as the
coaches instructed him to. Stephen cheered him on as if the state
championship were on the line. Blood always tells, dork or no.

12

Marko Meglich was a symphony in charcoal gray this morning, including the circles under his eyes. I suppose he hadn't slept much. For the second evening in a row I had interrupted his dinner, or his evening with Brenda or some other bimbette, with the discovery of a dead body. This time I'd even supplied him with a suspect.

"You might as well get back on the force," he said, "if you're going to be doing all our work for us. I mean, think of the pension and the paid vacations, if nothing else."

He waved me to a seat opposite his desk and I took it, thinking of what I'd done last night that was strictly by the book, and what I'd done that wasn't. I had called headquarters from Adams's telephone and asked for Marko, and when he'd called me back a few minutes later I told him not only about Adams's body but about the Parma Automotive truck leaving the scene as though it had been on fire. He had immediately dispatched some of the west side homicide cops to intercept Earl Faggerty, and they had read him his Miranda and brought him downtown kicking and screaming, wearing cuffs on his wrists and plastic bags taped over his hands to preserve any evidence, and even though they couldn't find the murder weapon, they'd booked him on suspicion of murder one.

What I'd left out was the presence of Buddy Bustamente at the crime scene. I had no worries they'd try to pin the murder on Buddy; except for one or the other of us using the bathroom, he hadn't been out of my sight since the dancing school that morning. But Buddy was a convicted felon, out on parole, and letting the authorities know of his involvement in this whole business wasn't going to do either of our reputations any good. So as soon as I'd finished making my phone report to Marko I told Buddy to go home. Then I called Avis and rented a tan Ford Escort, for until my car was operative again. That made me one of about twelve people in the greater Cleveland area under the age of fifty who were not driving a bright red car.

"Someone is killing the executive staff of *North Coast Magazine*," Marko said, fixing coffee for both of us. "One by one." He handed me a foam coffee cup and sipped out of his with some distaste. His lieutenancy still hadn't gotten him his own personal mug.

"Same weapon both times?"

Marko nodded. "Looks like it. A nine can get mean."

"Anything's mean when you get that close."

"I like Faggerty for it."

I shrugged. "I haven't made up my mind about that."

"He does have a sheet, Milan. I looked it up. Grand theft auto in Detroit, receiving stolen property in Dayton, armed robbery in Akron that got thrown out of court on a technicality. He falls for this one, he books a permanent room in the joint." His lip curled. "The little rat. God, he's a scuzz ball."

"Like you said, Marko, lots of people have records."

"Yeah, but lots of people don't have a motive. *North Coast*

Magazine skinned him out of a couple of bucks, and they were apparently trying to milk him for more. Plus yesterday he came after you with intent, which would indicate a violent nature and/or a disturbed mental state. You yourself saw him leaving the vicinity of the murder minutes after it happened. And"—he laid a finger aside of his nose, like jolly old St. Nicholas—"we ran a gunshot residue test on him last night as soon as we brought him in. We'd bagged up his hands when we collared him, just to make sure, and we found deposits of barium, antimony, and lead on both palms. Pretty good evidence he'd recently fired a weapon. What more do you want? Home movies?"

"Both hands?" I said.

Marko pantomimed firing a gun in the two-handed style favored on so many television cop shows. "Just like *Hill Street Blues*."

"It sounds perfect—if he's your man."

"You're not going to turn into a pain in the ass, are you, Milan?"

"When was I ever not? Come on, you have some tapes to play me."

He stood up. "As I told you, we haven't heard them yet. Might be Mantovani Plays Footlight Favorites, for all I know."

I laughed. "I hope you don't talk about Mantovani when you're with Brenda."

"Hell, no. We discuss Whitney Houston and Bon Jovi and the Plasmatics. And I don't know what I'm talking about."

Marko's tape deck was wall-mounted. He slipped in a cassette and pushed a few buttons, and the first thing we heard was Jay Adams talking. "Kukla restaurant, Peter Kazakis." The dead man's voice on the tape gave me a shiver. Marko noticed it and grimaced.

We heard some dishes rattling and then Adams asked a few innocuous questions about the restaurant: how long it had been in business, what kind of experience in the food industry Kazakis had. The restaurateur's answers were one long commercial, similar to the sales pitch he'd given Buddy and me at lunch the day before. Kazakis loved to talk about food, and specifically the food in his restaurant. The whole thing took about ten minutes.

"That was fascinating," I said when the tape ended. "I may not stay awake through all this shit."

"Z city, no question," Marko said, making a few notes on a yellow legal pad.

"Z city? I'll bet you got that from Brenda, too."

"Let's see what the others sound like." He took the Kazakis tape out and replaced it with another one.

This was a new male voice, rich and resonant, with a breathy, almost sexual quality, like a late night disc jockey. It said, "Merlys Mercer School of Dance," and then there was a rattling sound as someone put the microphone down on a wooden table.

"Who's this?" Marko said.

"Merlys Mercer told me that Leonard Pursglove had interviewed her for the magazine."

"With a voice like that, he should be on the radio at four o'clock in the morning."

"Maybe he is," I said. I leaned forward to listen.

PURSGLOVE: Tell us about your school, Merlys.

MERCER: . . . Mr. Pursglove, I really don't want to do this.

PURSGLOVE: Now, we've been all through this with your mother, Merlys. Let's just do this as easily as possible, all right?

MERCER: What do you want to know?

PURSGLOVE: Well, let's see. How early should a kid begin taking dancing lessons?

MERCER: Five years old is about right.

PURSGLOVE: Is that how old you were when you started?

MERCER: Yes.

PURSGLOVE: Can anyone learn to dance?

MERCER: Yes. I'm not saying anyone can be a good dancer, but if you can walk, you can dance.

PURSGLOVE: Have you found any kids in the neighborhood here who have real talent?

MERCER: A few, I suppose. Look, I'm not really comfortable with this. Why don't you just write whatever you want?

PURSGLOVE: Merlys, as long as we're doing this anyway, we might as well make it so it'll do you some good. Why don't you just relax? It isn't so terrible.

MERCER: It is terrible! Could you turn that thing off?

There was a pause, and then the audio presence on the recording clicked off and there was only the sound of the tape running through the heads. Marko got up and pushed the rewind button, raising his eyebrows at me.

"What do you think?"

"She seemed awfully reluctant," I said. "She was so uptight about spending the money, you'd think she'd want the story to be a sales pitch, wouldn't you?"

He nodded and put in another cassette.

PURSGLOVE: The Mentor Academy, Mr. Alex Malleson. Alex, you're the director of this school, are you not?

MALLESON: Oh, cut the shit, Mr. Pursglove, you know damn well I am.

PURSGLOVE: Alex, I'm *trying* to make this sound like an interview. [He sounded wounded.]

MALLESON: Well, we both know what it is, so why are we going through this grotesque charade?

PURSGLOVE: To make it sound legitimate. We want to write about your school.

MALLESON: You know about the school. It's a private academy for rich kids, and that's what it is.

PURSGLOVE: You want me to write that?

MALLESON: Write what you fucking please. Look, we don't hustle business here at Mentor. I don't want a bunch of truck drivers calling up and applying their runny-nosed kids to our school. This is bullshit!

PURSGLOVE: What do you want me to say?

MALLESON: Describe the grounds, say that some of our graduates have wound up at Harvard and Yale. Talk about our science fair.

PURSGLOVE: I don't know about your science fair. [There was the sound of a metallic drawer being opened, then closed.]

MALLESON: Here, here's a brochure. You can copy it.

PURSGLOVE: And what should I write about you?

MALLESON: Nothing!

PURSGLOVE: This isn't much of an interview, Alex.

MALLESON: That's too fucking bad.

Marko switched off the tape deck. "A pattern is forming here. None of these people seem to want the publicity they've paid for."

"Except Peter Kazakis," I said. "He sounded happy as a lark."

"You want to hear more?"

I shrugged. "As long as I'm here."

The next three tapes were with a chiropractor from Mayfield Heights named Edgar DeVille, the owner of a Serbian bakery on St. Clair Avenue, and a gymnastics teacher in Ohio City. All three interviews were conducted by Jay Adams, and missing from all of them was the rancor or reluctance that had characterized the interviews with Malleson and Ms. Mercer.

When I commented on it, Marko observed, "Maybe it's this Leonard Pursglove that rubs people the wrong way. Seems all the tapes he's on get ugly."

"You have any more?"

"A bucketful," Marko said.

We listened to the rest of the tapes. A caterer from Beachwood, a private exercise coach from University Heights, a guy who had a recording studio near downtown, a wedding photographer from Berea, all droning about their services to Jay Adams. A dog trainer, an aquarium store, a guy who collected and sold baseball cards. If someone hadn't shot Adams he might very well have died of boredom: as the afternoon wore on, I very nearly did so.

Then we got to the last tape.

PURSGLOVE: Interview with Emerson Judd Cowper, M.S.W. Dr. Cowper, how long have you been practicing here in Cleveland?
COWPER: That's a stupid question, Pursglove. If you're going to do it, do it right. And I'm not a doctor, I told you that. Why don't I just talk about my practice?
PURSGLOVE: It's your nickel.

And Emerson Judd Cowper proceeded to talk about his practice—ad infinitum: about families in crisis, about relationships in crisis, about marriages in crisis. And about how wonderful he was at "lancing the boil," as he put it, and easing the pressures. Apart from an occasional "I see," or "Uh-huh," Pursglove never got another word in until Cowper finally ran down some twenty minutes later. Pursglove asked him, "Is that it?" If it had been someone else talking about him, Cowper would have come off like a combination of King Solomon and Saint Francis. Since he was talking about himself, the entire interview seemed self-serving and was pretty distasteful. I wondered how Leonard Pursglove ever thought he would get a halfway decent article out of it.

Marko said, "Is there anything in these tapes that tells you who killed Adams and Mulkey?"

I shook my head. "But something isn't sitting right with me."

"Why don't you see if you can locate this Pursglove character?"

I looked up, amused. "Marko, I don't work for you."

"Hell, I know that, Milan. But I did share the tapes with you, didn't I?"

"You did," I said. "As a friend. Your gold shield doesn't impress me much."

"If you'd stuck around long enough to earn one yourself, you might feel different."

"If I'd stuck around that long I would have eaten my service revolver and you know it."

He put his feet up on the desk. The leather soles of his shoes were shiny, hardly worn at all. He didn't have the shoes of a cop anymore. "I've heard it all, Milan, and I don't want to fight with you about it."

"Good," I said. "In that case, I'll go find Pursglove. But it's *my* idea, okay?"

Marko Meglich laughed and shook his huge head. "Such a hard-ass, Milan."

My next visit to Pursglove's apartment did not result in a talk with Leonard Pursglove, but I did get to meet J. Rose. She said she worked days as a schoolteacher and four evenings a week as a cocktail waitress, which is why I hadn't found her in before. I suppose she needed the second job to support the expensive apartment. All she told me was that she didn't know Leonard Pursglove except to nod hello to, and that she thought he was a really attractive man, if you like older men, that is. I don't, so I wasn't very interested.

"When's the last time you saw him, Ms. Rose?" I didn't know her first name, and I couldn't very well call her J. I was standing in the second-floor hallway that ran between the two loft apartments, just outside her door. She was cute, lots of curly blond hair and startling blue eyes that peeked out through oversize glasses. Her pert nose wasn't quite big enough to support the frames. She was wearing a pair of jeans cut off at the top of the thighs to show her excellent legs, panty hose, and white sneakers with red socks. On top she had a scarlet sweatshirt with the ugly logo of the University of Arkansas Razorbacks.

"Last week sometime," she said. "He's home even less than I am. But when he is, he's usually typing."

"Typing?"

"Till all hours. It doesn't bother me—I sleep with the lights

141

and the TV on anyway. But I hear him typing all night long sometimes. I got the idea he's probably writing a book."

That was J. Rose. Still no Pursglove.

Mary came over for dinner that evening. Saturdays we usually spend at my place because she doesn't have to get up and go to work in the morning. I'm not much of a chef, but I had brought a pizza from Little Italy, with everything on it except onion and anchovies, and a bottle of retsina. We sat in the living room, a Slovenian and a Swede eating Sicilian pizza and drinking Greek wine. That's the kind of thing that makes America great.

One of my more recent purchases had been a videotape recorder and player, which I used mostly to keep my sons happy on long, snowy Sundays. But I had rented a movie for Mary and me, *The African Queen*, and as we watched it, munching our overloaded and messy pizzas, I reflected that my life was a lot like the river Kate and Bogey had to navigate, slow and peaceful and sleepy sometimes, and then all of a sudden fast and dangerous and somewhat breathtaking. That was how the Greg Shane case was going, anyway. It's not a bad way to live. At least it's never boring.

"Don't you like the movie, Milan?"

"I'm sorry," I said, coming back from a million miles away. "It's hard to leave things in the drawer sometimes."

"You still haven't gotten on track, hmm?"

"Yes and no," I said vaguely. I hadn't told her about the murders of Mulkey and Adams, and I had neglected to mention someone using me for a shooting gallery duck, either. That kind of thing tends to upset Mary.

She pointed the remote control at the TV and Miss Hepburn froze in the process of swatting a cloud of fierce mosquitoes. Mary said, "You want to talk about it?"

"I don't know," I said. "Mary, when you sell advertising to someone, are they usually happy about it?"

She laughed. "Nobody's happy when they have to write a check, but when people buy time they usually feel it's necessary, and they're pleased to be getting their message across. Why?"

"Nobody ever grumps about it?"

"You're the only grump I know," she said. "Oh, there are occasions when someone's commercial gets cut short or gets put on in the wrong time slot and the advertiser bitches. But for the most part I'd say they were happy."

"That's what I thought," I said. I took the remote from her and *The African Queen* continued its voyage.

We made love on the sofa first. I guess in the course of our relationship we'd done it more than half the time someplace other than a bed. Her sofa, my sofa, my easy chair, on the rug in front of her fireplace, and once even in my car. Mary was an exciting, sensual woman. That was, I suppose, the difference between her and Lila. In all our years of marriage my wife and I had confined the sex act to our bed, at night, and once in a great while in the morning. Sex was something that was taken care of after the kids, the house, the dinner, the family, and the PTA had been dealt with and put in their proper places.

The night had turned somewhat cool, and Mary was wearing my shirt. I had put on the velour bathrobe she had given me for my birthday. It was one of those one-size-fits-all robes, and as big as I was it only came to just above my knees, but I always wore it when Mary was over. When I was alone I preferred my old terrycloth with most of the nap worn away.

The film had long been over, the retsina was gone, and I was working on a beer while Mary sipped a cognac, which I stocked just for her. The stereo was playing cool, almost detached jazz, and the only light in the living room was from the streetlamp on Cedar Road shining in through the window. It was just before midnight. A warm, quiet, sexy time. It made the sudden stridency of the doorbell that much worse. Mary almost jumped out of her skin.

I went to my desk and put the .357 Magnum that lives in the top drawer into the pocket of my robe. The weapon was bigger than the pocket and the butt hung out precariously. Mary's eyes grew wide. She didn't know about the attempted

143

shooting two nights before, and I didn't have time to explain it to her.

I looked through the fish-eye peephole in the apartment door; in the dim light of the hallway I could see a man. He was wearing a sky blue jogging suit, and other than that I couldn't tell much about him due to the distortion of the lens. "Yes?" I called out.

"Milan Jacovich?" The voice sounded hoarse and shaky. "I gotta talk to you. Please!"

The urgency made me incautious enough to unlock and open the door, my right hand lightly touching the Magnum. The man on my threshold was six feet tall, about fifty, with a balding crown and long unkempt curly gray hair. A network of red lines crazed the whites of his blue eyes. He was developing a potbelly and had a bulbous nose hanging over a girlish mouth that worked constantly, the tongue flicking out, the lips pursing and stretching. He kept looking over his shoulder. He could have sat for a portrait of a terrified man.

"Jacovich?" he said again. I nodded, and he brushed past me into the living room. Mary stood up quickly, pulling the tails of my shirt down over her thighs, as she wasn't wearing anything else. My visitor was in such a bad way that he didn't even glance at her. He turned as I followed him in.

"What do you want?" I said.

The tongue darted out and collected a fleck of white saliva on his lower lip. "I hear you've been looking for me. I'm Greg Shane," he said.

13

The man must have had a hollow leg. Within half an hour he had half finished the bottle of Courvoisier that Mary had only started the evening before. He paced my living room as if it were a cage, swirling the brandy nervously in the snifter, occasionally standing with the snifter in one hand and the bottle in the other while he told his story. In a way he reminded me of Buddy. He was one of those childish men whose seeming lack of guile conveyed a certain charm. He would have been at home on the sales floor of a Dodge dealership.

"Look, I'm a hustler," he said. "I admit it. I've been a hustler all my life, looking for the angle. So I come to Cleveland, I start looking around, and I get the idea for the magazine. It's a good idea; it's the kind of thing Cleveland needs. So who says a guy can't make a buck? I'm entitled, no? My idea. I break my back, that's it. Strictly on the up-and-up." His eyes filled with tears. "I swear to God it was on the up-and-up, Mike."

"Milan," I said.

He gave a comical shrug. "You oughta call yourself Mike. Americanize it. It's tough enough surviving out there without being saddled with a Jew name."

"It's a Yugoslavian name," I said.

"Not you, me. Harvey Schoenstein, that's my real name. Do I look to you like a Harvey Schoenstein? Harvey is a name for a dentist, for Christ's sake! Guys don't want to do business with a Harvey—or a Milan. Greg. Mike. Good, solid names. The good guys are named that."

Mary, who had gone in and put her clothes on before Shane began talking, stood up with a barely concealed smile. "Want a beer, Mike?" she said.

"So," Shane went on. "I want to do a magazine, but I can't do it alone. What do I know from magazines, right? Let's face it, Mike, I'm no rocket scientist. I'm a salesman, that's what I do best. So I figure I'd better bring some people on board who can find their ass with either hand, right? I ask around for an editor, I get the name Jay Adams from ten different people. I call him up, I meet with him. So he's a fat, ugly little fageleh, so what? He knows lots of people in the artsy-craftsy set. Got no less than Ms. Edna Warriner to write a story for our premier issue. Not bad for openers, huh?" He waited for me to nod an affirmation before going on. "I judge a guy on what he can produce. And the man is fantastic. I mean he used to literally *shit* ideas." He poured himself another slug and made it disappear. No one ever told him you're supposed to sip cognac.

"So you hired him?" I said.

He wagged his head from side to side. "Hired, no. What was I going to pay him with, Monopoly money? He knew I didn't have the bread to hire him. I took him in as a partner. My wife Nettie would do the cold-calling—she's great at that—I'd do the selling, he'd do the writing. Fair or not fair, I ask you?"

146

He didn't wait for an answer. "Then when the little fag tried to hold me up for money, I told him to go fuck himself."

"You're getting ahead of the story, Mr. Shane."

"Greg. Call me Greg. I interrupt your fooling around, I drink your booze, I open up my heart to you, and you're gonna call me mister? Yeah, all right, so?"

"Where did Dan Mulkey come into the picture?"

"Mulkey knew everyone in this town, the politicians and the show business and the sports people. He could get us in places I couldn't go alone, or Jay Adams, either."

"And was he also a partner?"

Greg Shane drew himself up straight and looked at me with his chin on his chest, a gesture made less pixielike by the roll of fat under his chin. "I let him have a little taste, sure. Why not?"

"How did Jay Adams feel about that?"

"I didn't ask him. It was my magazine."

Mary came back with a beer and said, "Here you are, Mike."

I let her know by my look that she was going to have to stop that. To Shane, I said, "And Leonard Pursglove?"

"Ah," he sighed. "Leonard Pursglove. A class act, believe me. A handsome guy, he could get elected president of the United States on his looks alone. He's the kind of guy you want up front. The kind of guy can go in and talk to a Vivian Truscott, to a governor, to a movie star. You're not ashamed of him, you know what I mean? You need a guy looks like that, that presents himself like a mensch, up front. So I brought him along to handle the big stuff, to give the magazine class. Is it class, a fat little fairy wearing a dress going around saying he's the editor?"

"Editor in chief," I reminded him.

"Listen, he could call himself the mahatma for all I give a damn. It was my magazine."

I was reminded of a child refusing to share a new toy with his brothers and sisters. I said, "So what happened?"

"We started selling ads. It didn't go like I thought it would at first. A couple of bucks here, a couple of bucks there, the money just wasn't coming in. It was going *out,* all right. You wanna know what my phone bill was for those two months? Twenty-eight hundred and something dollars, seventy-two dollars or something, was my phone bill those two months. And the printer wanted money and the photography lab wanted money and—"

"How were you going to distribute this magazine?"

He affected a coy look. "Well, I found out there was no way I could have ten thousand copies printed up; I couldn't afford it. Best-case scenario, I couldn't afford it. So what I was going to do—just for the first issue, mind you, after that it was going to be strictly legit—was to have a print run of a thousand copies, and we'd all take them around by hand—me, Nettie, Danny, Lenny, and Adams—to the little convenience stores and markets near where the advertisers lived and ask the store owners to put them on the shelves, free, and whatever they sold they could keep the money." He sensed my disapproval. "Mike, it was short-hairs time." He got all teary again. "This was my dream, Mike, nobody was going to crap on my dream."

"So what happened?"

"*Oy.* What didn't happen? So Jay Adams and his little friend have the boards made up, and when I go to get them he tells me he won't give them to me unless I fire Pursglove and come up with twenty-two hundred dollars. I don't know where he got that figure."

"And?"

"And?" he said, outraged. "I don't have a fucking magazine and I don't have the money to pay him and I don't have the money to give back to the advertisers."

"Where did the money go?"

"I spent it! I had to eat, I had to live! My wife isn't well, there were doctors, lawyers. God knows what all." His voice started quivering again and he had to take a deep breath to get himself under control. He'd taken so many of them during his little recitation, the room was running out of oxygen. "I ran, Mike. Like a thief, I ran. I had to. I had nothing else I could do.

They were going to put me in jail. For a lousy eighteen thousand and change. I swear to God, on my wife's life, I didn't want to do that. I started out with a legitimate proposition."

"Eighteen thousand?" I said, feeling the back of my neck prickle.

"Sure, and that was gross! Never mind what I paid out for phones, for gas, for copying. All that ad money, it was nickels and dimes. The biggest ad we sold was for four hundred dollars."

"To whom?"

"The big hotel out on the west side."

I stood up, jamming my fists into the pockets of my robe. "Are you sure?"

"Sure I'm sure, what do you think? It was my fucking magazine." He turned to Mary. "Sorry, darling, I've got a mouth like a sailor when I get excited, I didn't mean offense to you." He crossed the room in three long strides, from the window to the door and then back again, his rage threatening to break out of its box. "If I get my hands on that little fag Adams I'll make it so he likes women!"

"What?" I was beginning to feel like the guest of honor at a mad tea party.

He smiled sadly, if indeed it can be called a smile when the corners of the mouth are pulled straight down. "Just a way of talking, Mike. I'm not a violent man."

"When you ran, Mr.—Greg. When you ran, Greg, where did you run to?"

"I don't know if I can trust you with that, Mike. I know you're after me. I'm in the area, let's say."

"Who told you I was looking for you?"

The Cheshire Cat in him said, "That's my little secret."

"And you haven't talked to Adams since?"

"No," he said, "or Mulkey or Pursglove, either. And I've tried. Been calling for two days now."

I looked at Mary. This was going to be a biggie for both of them. "Greg," I said. "Sit down."

"*Oy!*" he said. "When it's 'Greg, sit down' that means I'm

not going to like this part. What? What else could happen to me?" He poured and drank another two fingers of cognac. "What gives, Mike?"

"Greg . . . Jay Adams and Dan Mulkey are dead."

Beneath the one-day growth of beard his face turned the color of buttermilk. I've never seen a man so terror-stricken.

I kept my voice level. "Shot to death. Both of them. And someone who thought I was getting too close took a potshot at me last night."

He staggered to a chair and sat down heavily, his palm pressed to his chest as though he were pledging allegiance. I was afraid he was going to check out right there. Mary had her hand to her mouth, and her eyes drilling into me were the size and color of delft dessert plates. When this Shane business was over, Mary and I were going to have a talk about murder. I felt it coming.

"Jesus," Shane said. He was hyperventilating.

I lit a cigarette so I'd have something to do with my hands. Anything I would have said to him he wouldn't have heard anyway. And I couldn't think of anything to say to Mary.

Finally Shane said, "Who would do that?"

"I was hoping you'd know. The police are hoping the same thing."

He shrank back, once more the hunted prey. "What police? What do they want with me?"

"The bunco squad wants to talk to you about all the money you stole," I said.

"I didn't steal it! It was my money!"

I let that go. "And homicide finds it very strange that your former employees keep dying. They're wondering if you have any thoughts on that."

He leapt out of his chair as if fifty thousand volts had just hit his butt. "I'm not taking any murder fall," he said. "You can't make me, Mike!" And all of a sudden there was a gun in his hand, a little nickel-plated twenty-two that you'd use to shoot mice. Mary made a funny noise across the room, but he didn't even look at her. He waved the gun in front of my face,

150

making a breeze. "I should have known better than to trust you," he said. "I came to you for help and you're trying to pin a murder rap on me." There were little bubbles of spit at the corners of his mouth.

I reached out and batted the gun out of his hand with one swipe. He hadn't even had his finger through the trigger guard. Then I slapped him across the face three times, the kind of slaps that sting and humiliate but don't injure. "You little shit," I said, "you ever pull a gun on me again you'll wear it home!"

I pushed him backward and he stumbled and fell onto the couch. He fingered the red marks on his face where I'd hit him, and then he started to cry, rolling over onto his side on the couch and drawing his knees up against his chest. He was sobbing full out, in loud, elongated wails. If it was an act, he belonged on the stage of the Playhouse.

Mary had stopped being frightened and was staring at Shane with something that looked like pity. I said, "Mary, maybe you'd better go on home."

"From the motion picture *Fat Chance*," she said.

I picked up Shane's toy gun and unloaded it, putting the bullets in my pocket. Then I tossed it on the couch next to him. He was moaning, "Oh, God!" through the fingers he'd spread across his face, rocking himself back and forth like an Orthodox Jew at prayer. I let him sob it out.

Finally he sat up. "Sorry," he said. "I lost it there for a minute."

Mary said, "Have another drink, Mr. Shane."

"No. Thanks. Too late for that. Mike—Milan. Help me."

"I don't know what I can do, Greg," I said. "I already have a client, and my job was to find you. I guess I did that. Now, are you ready to talk to my client, to make some sort of restitution?"

"With what?" he said. "I have six hundred dollars in the bank. With what I owe on my car you couldn't get more than another twelve hundred out of it."

I shrugged.

"I'm not going to jail," he said, as firm as he'd been since he got there. "Not for fraud and not for murder. I didn't kill anybody."

"For what it's worth," I said, "I believe you."

"Look," he said, "give me some time. Give me forty-eight hours. To raise the money. Part of it, anyway."

I looked at him skeptically. He put his hand over his heart, pledging allegiance again. "You've got my word."

"Where are you, Greg? Where are you staying?"

His smile was sickly. "I can't tell you that," he said.

"I see. I'm supposed to trust your word, but you can't tell me where I can find you. In forty-eight hours you could be in South America."

He took another one of those vacuum-cleaner deep breaths. "Okay," he said. "I have a friend out in Madison who's away for the summer. We're staying there."

I took a pad and pencil from my desk and handed it to him. "Write down the address and phone number," I said. "And you'd better be there. You screw me, Greg, and you're going to wish I gave you to the cops."

"I swear to God, on my wife's life," he said, jotting some numbers on the pad before handing it back to me. He looked at Mary and smiled weakly. "I'm sorry, honey," he said. "I didn't mean to ruin your evening."

"Monday night," I said, "nine o'clock. Be here."

After he'd left neither Mary or I said anything for a while. She fixed herself another drink, and I went to the refrigerator for a Stroh's. I came back out and said, "Someone is lying. He claims he only collected a total of eighteen grand; Richardson Hippsley-Tate says Shane took forty-two grand from the Lake Shore Hotel alone. Damn, this is getting complicated."

It was as if I hadn't spoken at all. She didn't answer or make any acknowledgment, but just held her gaze level with mine, cradling the snifter in both hands. Finally she said, "Milan, what's this about you getting shot at?"

"I guess it slipped my mind," I said. "Look, Mary, I know how you feel, but—"

"No, I don't think you do," she said. "I'm just a simple kid

152

from Boston. I put on a power suit every morning and go in to sit at my desk and do my job. Not much shooting goes on down at Channel Twelve. I don't like it, and I'm having trouble handling it—people shooting at you, waving guns at you, people getting murdered. My God, I never thought I'd ever have to use that word in my life! Is this the way of things with you? Is this always how it's going to be? Every time you leave my bed am I going to have to worry you're never coming back?"

"Mary, this is how I make my living. It's what I've been trained to do. For every time it gets rough, there are a hundred other times it doesn't. I set up industrial security systems, once in a while I look for a missing spouse or a partner who took off with the cash receipts. It's a job, like anything else. If it gets hairy sometimes, it's not much more dangerous than driving the freeways in a snowstorm during rush hour."

She sipped her cognac. "I've never seen anyone wave a loaded pistol around before. Only on TV. He could have killed you, Milan. He could have killed *me*."

"He didn't, though. And he wouldn't have."

"How can you be so sure?"

"You saw him, Mary. He's no killer. He's a scared little guy who talks fast so no one can keep up with him."

"*Somebody* killed those other two men," she said.

"Yeah. But I don't think it was Shane. First of all, the other two killings were done with a much bigger gun. You think he's got a whole collection but he decided to bring the little one tonight? Besides." I walked over to the sofa and pointed at Shane's little nickel-plated popgun. "Killers don't leave their guns behind."

"Not very comforting, is it?"

"I can't give you any comfort, Mary, other than to tell you the police have a suspect in custody. A car mechanic named Earl Faggerty."

She laughed in spite of herself. "If my name were Faggerty I'd want to kill somebody, too."

"But I don't think he's the one, either. He's just another scared little guy who got caught in a squeeze."

She shrugged. "There goes the last of my comfort."

"I don't know what else I can tell you," I said.

"I don't know, either. But your business scares me, Milan, more than I can say." When her blue eyes got wet they looked even more beautiful than usual. "I'm not sure I can live like this."

She put down her drink and picked up her purse. "I think I'd like to go home now, Milan. I don't much feel like making love again, and I'd be pretty rotten company. I'm sorry, but I need some alone time, to think." She cupped my face in one hand and kissed me on the mouth quickly and without passion. "I'll call you next week," she said.

And she was out of the apartment and gone.

I stood there looking at the closed door, the way people sometimes stare at inanimate objects as though waiting for the objects to do something. Then I moved heavily to the couch and sat down. Greg Shane's gun dug into my left buttock and I shifted a little and pulled it out from under me. I looked at it and tossed it to the other end of the sofa.

Now I had some alone time of my own.

14

Never again.

Isn't that what every drunk in the world says when he wakes up with an old gym sock in his mouth and battery acid eating into his gray matter and curare-tipped darts in his eyeballs? Hangovers are so vividly unpleasant that it makes me wonder why the alcohol industry didn't go belly-up years ago, along with the manufacturers of whalebone corsets and buggy whips. My knowledge of my own body and the way it rebels against an overabundance of spirits should have stilled my pouring hand, but Saturday night had been special. The bottle of retsina I'd shared with Mary at dinner, followed by a six-pack and change and capped off by a third of a bottle of Courvoisier after Mary's abrupt departure, had done its dirty work and put me to sleep when all else had failed, but I was paying for it in the morning. Even my hair hurt.

I had slept in my underwear, which is not my habit, and I felt scummy and rank as well as sick, so I staggered to the shower and stayed under it until the hot water ran out, and for a few minutes after that. The icy spray I considered part of my penance. I blotted myself dry and lurched to the basin to shave. A debauched and dying monster glowered out at me from the mirror. It's not easy being green.

I'd always heard a bloody Mary is good for what ails you the morning after, but I was short both vodka and tomato juice, and I didn't think drinking the Worcestershire sauce straight would be much help, so I settled for a pot of strong coffee, which made my stomach do triple somersaults in the tuck position. I suppose I could have gone out for a bloody Mary, but my eyes weren't ready for the light of the sun just yet, and besides, I was damned if I would be caught in some sleazy bar on a Sunday morning. I tried to get my thoughts in order, but it was just too soon.

I went to the door to pick up my newspaper, but it wasn't there. Not unusual. At least four times a month they either forget to deliver it or one of my neighbors snags it. I groaned. I could live without the Sunday edition of the *Plain Dealer;* it was just that it was one more portent for a bad day. I went back to my kitchen and finished the pot of coffee and lit up my first cigarette of the morning. It tasted like burning hemp. I stubbed it out, but five minutes later I lit another one. It was not yet nine o'clock.

The telephone sounded like fingernails on a blackboard.

"Buddy here, Milan," he chirped. "Are we working today?"

I took the verb to mean "functional," and since I wasn't, I started to laugh.

He sounded almost hurt. "What's so funny, Milan?"

I got my laughter under control—it hurt too much. I mean *physically* hurt. I said, "Buddy, I'm paying another police station visit this morning."

156

"Gee," he said. "You hang out with the cops a lot."

"I'm not sure I'd like your friends, either," I said. "Why don't you meet me at DiPoo's at one o'clock, and we'll go from there?"

"Sounds like a fag bar," he said.

"Well it's not." I gave him directions to get there and hung up, sitting with my hand on the phone until the vertigo went away. Then I dialed Marko Meglich's home number. It rang five times before he picked it up. He was breathing heavily.

"Milan, for Christ's sake," he said, "it's Sunday."

"Damn, I'm going to be late for church," I said. It wasn't terribly witty, but considering the pain I was in, it was Eddie Murphy on one of his good nights. "Marko, I want to talk to your prisoner. Can do?"

"What prisoner?"

"What prisoner do you think? Earl Faggerty."

I heard another voice in the background before Marko put his hand over the mouthpiece. It was a feminine voice, and sounded about eight years old. "Milan, this is my day off. I don't want to get out of bed and go down to the store."

"I don't blame you, under the circumstances."

He got defensive. "What's that supposed to mean?"

"Marko, I don't give a damn about your sex life. I cheer for you. But I had a visitor last night."

"The tooth fairy?"

"It was Greg Shane."

There was a pause and then a whistle. Marko evidently didn't know that when you whistle into a telephone it sounds like Hurricane Hattie on the other end. I held the receiver away from my head until the gale subsided. He said, "I guess we need to talk."

"I see Faggerty first, Marko. Quid pro quo."

"Don't talk dirty on the phone," he said. "When do you want to do this?"

I looked at my watch. "An hour?"

He muffled his end with his hand again and said something

157

to his companion. Then he came back. "Make it two hours, okay?"

I smiled to myself. One for the road. "I'll see you at eleven, Marko."

"Yeah," he said before he hung up. "It just might be useful."

The way my head felt, I was as useful as a prima ballerina on third and goal from the two. But I wasn't going to argue with him.

I stopped at the corner and spent some quarters getting a newspaper out of one of those boxes. I took the second one from the top. Like everyone else, I always do that when I buy a newspaper from a machine. I don't know why. There aren't any more germs on the top one as on the one underneath. Maybe it's some sort of primal memory we all develop from not taking the end slice of bread from the loaf because the ones in the middle are fresher. Leave the stale ones for the next guy. I carried the paper to Corky and Lenny's Deli on Cedar Road and ordered a grapefruit juice and scrambled eggs with a bagel and cream cheese. And of course, coffee. The way my head was pounding, I should have had the chicken soup, although I don't know if its fabled medicinal properties extend to hangovers. And reading about the Indians' fifth whipping in six games didn't make me perk up much, either.

An hour later I pushed through the big wood and glass doors of the downtown police station and wondered how people who weren't as big as I am and who never played football managed to get in. Those are heavy doors. I was spending too much time at the cop house lately, and I didn't even have a retirement pension working for me. I was going to have to go back to industrial security, where the hours were regular. The kid at the desk had a custom-tailored uniform and looked like he spent most of his evenings in Shooters or some other upscale pickup joint. He probably did pretty well, too. Flat-assed and flat-eyed, with a neat blond mustache to match his helmet of well-barbered hair. Probably a year out of the academy. I wondered if after fifteen years behind a badge he'd develop a potbelly and a taste for teen-age girls like his lieutenant. He was exceedingly polite when he asked me to sign in, and he gave me a visitor's badge and directions to Marko Meglich's office that I didn't need. He even called me "sir." I didn't like that. It meant that I must look as old as I felt.

Marko met me at the door to his office wearing a Browns sweatshirt with a hood. It showed off his paunch. He was scowling, probably because he'd left Brenda, or a Brenda-clone, in bed to meet me here. I was jealous. All I'd left in bed that morning was one of my socks. He led me downstairs into the holding area where they kept the prisoners, as if I didn't already know the way, and told the sergeant in charge to bring Faggerty to an interrogation room.

"I want to talk to him alone, Marko."

"That wasn't part of the deal. You're not his attorney, you know."

"If you're in the room, he'll clam up. You know these red-neck types, they won't talk to a badge. It's in their genes from when their granddaddies made moonshine hooch."

"I can't do it, Milan."

"Then I can't talk about Shane."

He stood there in front of the sergeant's desk, his hands on his hips, breathing through his teeth. "That's withholding evidence," he said. "In a murder investigation."

"It's not evidence," I said. "It's a favor—for a favor."

He patted his hair down. It was thinning almost as much as mine was. Slovenians have a tendency to lose their hair early, as opposed to Croats and Serbs, who usually sport a thick dark mane until they hit fifty, at which time it turns white and looks like Marlon Brando's in *Superman: The Movie*.

"All right, Milan," he said. "But if my ass goes in the vise I'm taking you over the side with me."

"Don't mix your metaphors," I said.

"Tell me about Shane."

"Okay. Either he didn't know Adams and Mulkey were dead or he's the best actor I've ever seen."

"Why's he hiding, then?"

"He was hiding before the murders, Marko. He got caught in the squeeze of big ambition and small talent. He collected all this money from his advertisers and was buying groceries with it, hoping the magazine would go. When it didn't, he ran."

I didn't tell him about the discrepancy in the amount of money he said he collected from the Lake Shore Hotel and the sum Richardson Hippsley-Tate said he paid. I hadn't figured that out yet.

"Where is he?" Marko said. "Where's he hiding out?"

"What's the difference?" I said. "You've got your killer behind bars now, don't you?"

Marko's ears got red. "I meant what I said before. When the fit hits the shan, I'm not hanging alone."

"Just like high school, huh?"

"What do you mean?"

"Oh, come on, Marko, you remember our junior year. You were booking bets on the college football games, nickel-and-dime stuff. You got caught and they asked you the names of the kids who were betting with you. You sang like Bruce Springsteen on tour."

He shook his head. "Jesus, we were fifteen years old, Milan. Are you still pissed off?"

I had to laugh, even though it hurt my head. "No," I said, "but for twenty-five years I've been meaning to tell you I thought it stunk. Where's Faggerty?"

The interrogation room had all the ambience of a burial crypt. The walls were covered with that institutional green paint that all city treasurers seem to get on sale, and there was a folding aluminum table and two chairs. The one window was seven feet above the floor and barred on the outside. Two of those six-inch aluminum foil ashtrays were on the table, one on either side. They had recently been dumped, but I don't think they'd actually been cleaned since the building was erected.

When a uniformed sergeant brought Faggerty in, the wiry little mechanic took one look at me and turned to go—he remembered I had been at his shop with Buddy Bustamente, and I guess he figured he'd be happier in his cell. But the harness bull growled at him in a voice like a jackhammer to sit down. He sat down. I would have, too, if I'd been he.

When we were alone, Faggerty hunched in his chair with his head down, expecting the rubber-hose treatment, I suppose. I said gently, "You want a cigarette, Earl?"

He jerked his head up and down, and I took it for an affirmative. I gave him a Winston and lit one of my own. He sucked in the smoke; it was probably his first cigarette since his arrest.

"Remember me?"

He made a sound.

"Earl, I'd like to help you if I could."

"Why?"

"Because I think they've got the wrong guy."

"Fuckin' A," he said.

"But you've got to help me a little, too."

"They got me locked up, man," he said. "I can't help nobody."

"Let's find out. Let's talk a little. You know I'm not a cop, right?"

"Naw, I don't know that."

"I gave you my card the other day. Didn't you look at it?"

He looked down again, and his prominent ears reddened. "I don't read so good," he said.

"Okay. Well, my name's Milan Jacovich and I'm a private investigator. I'm not with the police."

"Then what you doin' here?"

"Trying to help you, if you'll let me. Remember on Friday I came by the garage and asked you about Greg Shane?"

His head jerked up and down again.

"You must have thought Shane sent me, right? And you said I wasn't going to get another nickel. Right? What did you mean by that, Earl?"

"I didn't say that." His lie didn't fool either of us.

"Come on, Earl. What did you mean?"

"I can't talk about it."

"Why not?"

He looked around the room, searching for hidden cameras or microphones or two-way mirrors. I assured him there were none, hoping I was right.

"Still can't say."

"Earl, I don't know what you're hiding, but it's sure as hell not as bad as murder one. The cops have a nice little room with steel walls and a bucket to piss in all reserved for you—for permanently. Now, whatever your problem is, it couldn't be as bad as all that." I reached out and touched his shoulder, and he jumped a mile. I had the feeling that in his whole life, every time anyone had touched Earl Faggerty it had been with intent to hurt. I took my hand away. "You may not know it, Earl, but I'm your friend. Maybe the only one you've got that can help you."

"Aw, jeez," he said. He put his hand over his eyes. "Aw, jeez!" Then he looked up at me. "Do you swear to God that if I talk to you, it's just between us? 'Cause I'm doing no more time."

"Cross my heart," I said. "You tell me you didn't kill Jay Adams, and I'll only use what I need to help you out of here. How's that?"

He hesitated. "I don't know," he said.

It took me another five minutes or so to convince him. The room was airless, stuffy, and by the time he was ready to talk I felt like I ought to be in intensive care.

"Start at the beginning," I said.

"All right, then. First off, I get a call from this lady 'bout some magazine or somethin'. I say I'm not interested. Say I got all the business I need. The next day some dude comes around and puts the arm on me for two thousand bucks."

"Two thousand dollars?"

"Fuckin' A."

"He slapped you around?"

He gave me a disgusted look. "Shit, nobody messes with me that way—'cept that fuckin' *ox* you brung around."

"Well, what do you mean, he put the arm on you?"

"Said he'd . . . tell the cops certain things about me if I didn't take an advertisement in his shit-rag paper." He pronounced *advertisement* with the accent on the second syllable.

"What things?"

Faggerty checked the room over again for spies in the woodwork. He said, "Running your own business ain't easy, okay? Sometimes to put the bread on your table you got to do certain stuff."

"What stuff?"

He slumped, defeated. "You know what a chop shop is?"

"Sure," I said. "It's a place that takes in stolen cars, strips the parts off, and sells them. A good chop man can take a car apart in an hour so the owner wouldn't even recognize it."

"Well . . ."

"Are you telling me Parma Automotive is a chop shop?"

"Not all the time!" he protested. "I do good work, got lotsa good customers wouldn't trust their wheels to no one else. But every so often . . . sure. I'd do a job now and again."

"Where do you get the cars?"

He set his mouth in a thin line and shook his head.

"Okay, Earl, I like that, not ratting on your friends. Let's talk about this guy, now. You gave him two thousand dollars to keep quiet?"

"He didn't put it just like that. He said he'd give me an ad in the paper and then do a story about me."

"Was this Mr. Shane?"

"Uh-uh," he said.

"You remember his name, this guy?"

"Uh-uh."

"Was it Jay Adams? A little fat man?"

"Naw, he come out later to talk to me. Had a recording machine going. They was gonna write up a story for the magazine. I wouldn't talk to him."

"What did this man—the first man—look like?"

He shrugged. "I don't know. Older guy, maybe forty-five. Silver hair. Good suit. Talk like a movie star."

"Okay. Okay, Earl, now tell me what you were doing at Jay Adams's house on Friday."

"I didn't kill him, I swear to Jesus! I never killed nobody."

"I know, Earl. Just tell me, nice and easy."

I sat opposite Marko's desk. Because of the heat of the day we were drinking RC Cola out of cans and didn't have to worry about foam-particle poisoning. I said, "So when I showed up at Faggerty's place Friday, he thought I was from the magazine and wanted to bite him some more. He says he didn't know where to find Shane or the guy he talked to, who I assume was Leonard Pursglove, but when Adams did the interview for the story, being the egotist that he was, he left Earl one of his cards that said 'editor in chief' on it. After I saw him on Friday, Faggerty figured he had to talk to someone who wasn't bigger than he was, get them to let him up, and he drove out to the east side and went to Adams's apartment. He says Adams was dead when he found him, and he panicked and ran. Wouldn't you, if you were Faggerty and had a criminal record?"

"That story sucks," Marko said.

"It has the absolute ring of truth from where I sit."

"Why do you have a hard-on about this, Milan? What's Earl Faggerty to you besides a guy who tried to part your skull with a wrench?"

"Faggerty's no killer," I said. "Not premeditated. He might kill somebody with his fists or a blunt instrument in a fit of anger; he wouldn't shoot somebody in the head. You know the type, Marko. He's from down south someplace, still has pig shit on his boots. And you didn't find a gun on him anywhere."

"He probably chucked it out the window in fright," Marko said.

"He's a poor man. He wouldn't throw away something expensive like a nine-millimeter."

"Okay, fine," he said, draining his RC. "But remember, we picked him up when he got back to his shop, and we bagged his hands before we brought him in. We ran a GSR on him and found traces of barium, antimony, and lead on both hands, like I told you."

"Marko, the man is a mechanic."

"So?"

"So he does brake jobs."

"I take mine to the Honda dealer. What the hell are you talking—"

"If you do a brake job you are likely to get your hands in contact with brake fluid, right?"

"Sure, but—"

"Barium, antimony, and lead," I said. "He probably has it all over his hands every day. Makes a hell of a lot more sense than your two-handed shooter scenario."

Marko raised his own hands to indicate his helplessness. "He's all I've got. You want me to let him go? They'll have me directing traffic in Sandusky by morning."

"No, I guess you have to keep him for a while. But when I bring you the real perp, then Faggerty walks."

"What about—"

"The chop-shop rap? Forget it. That was in confidence; I gave my word."

He slammed the soft drink can down onto his desk. "You had no right to do that! God, I'm getting sick of you, Milan."

"Why?"

"Who in hell you think you are? The goddamn DA or something?" He was at a rolling boil. "I break rules for you right and left because we've been friends for thirty years, and because you used to be a good cop. But you come tromping in here, you compromise my investigation—you make promises to my prisoners on my behalf and then expect me to live up to them. You're overstepping yourself and you're doing it on my turf."

I shook my head. "Boy, you get interrupted in mid screw and you really turn into a bear, don't you?"

"Milan, I want you out!" he barked. I could see he wasn't kidding.

"What?"

"I want you off this case. I'll go along and pretend I never heard about Faggerty's chop shop, but that's it. From now on you and I don't know each other as far as these murders are concerned. I'll see you sometime for a drink, some laughs. But you're on your own as far as the rest of it goes."

"And how about the fact that an attempt was made on my life the other night, Marko?"

"That's been duly reported and recorded and is being looked into," he said coldly. "If anybody tries it again, let me know."

"Marko—"

"It's Mark, God damn it! It's been Mark for ten years, and you know it! Now get out of here and let me finish my day off in peace."

I stared at him. My headache was getting worse.

"I mean it, Milan," he said.

I dropped off my visitor's badge with the young cop at the front desk, and he said, "Thank you, sir." It didn't make me feel any better the second time. But it didn't make me feel worse than having a guy I'd known since we were kids toss me out of his office as if I were something that had come in on the bottom of someone's shoe.

15

There's not much doing in the Flats on Sunday mornings. The only people around are the brunch eaters and the hard-core drinkers. Everyone else either sleeps in or goes to church. So I found a parking place very close to DiPoo's, and I noticed Buddy's Celica in the same lot.

Inside DiPoo's it was quiet. Gone were the weekday happy-hour middle-management guys hustling and networking. The only people at the bar were the serious alkies. You can always spot the bottle babies. They hunker over the bar, their hands cupped around their drinks as if they're guarding a rare treasure, their cigarettes in the ashtrays in front of them sending up wispy Apache smoke signals, their eyes glued to the television set as if they only came by to watch the game and not just to drink alone.

Buddy was at a booth in the dining room, digging into a breakfast of steak and eggs. In my condition it made me ill just to look at him.

"Hey, Milan," he said. "Isn't it a beautiful morning?"

"Just a slice of heaven," I said, sliding in next to him. I ordered coffee that I didn't want and sat back to ease the pounding in my head.

"How'd it go at police headquarters?" he said.

"Okay. I listened to the tapes, but I didn't get much out of them. You didn't miss much."

He chewed vigorously for a moment. "What else is new?"

I wasn't going to relate the particulars of Greg Shane's visit the night before. I had foolishly promised Shane forty-eight hours, and I was not about to go back on my word. I also wasn't going to discuss the contents of Dan Mulkey's tapes with Buddy until I had figured out what they meant. I didn't want Victor Gaimari to go off half cocked and do something silly.

"Not much," I said.

"You look like hell," he said mildly.

"Compared with how I feel, I look terrific."

"You know, some guys just shouldn't drink. They can't handle it. I knew a guy in Buffalo once, name of Guggie. Man, two beers and he was flat on his—"

"Save it, will you, Buddy."

"Oh, sure, Milan." He went on eating. "Where we going now?"

"To church," I said.

The Mayfield Heights Foursquare Gospel Church was located halfway up a hill, overlooking one of the less lovely spots in town, the east side industrial section. The church itself was white clapboard, with a steeple that tried to soar skyward but didn't quite make it. In the glaring sunshine the heat seemed to be rising from the building in shimmering waves. A sign outside proclaimed the title of that morning's sermon: JESUS WAS A STRAIGHT SHOOTER. I was sorry we'd arrived too late to hear it.

There were several cars in the parking lot, and quite a few

people dressed in their churchgoing finery were working inside, straightening hymnals and picking up discarded orders of service from the floor. When we inquired after the pastor, we were directed to a small office near the front of the church.

"Hello, there, brothers," the pastor said, a tall, cadaverous-looking man dressed in a dark gray three-piece suit despite the heat, with a blinding white stiff-collared shirt and a tie in three shades of blue. In his left lapel was a shiny silver cross. He was working at a cluttered desk when we came in, and I couldn't help noticing that what he was going over were financial statements. He stood and offered us both a professionally hearty handshake as I introduced Buddy and myself.

"Welcome to Foursquare," he said, "although you're a bit late for Sunday morning worship. I'm Reverend Simms." He looked at Buddy, then back at me. "A couple of Catholic boys, from your names. And backslid, I'd wager, if I was a wagering man, which of course I'm not."

Buddy shrugged. "I haven't been to church in I don't know when."

"That's all right," he said, "Foursquare embraces all comers with open arms." He spread his arms wide in illustration.

"Actually," I said, "we came here looking for a Mrs. Mercer. I believe she's your organist."

"Ah, Sister Gladys," he said. "Yes indeed, that lady has music in her heart. Don't know what I'd do without her. Of course, she isn't here now. She'll be back this evening for prayer meeting, though."

"We were rather hoping to talk to her privately," I said, "so as not to disrupt the church."

He smiled broadly, giving me a flash of white-on-white teeth. Toward the back of his mouth I caught a glimpse of the metal bands that anchored his dentures. "You know, Mr. Jacovich, when you've been in the religion business as long as I have, you learn to read people pretty well."

"I imagine you would."

"You also learn to spot a cop at thirty paces."

It was so abrupt and so unexpected coming from a minister

169

that I had to laugh. "Ex-cop," I said. "You're very good, Reverend." I handed him one of my cards, and he looked at it long enough to memorize it before putting it in the pocket of his vest next to his watch fob.

"I hope Miz Mercer isn't in any sort of trouble," he said.

"Not at all. Maybe she can help us, though."

"Because I would stand up for Miz Mercer at the Gates of Heaven on the day of Armageddon. She is one of the most pious, upstanding women I've ever met." And then he remembered that this was the age of raised consciousness and he amended, "One of the most upstanding *people*, of any gender."

I wanted to ask him how many genders he knew about. Instead I said, "Has Mrs. Mercer been with the church long?"

"Oh my," he said, "I've been here going on eleven years, and she was with us when I arrived. Her knowledge of sacred music, her feel for the melodies, is quite remarkable. She used to be in show business, you know—but that was before she put aside all that worldliness and gave her life over to Jesus Christ. That show business, it's no life for a woman like Sister Gladys."

"Well," I said, "if you could tell us where we might find her this afternoon, I'd be most appreciative."

"Would you?" Reverend Simms said. "Would you, Mr. Jacovich? Well, that's the kind of information we don't normally give out to strangers, the home addresses of our people."

I nodded and sighed. My headache had faded to a distant and muffled drumbeat, but I felt it coming back again. "I would certainly be willing to demonstrate my appreciation, Reverend Simms. In the form of a charitable donation to the church fund."

"Ah. And how much of a donation did you have in mind, sir?"

I peeled five twenty-dollar bills from my roll. "Would one hundred dollars be sufficient?"

His hand moved faster than a striking timber rattler and the money disappeared into the pocket where he'd put my card. "You'll be blessed, sir. Jesus will bless you. You'll be down in His books. He keeps careful records, you know."

Apparently during His gunslinging days Jesus had found the time to take a few accounting courses at Cleveland State. "And Mrs. Mercer's address?" I said.

He flipped expertly through a Rolodex on his desk and jotted down a number on a pad imprinted on every page with the legend GOD LOVES YOU. "It's not too far from here," he said. "Sister Gladys likes to be near her spiritual roots."

"Thank you, Reverend Simms. You've been a big help."

He rose and shook hands again, telling us we'd be welcome back any time. All three of us knew he didn't mean it.

When we got back into the car Buddy shivered. "I'm glad to get out of there, Milan."

"Why?"

"Churches give me the creeps."

It was my first inkling that churches and police stations had something in common.

The address Simms gave me for Gladys Mercer was located in a run-down neighborhood about a mile from the church. On one corner was an auto salvage yard. The rusted hulks of Detroit's finest grinned out at us through the cyclone fence with blind eyes. Across the street between two ramshackle houses was a mom-and-pop grocery store with a tin 7-Up sign in the window. Close by was a television repair shop; a folding iron grille stretched across its door and window to stave off vandalism or theft, both of which were probably business as usual on this block.

I parked in front of the house and got out, stepping on the spidery outlines of a game of hopscotch scratched onto the sidewalk with a sharp stone. We went up onto the sagging porch and I rang the doorbell, but no sound issued from inside the house. All I could hear was the roaring of the vintage air conditioner in the front window. A brownish wet stain ran from the condenser beneath it down the dirty yellow facade of the house into a dried-up flower bed that hadn't seen a flower in many years. I rang again, and then knocked hard.

After my second knock the yellowing net curtains covering

171

the glass in the top half of the door were pulled aside and a gray-haired woman peered out at us. I saw her mouth *Yes?* but I couldn't hear anything.

"My name is Milan Jacovich, Mrs. Mercer," I yelled. "Reverend Simms told us we could find you here."

She frowned, not hearing, and pressed the side of her head up against the glass, mashing her ear and some gray curls against the window. She had small earlobes, pierced but unadorned. I repeated myself, loudly. She took her head away, the netting fell back into place, and I heard her unlocking three locks. She opened the door about four inches, the limit of the chain lock. I often wonder why people bother with those things. A medium-size child could easily rip one of them out of the woodwork. I felt a blast of icy air from inside the house.

"What is it?" she said.

I handed her a card through the opening, and she held it almost at arm's length to look at it. "Oh, my stars," she said. "Well, if Reverend Simms sent you—just a minute."

She shut the door, undid the chain, and opened it wide for us to enter. I felt guilty allowing her misapprehension to stand, but not very. I smiled and nodded as I walked by her. She was an older version of her daughter. She had the same long neck, the skinny butt, the lank and lifeless hair, and the same whipped look about her.

Inside, the house was dark, and the sound of the air conditioner bounced off the walls. The furniture was faded, the woods were dark, and there were dainty knitted antimacassars on the backs of all the chairs, though I figured Buddy was the first man who wore grease on his hair to enter this room in twenty years. All over the walls were pictures of Jesus Christ: Jesus and Mary in the manger, Jesus riding into Jerusalem, Jesus on the Mount, Jesus in Gethsemane, Jesus ascending from the tomb. Against the wall was an old Hammond organ, and on its top were three pictures in cheap silvered frames. One was of a child of about eleven, probably Merlys, in a satiny dancing costume, her knobby knees making the photo somehow touching. Another was of more recent vintage, Merlys in a flowered dress, with her tired eyes and defeated expression. The third was, of course, Jesus again, doing His number with Lazarus.

Mrs. Mercer said, "Please excuse the house. I didn't have time to clean up today."

I looked around. There was nothing to excuse; the room looked as if no one had ever lived there. From the back of the house, probably the kitchen, a radio played sacred music.

Mrs. Mercer indicated the sofa. "Won't you sit down, gentlemen? I'm afraid I have nothing to offer you except some sun tea."

"No, thank you," I said before Buddy could accept. "I just need a few moments of your time. I spoke to your daughter—"

"Merlys?"

"Do you have another one?"

"Oh, no," she said. She sat down on the organ bench, her knees pressed tightly together in their support stockings, her heels hooked over the rung beneath the bench, her toes pointed at the floor. I could tell that her legs were still slim and muscular. She wore steel-framed spectacles with thick lenses. "How do you know Merlys?"

I cleared my throat. "I talked to her the other day. I'm looking into the *North Coast Magazine* situation."

Mrs. Mercer bobbed her head and the light flashed off her glasses. "What situation is that?" she said weakly.

"Apparently there is no magazine, and the publishers have disappeared with all the advertising money."

Her hand went to her neck, and she pulled at the loose flesh. "Oh," she breathed.

"Merlys tells me that advertising in the magazine was your idea."

"Oh," she said. "There's no telling Merlys anything. Never was. She never did listen to me. If she had . . . well. You know, she just barely gets by with that dancing school."

"Uh-huh."

"The Lord never saw fit to bless her with any great talent. She learned the steps all right, but she just didn't have the flair, the sparkle that I had. I was a dancer, too, you know."

173

"I'll bet you were a good one," Buddy said, and either missed the look I shot him or chose to ignore it.

"But I got married instead, and when Merlys was born I tried to give her the career that I couldn't have. It didn't pan out, though."

"Mrs. Mercer," I said, "with Merlys doing so poorly at her studio, how is it that you advised her to spend all that money on an ad?"

Her eyes batted behind the thick lenses. "It was a business decision," she said. "Merlys never had much of a head for business, either. I prayed hard over it, and the Lord seemed to want— Well, I just thought it was a good idea."

"Did you know that Dan Mulkey, who used to produce the TV show Merlys was on when she was younger, was one of the *North Coast* executives?"

She pursed her mouth up, and the lines that appeared around it looked like a full set of false eyelashes. She didn't answer me. Her right hand fluttered in front of her face like a hummingbird until finally she put it in her lap again. Willed it there.

I said, "Did Mr. Mulkey try to pressure you in any way? Did he try to get you to use your influence with Merlys so she'd take that ad out in the magazine?"

"How could he pressure me?" she said. Her voice sounded far away.

"I don't know, Mrs. Mercer. You tell me."

All of a sudden her skin got very white, and then red, and something funny happened to her face. It seemed to wrinkle up like cheap material in the rain. She began rocking violently from the waist, bending forward almost double and then jerking her body backward so that her spine banged into the keyboard of the organ. "Oh, Lord!" she wailed. "He promised he wouldn't tell. He promised he wouldn't say anything if . . ."

"If what?"

And she started to cry, deep wracking sobs that were being torn from depths inside her I wouldn't have guessed were there.

Buddy looked at me strangely. He was distinctly uncomfortable with old ladies weeping. So was I, for that matter.

"I was trying to help my little girl," she cried. "I pushed her too hard, I wanted for her what I never had, and I was willing to do anything, *anything* to make her a star. It was important that she be seen on television every week—it was important to her career. Oh, Lord, he promised he'd never tell!"

"Mrs. Mercer," I said as gently as I could, "Dan Mulkey is dead."

"It's the Lord's judgment!" she moaned. "For his sins. And for mine! Oh, Jesus . . ." The way she said it, it was a prayer and not a blasphemy.

"What sins, ma'am?"

"I'm too ashamed to say!"

Buddy was at sea, shifting from one giant ham to the other on the uncomfortable sofa. If police stations and churches made him uneasy, Gladys Mercer's living room was driving him crazy. I didn't speak; I was waiting for her tears to stop.

Finally Mrs. Mercer got her breathing under control, although when she exhaled there was a catch in it. "The Lord understands," she said. "He's forgiven me, you know. It was a long time ago."

"How much did you give *North Coast* for the ad, Mrs. Mercer? Merlys gave them two hundred dollars. How much did you give them?"

She shook her head. "I don't want to talk about that. It doesn't matter how much. I don't want to talk about any of this anymore." Her glasses were streaked with tears, and she took them off and wiped them on the hem of her housedress. Her eyes were a pale blue, almost gray, and her lashes were short and light. "You gentlemen will have to excuse me now," she said. "It's Sunday, and that's my day to pray."

She stood up, and Buddy and I followed suit. She led us to the door and opened it, the heat from outside rushing into the room like floodwaters. I said, "I'm sorry to have troubled you, Mrs. Mercer."

"Jesus bears my troubles," she said, too brightly. "That's what He's for, you know."

I drove to a nearby coffee shop, installed Buddy at the counter, and went to the pay phone, where I called Edna Warriner's home. Her secretary answered.

"Ms. Warriner is taking a nap now," she said coldly, "and I can't possibly disturb her."

"That's all right, Ms. Menafee. It's you I wanted to talk to anyway."

"I?"

"Yes. Would it be possible for you to meet me? How about Cain Park, at the corner of Lee and Superior?"

"I have nothing to add to what Ms. Warriner's already told you, Mr. Jacovich."

"I'd really rather discuss this with you privately," I said. "I'd hate to have to bother Ms. Warriner with it."

I heard her sharp intake of breath. I felt like a shit.

"Very well," she said. "Half an hour?"

"I appreciate it, Ms. Menafee."

I went back to the counter, where Buddy had ordered two bacon cheeseburgers and a malted. He had torn his paper napkin into strips, impatient with waiting.

"Milan, did you understand what that old lady was crying about?"

"Yes," I said.

"Well, clue me in."

"Blackmail."

"Blackmail? She blackmailing somebody, a nice old lady like that?"

The waitress brought his food and glared at me for not ordering anything. There were twelve stools at the counter, and they were all empty except ours, but that didn't keep her from resenting it that I was taking up some prospective paying customer's space. "No, Buddy, she's not a blackmailer. She's a victim."

Buddy drowned his burgers with ketchup and started on the

first one without cutting it. The ketchup and dressing oozed out the sides of it when he took a bite. Some of it dropped onto the lapel of his leisure suit, but since he was wearing black it didn't show very much once he wiped off the excess with my napkin, having turned his own into confetti. "You know," he said around the food, "sometimes I think the world is made up of sharks and little fish and nothing in between."

"And which one are you, Buddy?"

He smiled at me, chewing, but his eyes went hard. He didn't need to answer.

We stopped at a convenience store so I could get Buddy a *Penthouse* to keep him occupied while I talked to Helene Menafee, and then we drove to Cain Park. Cain had been around for some fifty years, and its large outdoor amphitheater was the home of one of America's oldest municipal theaters. The amphitheater had fallen victim to the savagery of Ohio's winters until 1979, when a Hollywood company producing a film called *Those Lips, Those Eyes* had decided it was the ideal location for their shoot and spent more than a hundred thousand dollars sprucing the place up, replacing the rotted stage floor and leaving a good bit of the scenery behind as well. After that the city of Cleveland Heights got into the act and floated a five-million-dollar bond issue to revitalize the park and the theater, and there were now high hopes for it.

Being Sunday there were no workmen in evidence; just a few idle strollers and some mothers who had brought their little ones out for a day of fresh air someplace where there was a slight breeze blowing. Buddy took a bench about seventy feet into the park and watched the kids tossing a beach ball around over the top of his girlie magazine. I sat down on the bench nearest the corner and waited. The sun was hot enough to bake lasagna. Finally a late-model Chevrolet pulled into the parking lot and Helene Menafee got out and started walking toward where I sat. She was wearing dark slacks and another buttoned-to-the-neck blouse. She held her spine as if it had been starched and ironed.

"Thank you for coming," I said.

"As I told you, I can't imagine what we might have to say to one another, Mr. Jacovich. As far as Ms. Warriner is concerned, this whole magazine business is a closed chapter." She sat down next to me on the bench, being careful to keep several feet of space between us.

"Is it, Ms. Menafee? Ms. Warriner said that she only gave them the story because you urged her to. Is that right?"

She shrugged. She was facing away from the sun, and the backlight made a halo around her hair. "It never hurts to have a writer published anywhere," she said. "Ms. Warriner doesn't need the publicity, but exposure is always good. It's too bad it didn't work out, but it's no great loss. It was an old story. I didn't even retype it."

"Are you sure that's the only reason you let them have the story?"

"That and the fact that Jay Adams is an old friend." She shaded her eyes with her hand. "What are you driving at?"

"Ms. Menafee, several of the advertisers were coerced by threats of various kinds into giving the people at *North Coast* money. Legally it's called extortion. I thought perhaps the same thing might have happened to Ms. Warriner."

She turned away. Across the expanse of green grass Buddy was watching us over his magazine.

"Ms. Menafee," I said, "if I'm off base here, please excuse me, but were you being blackmailed by the people at *North Coast*?"

"Certainly not," she snapped, but I could tell her heart wasn't in it.

"It wouldn't do Ms. Warriner any good if word got out that the woman who writes those sexy romantic thrillers that can make a housewife forget about diapers and ironing and making dinner by transporting her into a world of love and adventure, was involved in a—forgive me, please—a lesbian relationship, would it?"

She recoiled as if I'd slapped her. "You filthy bastard! Are you in the blackmail business as well?"

"Not at all," I said. "But Dan Mulkey and Jay Adams are

both dead—murdered. I'm trying to find out what happened to them, and maybe prevent more killing. It wasn't just the story, was it? How much money did you give them, Ms. Menafee?"

There was no sound except the distant laughter of the kids at play, and out of sight somewhere a remote-controlled model plane droned noisily. Helene Menafee's chin suddenly dropped onto her chest as if someone had severed the muscles in her neck. "Oh, God," she said, "this will kill Edna. If she ever finds out, it will kill her. She's ill, you know. Emphysema. She's not a young woman." She was talking into her chest.

"They didn't approach Ms. Warriner directly because they knew she'd tell them to go to hell, is that right?"

She nodded.

"So they came to you instead. Was it Jay Adams?"

"No," she said, her voice muffled.

"Pursglove? Leonard Pursglove?"

She sighed, raising her chin a bit to get some air. "He said he'd contact that awful newspaper they sell in supermarkets, *The Tattle-Tale*? He would have made it sound so much worse than it is. He had a vivid imagination and quite a way with words."

"How much money did you give him?"

"A thousand," she said.

"You must have known that was only the beginning."

Her eyes widened in anger and her nostrils quivered. "I had no choice! I love Edna—I'd do anything to see she wasn't hurt!" Then her mouth curled in a sneer. "I don't expect *you* to understand that, though."

"Why not? I have people I love too. I'm not making any moral judgments here, Ms. Menafee. I sympathize with you, and I'm trying to help you."

For a moment her look shouted her disbelief, and then a tear rolled down her left cheek, the iron went out of her backbone, and she practically collapsed against my side, her face pressed against my shoulder, and I could feel the spasms in her body. "God," she said into my neck, "I feel so dirty!"

Awkwardly I put my arm around her shoulders and patted her. I felt like a big clumsy bear. "You're not the dirty one, Ms. Menafee," I said.

16

"I don't get it," Buddy was saying to me on the way back to the Flats to pick up his car. "You mean that broad you was talking to in the park is a dyke?"

"She's a lesbian, yes," I said.

He crinkled his nose. "Jeez, Milan. I mean, who'd wanna do that?"

"You've got me, Buddy," was all I said. It was just easier that way. There are more things in heaven and earth, Horatio, than were dreamt of in Buddy's philosophy.

"You're such a smart guy," he said, truly impressed, though for the life of me I couldn't figure out why. "I mean, you always know the right kinds of questions to ask and stuff. I'll bet it's 'cause you went to college and everything."

"I don't think college had much to do with it."

"I coulda gone to college," he said, "but I dropped out of high school when I was sixteen. I was too hungry for bucks, and I mean it was right now. I wasn't gonna wait no four years of college. So I bopped around for a while, doin' odd jobs. I was a big kid even then, and this guy, Mr. Bellomo, he seen me and asked if I wanted to fight." He put a hand on my arm. "Not fight *him*, Milan, he meant fight professionally. So I said sure, why not, and he got me a trainer and got me some fights. I was pretty good, but I never woulda gone noplace with it. I was a heavyweight, and all these guys they got now coulda put me away in two rounds, cause I wasn't so fast. But I could hit. It was my hitting got me in trouble back in Buffalo."

"Oh?"

"Mr. Bellomo was in the numbers, you understand, and he used me to make collections. I got carried away with my work one time, and the next thing I know I'm in the joint. Man, it's hard in there."

"I'll bet."

"You either get tough or die, you understand? So I started boxing in there, too, and I did my time that way. I didn't lose no fights at all inside, and nobody fucked with me, so it wasn't too bad. Then when I got out Mr. Bellomo said that Buffalo was too hot for me, so I come here to work for Mr. D'Allessandro and Mr. Gaimari, and so far it's workin' out pretty good. But I don't wanna go back inside, Milan. Not ever."

"Well, keep your nose clean," I said. I pulled up to the curb beside the parking lot on the river. Buddy squeezed my arm, and I could swear there were tears in his eyes.

"Thanks, Milan. For puttin' up with me. I'm really learning so much from you. And I'm tryin' to stay outta your way."

"I know, Buddy. It's all right."

"See you tomorrow." He loped over to where the nose of his car hung over the east bank of the Cuyahoga, turning to wave.

I shook my head. It would have been nice to be a role model for my kids, I guess, but being one for an ex-con with muscles where his brains should be was something I was having trouble dealing with.

I took one more swing by Leonard Pursglove's apartment building. He wasn't there, which didn't surprise me somehow. J. Rose wasn't there either. My rental car huffed its way up the hill out of the Flats and I drove home via Euclid Avenue as far as University Circle, passing by Channel 12, and the hurt of missing Mary was a coyote's sharp teeth in my guts.

Sunday nights alone are worse than a toothache. I was in no mood for watching *60 Minutes*, and especially not a rerun of *Murder She Wrote*. I longed for the old days when Sunday nights meant Ed Sullivan, and kicking back to watch the little Italian mouse or the comedy of Wayne and Shuster, or Señor Wences, the ventriloquist who would paint a face on his hand and make it talk. When we were in junior high school, my friend Alex Cerne used to break up the locker room with a funny routine about Señor Wences trying to talk his hand into going down on him. Now Ed Sullivan is dead, Alex is a periodontist in Euclid, and Señor Wences is probably back in Spain, still arguing with his hand.

I transfer all my case notes onto three-by-five cards, and now I spread these across my desk and shuffled them around, trying to make some sense out of them. It was a lonely game of Canfield played by an idiot. The pattern was sketchy; it needed more filling in.

I took down a book, a mystery about an Orange County, California, detective named Murdock. At least I was sure Murdock would solve *his* case. And he was well on his way when the telephone interrupted me. A long-distance collect call from Saxon Investigations in Los Angeles.

"Hey, I'm glad I caught you in, Milan," Saxon said. He sounded like he was around the corner instead of twenty-five hundred miles away. I could hear jazz playing in the background and remembered that he was a buff.

"I just decided to take the evening off from my many social obligations," I said with just a trace of bitterness. "Don't tell me you have something for me already?"

"Quite a lot, actually. Got a pencil?"

I fumbled in the drawer for a felt-tipped pen. It took me three tries before I found one that still wrote. "Shoot," I said, and pulled a yellow legal pad in front of me.

"Okay. First of all, Richie Hips."

"Who?"

"Richardson Hippsley-Tate, old boy," he said, faking a creditable upper-class British accent. I was willing to bet Saxon was a pretty good actor when he got going. "That's his nickname among our friends with the bent noses and the bulges under their suitcoats. The Manhattan Beach hotel he managed a few years ago is the Victorian Inn, about five miles from the airport. It only has sixty-eight rooms, but with the prices they charge they don't need any more. Also an expensive restaurant, and a lounge where Rémy costs six bucks a shot. Anyway, Richie ran things there for about eight months before he came to a parting of ways with the management. It seems some government type from Washington had a weakness for teenage hookers and smuggled one into his room. Somehow or other Richie got pictures of it and tried to put the squeeze on the guy, but the laugh was on Richie, because the guy wasn't married and everyone in Washington knew he liked young stuff and he didn't care who else knew what. Anyway, after that Richie drifted to Vegas and did some security work in one of the downtown casinos until he got the call to manage the hotel in Cleveland. And you know who that call came from. The word I get is that he's strictly small-time, but a good team player. That's why the boys keep him around."

"Where'd you get all of this on a weekend, Saxon?"

"A friend of mine, Alan Mack, used to play piano at the Victorian Inn back when Richie Hips was running the place. As a matter of fact, Richie fired him—he wanted a kickback out of Alan's salary and Alan wouldn't give it to him. And Alan knows some other musicians in Vegas, which is where I got the rest of this stuff."

"Let me hear it."

"You asked about a lady named Vivian Truscott."

"Yeah. She's the number-one television news hen here."

"That's what she was in Las Vegas too. But that's not how

183

she started out. She started out doing dirty things for money with visiting firemen in their hotel rooms. Worked the lounges at the Sands and the Dunes regularly."

Perhaps that explained why a journalist didn't know what a "slant" was. "I'm listening."

"Okay. One day she tricked with the owner of one of the smaller TV stations here in Vegas, and he got enamored, really hooked. Sending flowers, expensive presents, seeing her four or five times a week. At two hundred a pop, he figured it would be cheaper for him in the long run to put her on the station's payroll as the weekend weather girl, at a salary commensurate with her abilities. Well, she was really good on camera."

"Off camera too, I'll bet." I was scribbling frantically to keep up with him.

"That goes without saying. Anyway, she wound up as the six o'clock anchor for two years, when she got a better offer from you folks in Cleveland."

"Your friend Alan Mack has some interesting Vegas connections."

"All Vegas connections are interesting, Milan. Want some more?"

"All you've got."

"I asked the Vegas folks about Gregory Shane, but no one seems to have heard of him. At least, not under that name."

"That's what I was afraid of."

"But don't despair. I found out from a badge-toting acquaintance of mine that about eighteen months ago someone named Harry Sweet tried to start up a local magazine in the San Fernando Valley, which has a population of well over a million. It sounds very much like the same kind of deal this Shane was running in your town. He and his wife ran it themselves. Paid editorial, going after the small businessmen in the area—and I mean small. Caterers, hypnotherapists, chiropractors, pool supply stores, beauty shops, that kind of thing. I guess I don't need to tell you that the magazine never got off the ground, and that Mr. Sweet disappeared with some fourteen thousand bucks of other people's money."

"That doesn't sound like much of a score."

"It's not," Saxon said. "Sweet wasn't much of a crook. He certainly wasn't a very big one. The cops didn't even try that hard to find him. We have major drug dealers in L.A., people selling phoney stocks, pyramid schemes that net millions. This is the bunco capital of the world, because everyone out here wants to hit it big, fast. So a guy like Sweet who takes little two-hundred-buck bites out of shop owners and dentists doesn't even make a ripple."

I thought for a minute. "You speak any Yiddish, Saxon?"

"You can't survive ten minutes in Hollywood without knowing some Yiddish. Why?"

"You know what the word 'schoen' means in Yiddish?"

"I think so: beautiful, or nice?"

"Is it too much of a stretch to Sweet?"

"I don't follow."

"Greg Shane's real name is Harvey Schoenstein. Schoenstein, Sweet, Shane."

"Bingo!"

"But we're talking much bigger numbers here."

"Maybe he's decided to expand."

"I wonder." I wrote some more. "Is that it?"

"That's it, except for Alex Malleson."

"The headmaster."

"Right. It seems about six years ago one Alexander Malleson was running a school for rich kids in San Marino, which is a small township near Pasadena with a median income of about a billion dollars a year. Nobody knows exactly what happened, but there were rumors of sexual games with some of the little girls there, seven and eight years old, lifting their skirts, putting his hand inside their panties. What the papers euphemistically call 'bad touching.'"

"Jesus," I said.

"Nothing was ever proved conclusively, and there were no indictments brought, but the parents were rich and influential, and Alex Malleson very quietly resigned and went away. As far as I could dig, he hasn't been heard from in the state since."

"God, Saxon, where did you get all that?"

"A very hard cop by the name of Joe DiMattia, whose wife I used to go out with—and I'm charging you extra for all the verbal abuse I had to take to get it."

I didn't care. What Saxon had managed to dig up fit perfectly. I'd not only pay him for his time, I'd have a case of that weird Scotch he liked shipped to him. It would all be added to Richie Hips's final bill, including the collect phone call.

Now the three-by-five cards were starting to make more sense. The staff of *North Coast* had an interesting history. Greg Shane, it would appear, had pulled a similar con out in the Los Angeles area—for small change, to be sure, but still the same con. His wife Nettie had been a Las Vegas hooker. And Dan Mulkey, once a prestigious recording executive, had lost that job for taking kickbacks.

Some of the people who'd been stung by *North Coast Magazine*, like Peter Kazakis and his Kukla restaurant, seemed to be legitimate, guilty only of poor judgment when they took an ad out with Greg Shane and his minions. But some of the others were evidently not really advertising but paying hush money. For instance, Gladys Mercer did not want her position in the Foursquare Gospel Church jeopardized by it becoming known that she once slept with Dan Mulkey so he'd put her teenage daughter on television, and she'd talked Merlys into taking an ad. Vivian Truscott certainly didn't want the good burghers of Cleveland to know she had gotten her start as a two-hundred-dollar call girl in Las Vegas casinos before coming to our town and looking earnestly into the camera to deliver reports about peace talks in the Middle East. She'd broken her rule about giving interviews to keep it quiet, hoping for a chance at superstardom with one of the networks. Alex Malleson had been the subject of rumors regarding his conduct with little girls—not exactly the best recommendation for a headmaster at an exclusive private school. Earl Faggerty was a two-time loser who couldn't afford another conviction for dealing in stolen cars. And Helene Menafee was willing to pay to keep her elderly female lover's career from being destroyed. Any one of them had good reason to dispose of Dan Mulkey and Jay Adams, to say nothing of the remainder of the *North Coast* staff. It was no wonder Shane had run for cover, and probably Leonard Pursglove, too.

A motive doesn't mean much. We all have motives for murder at one time or another: the TV repairman replaces tubes that were perfectly good to begin with, the dry cleaner ruins an expensive dress, Jehovah's Witnesses get you out of the shower or wake you from a nap. And those are just the everyday ones. Most of us don't kill anyone even when we've got a heavy-duty motive, because we have a little safety valve that lets us blow off steam without bodily harm coming to anyone. But once in a while a person comes along whose safety valve is out of order, and then someone gets hurt. Bad hurt, like Jay Adams and Dan Mulkey. It could be any one of the people they were blackmailing, or it could be Greg Shane himself. That's why I was shuffling index cards on my desk instead of reading a good book, to try and figure out who it was.

Looking at my cards, one thing didn't seem to fit. When Greg Shane had run the same magazine scam in California, if indeed Shane and Sweet were the same man, he had merely absconded with some penny-ante advertising money. There was no blackmail, no high-level crime. A few little people who couldn't afford it got nicked for a couple of hundred dollars, which, while admittedly not legal and certainly not nice, hardly made Shane a master criminal.

And why did Richie Hips kick in with forty-two thousand dollars of the hotel's money? Certainly Hippsley-Tate's past sins and criminal connections would not cost him his job with the Cleveland branch of that same mob. And though Victor Gaimari might not want it on the front page of the *Plain Dealer* that it was his own and D'Allessandro's money that had built the hotel, a good investigative reporter like Ed Stahl could ferret that out with no trouble at all. And if he did, no one in Cleveland would do much more than shake their heads sadly and cluck their tongues about it. The hotel was providing a lot of jobs for the local citizenry in an otherwise depressed time and attracting a lot of money into the area as well, and people's morals often tend to come to a screeching halt at their wallets.

The hammering on my front door was so loud and forceful it made me spill the cards all over my desk. I was annoyed; whoever it was had better be on fire. I took the big gun out of my desk drawer and stuck it in the waistband of my slacks. Maybe the guy who'd taken a shot at me on the street the other night had grown bolder.

I saw Greg Shane through the peephole, and he banged on the door again while I had my eye to it, making me jump. I opened the door. He was wearing a dark blue velour shirt, a pair of baggy Wrangler jeans frayed at the cuffs, and dirty white running shoes with Velcro fasteners, and his hair, the long gray fringe around his bald head, was in wild disarray. He blasted past me, and when I had shut and locked the door he whirled around to face me. His eyes were crazy; I'd never seen anyone that agitated.

"You fucker!" he screamed.

"Good evening to you too."

"God damn you, Jacovich. God damn you!"

"Hey, slow down, Greg. What's this all about?"

"You couldn't wait, could you? You lied to me, you fucker!"

"Greg, I don't know what you're—"

"You turned me in, didn't you? You told them where I was, didn't you?" His voice was shrill and hysterical.

"Told *who* where you were?"

"I don't know," he said, and burst into tears. "But they came for me! I was out at the store getting booze and they came for me—*and they got Nettie*." He collapsed onto the sofa blubbering, and I let him. An awful lot of people had been crying in my presence in the last few days. I was getting tired of it, maybe because I couldn't do anything about their tears, and maybe because I had a few of my own to shed and nobody seemed ready to let me.

He finally cried himself out and put his head back on the cushions, eyes closed, hyperventilating at first and then calming down, or as down as Greg Shane could calm under stress. I went to get him a brandy, too late remembering I had finished the bottle during my debauch of the night before. He'd have to settle for a Stroh's—my last one.

But he waved the proffered beer away and just lay there breathing loudly, staring up at the ceiling. His face was the color of four-day-old snow. I was worried he was going to check out right there in my living room. I'd seen enough dead bodies to last me for a while.

"Come on, now. Sit up and tell me what happened."

"She's dead, Mike," he said in a tone from the crypt. "I wasn't gone fifteen minutes and they got her. Shot through the head. She was taking a nap."

"God, I'm so sorry."

He dug at his eyes with his thumb. "She had a tough life, you know? I took her out of Vegas and tried to make it up to her, all the things she'd gone through, all the stuff she'd had to do. And then—" He snapped his fingers and then looked at them, as if making the noise had been their own idea. He started to cry again, but this time it was quiet crying, only from the eyes.

"When did this happen?"

"Tonight—about six o'clock or so. I don't even know any more." He looked up at me, accusation lasering out of his eyes. "You were the only one who knew where I was, Mike. You told them. Nettie'd be alive now if it wasn't for you. I could kill you for that, Mike. Maybe I will."

"Greg, I haven't told anyone, not even the police. I promised you forty-eight hours and I meant it."

"How'd they find us, then? How'd they know where to come and get poor Nettie?"

I went behind my desk and put the gun back in the drawer. Then I sat down and looked at the index cards. The one with the record of the attempted shooting of me jumped up and bit me on the ass.

"Someone tried to kill me Friday night," I said. "I don't know who and I don't know why. But they knew me, knew I was on the case and getting close. It's possible they were watching this apartment last night, waiting for me to be alone so they could try again. And they saw you instead. Were you driving your own car?"

"A black eighty-seven Vette," he said glumly.

"That's pretty conspicuous. They must have seen you drive up here and then tailed you back to Madison."

"Why didn't they just shoot me then?" he wailed. "Then Nettie—"

"Because they wanted you both, Greg. Whoever it was wanted to get rid of you both."

He grunted three times as if he'd been punched in the stomach. "Useless," he said. "Cruel and heartless and useless. Nettie was no threat to anybody, hasn't been in years."

"What do you mean?"

He sighed. "Just what I said. The only thing Nettie might do to hurt anyone was to forget they didn't have a coffee cup in their hands and pour scalding coffee all over their lap."

"Huh?"

"Alzheimer's. You know what that is? They used to call it senility. The brain turns to oatmeal. It started about four years ago, and it's been getting progressively worse ever since. Oh, she had her good moments. Most of the time, as a matter of fact. People who knew us well never suspected. And even when she'd do something strange they'd think she'd just had too much to drink. She was a hell of a saleslady on the phone—nobody could ever say no to her. But then there were other times she didn't know who I was, what she was doing. Sometimes she couldn't even remember where the bathroom was. Why kill a poor sick lady like that? Jesus!"

"Did you call the police?"

"What are you, crazy? Of course I didn't call the police! They'll say I did it—and then they'll lock me up for fraud."

"Greg, you just can't leave her there."

He sat up, his hands in front of him, palms outward. "I don't want to get involved."

"Get involved? Your wife has been killed, man!"

"The police . . ." Greg Shane said, shaking his head.

"Jail is the safest place in the world for you right now."

"No, it isn't. This is."

"What?"

"Right here. You'll protect me, Mike, I know you will. Listen, I did some checking before I decided to come here last night, and I know your reputation. You're smart, tough, honest, fair—"

"You make me sound like the Boy Scout pledge."

"You'll be my bodyguard. I'll hire you, name your price. Of course, I can't pay you right away . . ."

"You can't stay here, Greg. I don't want the responsibility. Besides, it would cost me my license."

"Who'll know? Mike, I'm scared, really scared, for the first time in my life. I've had run-ins with the police, I've been beaten up in Vegas a time or two, but this isn't fucking around any more, this is—well, look what happened to Nettie."

"Greg, you aren't my responsibility."

"We're all responsible for each other. That's the way it works. You know that, you're a decent man. Listen, you gave me till tomorrow night. Don't go back on your word now. Tomorrow night I'll surrender to you personally. You can hand me over to the cops, shoot me, do whatever you want. But give me till tomorrow night, like you promised."

"The police—"

"Don't ever have to know."

I hate it when people finish my sentences for me, especially if they don't finish them the way I would have.

"I won't tell them I was here," he went on. "I'll say that I was hiding. I swear to God I won't cross you. Look, I'll be here, right here. Where the hell am I gonna go? I stick my nose out that door, I'm history."

It struck me that Greg Shane had gotten over the tragic death of his wife pretty quickly, and now all he was thinking about was saving his ass.

"I can't do that," I said.

"Sure you can. And it'll be to our mutual advantage."

"How do you figure?"

"Because I'll talk to you about the magazine. About the people, about what went on. And maybe I'll say something that will trigger something that might help you."

"Help me what?"

"Do your job, Mike," he said, as if we held these truths to be self-evident.

"My name," I said, "is Milan, not Mike. And my job was to find you."

What the sniveling little bastard said made sense, though, I had to give him that. The minute someone put a bullet through my car window, finding Greg Shane didn't mean any more to me than a bucket of steam. I don't like getting shot at. It's bad for the digestion, it tends to cause insomnia, it came within inches of being fatal, and it might have already cost me Mary, the only good thing that'd happened to me in years. So before it was too late, I wanted to find out who did it and why, and to make sure he or she didn't do it again. Maybe Greg Shane could help me figure out how.

In the meantime I left him in my apartment to use the shower, stuck my .357 magnum under a lightweight jacket—more to keep Shane away from it than for my own protection—and went to the liquor store across the street and bought some more Stroh's and another bottle of cognac. Then I got into my rental car and drove to a pay phone outside a closed-up gas station about two miles away, where I called in an anonymous tip to the Madison police that a murder had been committed.

Shane was all pink from his shower when I got back, sitting on the sofa wearing my velour robe and reading the Murdock mystery. I wondered if he was planning on sleeping in my bed, too, and wearing my clothes the next morning.

"Greg," I said, slamming the cognac on the coffee table in front of him, "let's you and me talk."

17

Fear loosens more tongues than alcohol, drugs, torture, or the noble and burning desire for truth. Greg Shane jabbered like the host of an all-night telethon, and I use the term *all-night* advisedly. He didn't wind down until five o'clock in the morning. Of course, he wasn't talking all the time. Sometimes he cried. Sometimes he paced the floor, the skirts of my robe swirling around his skinny legs. Sometimes he roared, and often he whimpered. It was a dazzling light show of emotions, which is the only thing that kept me attentive, because most of what he said was twaddle, self-serving garbage, reheated gossip, and his largely uninteresting life story. But in between the mood swings, he talked.

"Sure, we did this in Los Angeles, I won't deny that. But we didn't start out to hurt anybody—we didn't this time, either.

I really wanted a magazine, Milan, that was my dream," he whined. He had at least stopped calling me Mike. "You know, when you spend your whole life working for other people, you fantasize about doing your own thing and not having somebody else's boot on your neck every minute. That's all I wanted. You understand that; you're your own boss."

"Sure," I said, "but you always have to answer to somebody."

"Right," he agreed, moving from whiny to authoritative in one word. "And I would have to answer to the advertisers. But things backed up on me. The money wasn't coming in and the costs were mounting."

"But you knew that would happen, Greg. You'd done it before, in L.A."

"Yeah, but there was a difference. In L.A. I tried to do it all myself. It was a mistake. I'm a dummkopf, I'm no businessman. I'm the idea guy. So when I got here to Cleveland I went out and got some good people."

"Dan Mulkey?"

"Danny had contacts, he knew everybody in this town. And what he told me is, he could get some backup money for me if I started to run short." He grimaced. "That never happened, but it sounded good on paper, didn't it?"

"And Jay Adams?"

He shrugged. "I told you. Jay was a good editor, but I couldn't have someone who looked like that going out and talking to clients. That's why I brought in Pursglove. He was going to be my front man."

"Where did you find Pursglove?"

"Danny knew him. Recommended him. He was just what I needed. He could write, he knows important people, and he looks like a champ. He's everything Jay Adams wasn't." He rubbed his nose like Wallace Beery in *Min and Bill*. "I felt bad running out on Leonard," he said. "More than the others. Leonard and me, we could've whipped the ass off the world together. But it was me that was responsible for the money, and it was me that had to split before I got hung out to dry."

"Seems to me your advertisers got hung out, too."

"A hundred, two hundred bucks. Sure I felt bad, but that's part of the cost of doing business."

"What about the Lake Shore?"

"If they can't eat four hundred bucks without crying about it," he said, "they've got no business putting up an umpty-million dollar hotel."

"Four hundred bucks," I said levelly.

"Yeah. For the back page."

"Supposing I told you that your math and theirs are a little different?"

He stared at me. "I'd say you, or they, are full of it. Four hundred dollars, in fifties, delivered to Leonard Pursglove personally by the manager."

"Mr. Hippsley-Tate?"

"Some English guy, yeah."

"He's not English, he just has an English name."

"I don't care if he's Scandihoovian. Four hundred bucks." His blue eyes filled up again. "Nettie's life was worth more than that, Milan."

"You didn't receive any other large sums of money from your advertisers?"

"No, four hundred bucks for the back cover, that was our big one."

"Are you sure?"

"I've got books, records I can show you."

"Anybody can whip up a set of books."

He looked hurt. "Milan, don't you trust me?"

Finally at five o'clock he got sleepy, or punchy from crying and screaming or worn out from thinking up lies to tell me, and dozed off on the sofa. I fell asleep in the chair opposite. I had a perfectly good bed in the other room, but somehow I didn't want to leave Greg Shane alone to wander around my apartment. It wasn't that I thought he'd steal my television set or my stereo or the family silver; I just felt more comfortable being where I could keep an eye on him.

We were both jolted awake by the doorbell a few minutes

before nine o'clock. Shane leapt from the sofa and began running around like a rat in a maze, his eyes wide with fright and the saliva flecking his mouth. "Oh, God. Oh, Jesus, who's that? Who is it?"

"Greg," I whispered, "get into the bedroom and stay there, you understand? Don't come out, no matter what. And don't make any noise."

He scurried into the other room, emitting a high-pitched hum of terror, and I went to the front door to admit my associate, Buddy Bustamente.

"Hey, Milan," he said. The leisure suit was dark brown today. He looked at me. "Were you out all night?"

"Why?"

"That's the same clothes you had on yesterday. What'd you, sleep in them?"

"Yeah," I said.

He guffawed. "Pretty good, huh? I should of been a detective."

I picked up the bottle of cognac and Shane's glass and took them into the kitchen. Buddy followed me.

"Shall I make some coffee?" he said.

"No. Let's have breakfast out."

"How come?"

"I just feel like it, Buddy. Let me get my jacket, okay?" I went into the bedroom. For a moment I didn't see Greg Shane; then I caught a glimpse of the top of his head. He was crouched on the floor cowering on the other side of the bed.

"Who's that?" he hissed.

"Never mind," I said, "We're leaving. You stay in this apartment, you hear me? You don't go out, you don't answer the phone, you don't open the door. You stay right where you are. I'll be back later."

He nodded, too scared to say more. He was still in his crouch when I left the room—for all I know, he stayed that way all day.

I got my gun out of the drawer and slipped it into the harness under my lightweight jacket. Buddy admired it openly. "That's some piece," he said.

"Gets the job done."

"When you wear one on your leg, you can't pack that much heat," he said. He lifted his right trouser leg to show me the .32 strapped to the side of his ankle.

"Have you been carrying that all along, Buddy?"

"It's a Justin."

"A what?"

"Justin Case." He cackled at his own joke.

"That's very amusing," I said.

Ed Stahl looks the way a reporter is supposed to—like Clark Kent. Except Ed's Clark Kent had gotten a little too close to some Kryptonite. He was tall, about six foot one, with black curly hair going to gray, and his face with its once sculpted jaw had become a bit jowly. The broad shoulders and chest were there, but were matched by an ever expanding waistline, and the horn-rimmed glasses were not for show but to aid a pair of eyes grown weak and tired from years of reading and editing his own copy. Since his Pulitzer Prize of several seasons ago Ed had been accorded the supreme accolade at the *Plain Dealer:* his own office. It didn't have any windows, to be sure—it didn't even have a door—but it was an office, and the desk that took up most of the floor space was cluttered with papers, notes, tear sheets, and today's editions of *The New York Times*, the *Washington Post*, and *The Wall Street Journal*.

Ed was behind the desk, wearing a god-awful plaid shirt and a red knit tie. I hadn't seen a knit tie like that since the fifties. He was on the phone when we walked in, and at his elbow was a mug with the string of a tea bag hanging out of it. Ed had been warned off coffee several years before by a doctor who just didn't understand the pressures of a daily news deadline.

". . . so I assume you'd have no objections to letting someone on staff here examine your books, then, Mr. Walker?" Ed was saying into the phone. "After all, you are a publicly held company . . . I don't see it that way, sir, and I don't believe the district attorney will, either. It's up to you." He jotted something down on a sheet of copy paper. He always wrote with a yellow Faber pencil. "Fine, then, Mr. Walker, I'll have someone out there early this afternoon. Thank you, sir."

He hung up. "The malefactors of great wealth," he said. "Isn't that what Teddy Roosevelt used to call them?" He pronounced the president's name correctly, with a long *u* sound, as opposed to his cousin, Franklin Delano, who had preferred Roosevelt. "I call them a pain in the ass."

That seemed as good a cue as any to introduce Buddy to Ed. "He's . . . working with me for a few days."

The two men shook hands, and Ed's quick brown eyes behind his glasses sized Buddy up immediately, categorized him, and pigeonholed him. He glanced at me curiously. Everyone to whom I introduced Buddy gave us a peculiar look. Maybe it was his garish outfits, or his prison pallor, or his impressive size. Maybe it was because he didn't look like the kind of guy I would be palling around with. I had to admit I was getting used to him, though. He was not very bright, half the time he got in my way, and just thinking about the amount of food he consumed hourly made me sick to my stomach, but there was something about him, a kind of little-boy eagerness, that made him hard for me to dislike.

Ed gestured us into two uncomfortable metal chairs with plastic padding on the backs and seats and gulped the dregs of his tea, keeping the string of the tea bag on the other side of the mug with his forefinger. "God, I hate tea," he said. "Makes me feel like an English country vicar." He picked up a curved pipe from the filthy ashtray and lit it with a wooden kitchen match, and his head almost disappeared in a blue fog. "Well, Milan, to what do I owe the honor? If you've come to take me to lunch you're three hours early."

"Actually I wanted to take a look through your morgue," I said. "Just some background stuff."

"On *North Coast Magazine?*"

I shrugged, noncommittal. "Peripherally."

"Peripherally," he said. He gave a sidelong glance at Buddy, and stood up. "Come on outside for a minute," he said, and then to Buddy, "Excuse us, okay?"

"Sure," Buddy said, and reached for the copy of *The New York Times*. He was so easy to get along with that it made me sick. I followed Ed out into the city room, far enough away from the doorless entrance to his office that Buddy couldn't hear what we were saying. The noise in the room, the low mumble of twenty-five people on the telephone, bells ringing, computers spewing out reams of printout, was such that Buddy couldn't have heard us if he'd been standing four feet away.

Ed was puffing angrily on his pipe, and the blue smoke drifted toward the ceiling to be caught up in the draft of the central air conditioning and dispersed throughout the room. Probably some tight-assed nonsmoker in the city room would eventually file a grievance about it. Life used to be a lot simpler in the good old days, when smoking was not looked on as one short notch above pedophilia.

He turned on me. "Damn your Slovenian ass, Milan, we're talking a triple homicide here. Don't give me any of your 'peripheral' shit. Now, if you've got something, I want it."

"Ed, I don't know what I've got yet. And if it hits the street before it should, somebody else might get hurt as well."

"You ask a lot, but you don't give much."

"I'll give you all I've got, Ed—when it's right."

"And when is that going to be, I wonder?"

I sighed. "Would first thing tomorrow morning do it?"

"And if it's got to be top secret today, what makes you think it'll be okay to spread it around tomorrow?"

"I just know, that's all," I said. I didn't want to tell him that at that very moment Greg Shane was in my apartment, probably crouching behind my bed like a fox hiding from the hounds.

"Uh-huh. And who's your pal in there?"

"A visiting professor of English literature from Harvard. You ought to read his dissertation on *Beowulf*."

"Don't be that way. The guy's a hood and you know it. Whose payroll is he on, and why are you schlepping him around with you like he was your uncle from Pittsburgh?"

"Ed, I'll explain it all tomorrow."

He puffed on his pipe, took it out of his mouth, and put it back in again. I heard his teeth click against the mouthpiece. "All right, Milan, go on down to the morgue. I'll phone and tell them you're coming."

"Thanks, Ed," I said. "You're back in the will."

The morgue of a newspaper, that room where they file all their back clippings, used to be a Dickensian kind of place where the must and mildew hung in the air like a fine dry mist, together with that peculiar odor of yellowing paper and ink growing faded and dim with the attrition of time. Now, however, technology has robbed us of our time-honored traditions. Everything has been reduced, compressed and transistorized, and now the back issues of the papers have been transferred to microfilm.

The librarian had been expecting me, thanks to Ed's phone call, and I told her what I was looking for and she went away and sat at a computer and did some strange things at the keyboard, pushed a few more buttons, and then the orange text on the screen bounced and whirred and the computer made some funny knocking sounds inside itself, and then she went into another room and came back with a four-by-six plastic sheet and instructed me in the use of the viewer.

"Just the one?" I said.

"That's all that's on file," she told me.

The item was from the *P.D.* of September 13, 1981 and was only a small squib in the marriages column announcing the nuptials of one Sandra Wardlow Cronin to an Emerson Judd Cowper. It was apparently the only time in the last ten years Mr. Cowper had gotten his name in the paper. No criminal record, and apparently no deep dark secrets.

I went back to the librarian and asked her if she could run the name Sandra Wardlow Cronin through the computer and see what she came up with. In five minutes she was back with another small sheet representing an entire newspaper.

"There are two entries for Sandra Cronin," she said. "One you already have, and then there's this one."

I thanked her and went back to the machine. Buddy hovered over my shoulder. "What are you doing, Milan?"

"I'll be through in a minute," I said. The new microfilm was for the issue of July 24, 1981, and I looked around with the viewer for the coordinates the librarian had given me. The search led me to a column of legal notices. There it said that the marriage of Sandra Wardlow Cronin and Harry Cronin had been dissolved on that date in Superior Court, Cuyahoga County. I couldn't help noticing, a few entries down, the announcement, with the byline Harry J. Cronin, that he was "responsible for my debts only." I dutifully wrote all the information down in my notebook.

"So that shrink married a divorced woman," Buddy said when I shared my discovery with him. "So what?"

"I don't know yet," I said.

He squirmed like an eight-year-old in church. "This is boring."

"You've been seeing too many movies, Buddy. Now you know what a detective really does: goes over records and old newspaper stories, checking and rechecking. This is about as exciting as it gets."

I gave the materials back to the librarian and thanked her, and we headed for the parking lot.

"Where we going now, Milan?"

"To see a man about a divorce."

Harry Cronin was a real estate broker in Shaker Heights, working out of a storefront office on Chagrin Boulevard. We drove there in about twenty minutes. It was not a high-powered, glamorous office, but neither was it a mean one. Just the office of a guy trying to make a living, a sallow little fellow who was putting on weight, losing both his hair and the battle against middle age without much of a struggle. The kind of guy who smiled all the time, even though it was obvious when we walked in the door that Buddy and I were not there to purchase a house.

"Look, Mr. Jacovich," Cronin said after I'd told him who I was and why I was there, "I don't want to talk about my divorce. It's over, and I don't believe in looking back."

"I understand that," I said. "And I really don't care what happened to your last marriage. I'm just trying to find out about Judd Cowper."

He frowned, and a shadow of pain crossed his face like a cloud scudding across the sun. "Cowper is beneath my contempt," he said.

"Why?"

"I told you, I don't want to talk about it. Look, he's married to my ex-wife now, and I don't want to cause her any more problems. She's got her hands full with him, I'm sure, and frankly the two of them deserve each other."

"Mr. Cronin, I don't want to alarm you, but three people have been killed in the last few days and it seems Cowper knew one or more of them. I won't bore you with explanations, because they might be slanderous, but I would appreciate your answering two simple questions for me."

He grinned without much warmth. "I guess I can handle two questions."

"Did Judd Cowper have anything to do with your divorce?"

"That's a pretty humiliating question."

"Your answer will be held confidential, sir."

Cronin shuffled through a stack of listing sheets on the corner of his desk. He kept his eyes cast down. "Cowper and Sandra were . . . having an affair, yes." He shook his head. "Is the second question going to be that tough?"

"Let's see," I said. "Was Mrs. Cronin—Mrs. Cowper— seeing Cowper professionally at that time?"

Cronin looked up at me, his eyes bright. "It's the most despicable thing I ever heard of," he said. "For someone in his position—like a doctor—to take sexual advantage of a woman who had come to him for professional help. . . . Despicable. I wouldn't be surprised at anything that man might have done."

"Why was she seeing him professionally, Mr. Cronin?"

"Depression," he said. "Our marriage wasn't exactly made in heaven, Mr. Jacovich. I have a tough time making ends meet here. The big real estate companies with multiple offices are forcing little guys like me out on the fringes. I work hard; long hours for not much money, and even when I was home I was always worrying about business. We couldn't even go for a nice drive without my seeing a property I thought I might get a listing for. We didn't have any kids, and I'm not the most romantic guy in the world, and I guess it got to Sandra. She needed some help, and she found Cowper in the yellow pages. And the miserable shit took advantage . . ."

"Mr. Cronin, you could have had him brought up on charges before the licensing board. Why didn't you?"

He shrugged his thin shoulders. "I knew he and Sandra were going to be married as soon as the divorce was final. I didn't want to cause her any trouble." His eyes got red and he dug at them with his fingers. "I still loved her, you see."

"Milan, could we stop and eat?" Buddy said when we were rolling again. "I didn't get any breakfast."

I felt unreasonably guilty that I hadn't offered Buddy anything to eat at my house, but I couldn't very well have made him some toast while Greg Shane was in the fetal position on my bedroom floor. I fought down my annoyance and stopped at another doughnut shop. I didn't want any doughnuts. I wanted to think about what I'd learned that morning—that Judd Cowper was indeed among the ranks of those with something to hide. It wasn't unreasonable to think that someone at *North Coast* had found out what I had—that Cowper had engaged in sexual relations with a client who had come to him to be treated for depression—and was quietly blackmailing him to keep that fact from the state licensing board, which surely would have taken a dim view of such matters. Chalk up one more motive for murder, I supposed.

I decided to make one more try at Leonard Pursglove. I was beginning to worry about him. With the exception of Greg Shane, who was relatively safe in my apartment, Pursglove was the only staff member of *North Coast* still alive, and I wanted to keep him that way. At least, I hoped he was still alive. Maybe he wasn't answering the door or the telephone because he couldn't. It wasn't a happy prospect; the body count on this case was running way too high.

There weren't many places to park near Leonard Pursglove's apartment building; I had to settle for a place down the street about half a block. I was waiting for Buddy to finish a jelly doughnut; his lips were ringed with sugar and there was a dab of strawberry goo at the corner of his mouth, which he sought out and destroyed with his tongue. As I opened my car door a taxi cruised past me, stopped in front of Pursglove's building, and honked its horn twice.

I stayed where I was, putting my hand on Buddy's arm. "Hold it," I said.

After about a minute the door opened and a man came out. He was in his middle forties, casually but expensively dressed in a corduroy jacket, a dark blue shirt, and gray slacks. He was quite handsome and carried himself in that way men who possess a great self-image do. He ran a hand through his shock of smoke gray hair, looked furtively around, and climbed into the taxi. It could have been J. Rose's boyfriend, I suppose, but she taught school and had probably been gone for several hours. The description seemed to fit Leonard Pursglove.

I started the engine.

"What're you doing, Milan?"

"I'm going to follow that cab," I said, aware of the absurdity even as I said it. Life is sometimes like a bad movie. But Buddy seemed to recognize the tension in my voice, and observed the gravity of the occasion by closing up the box of doughnuts and putting them on the back seat.

The cab turned up Euclid and headed east. I hung back four car lengths—not that I had any choice; the midday traffic was heavy, as usual. But we didn't have far to go. The taxi stopped in front of the Euclid entrance to the Old Arcade, and Pursglove scrambled out, handed the driver a bill, and went inside.

I slammed on the brakes. "Park it," I said to Buddy, "and meet me by the entrance." I jumped out of the car, almost losing the rental car's door and my own life to a Cadillac that was trying to get around me, and hurried into the arcade after Pursglove.

18

The Old Arcade is one of Cleveland's most famous landmarks. Built in 1890, it boasts a skylight of eighteen hundred panes of glass one hundred feet above the floor, and six floors of balconies containing attractive shops and offices. Those who use it as a cut-through from Euclid to Superior often pause to raise their eyes to the magnificent trussed arches that hold the roof up, or the rows of gargoyles that look down on them, rivalling those of Notre Dame. There are several restaurants with tables out on the balconies, and lots of polished brass, hanging plants and ferns, banners that portray some of the other local spots of interest, and a gigantic American flag. Today it was crowded with midday shoppers and strollers, but it wasn't hard for me to keep Leonard Pursglove's thick gray hair in sight. The arcade is so open and uncluttered that it provides an unobstructed view in almost every direction. It's a good place for a tail.

When I caught up with Pursglove he was standing quietly, waiting for an elevator the way everyone waits for an elevator: staring at the closed door or up at the floor indicator, not making eye contact with anyone near him, all wrapped in that protective cocoon people wear in crowds that says "I know I'm standing too close to you but it isn't my fault; I'm just trying to mind my own business." It worked for me because he wasn't looking around and didn't see me. As far as I knew he'd never laid eyes on me before, but one could not be sure. I walked down to the end of the arcade and went up the stairway to the second level and then halfway up to the third and waited. When the elevator reached the second floor the door opened and several people debarked, but Pursglove wasn't one of them. I raced up the rest of the way to the third floor, but he didn't get out there either.

By the time I got to the fourth level there was a tightness in my chest—I wasn't used to running up the stairs. But I was not to be spared; Pursglove was evidently still in the elevator car. I doggedly walked up another flight, more slowly this time.

As I reached the fifth level I saw Pursglove walking purposefully along the east side of the arcade, obviously looking for something. I hung back to see where he was headed. He turned into one of the shops; from where I was standing I couldn't see which one. I waited about two minutes until I was sure he was not going to come right back out and then went on down the gallery.

Pursglove had gone into a place called Arcade Travel. He was seated with his back to the door across a desk from a red-haired woman, one of those pixyish middle-aged ladies whose husbands make a fine living in law or medicine, who go into the travel business to give themselves something to do and to take advantage of discount fares to Europe and Hawaii and Mexico. She and Pursglove were in earnest conversation about something, and the woman was nodding in that self-important way people have when they want you to think they are the only ones in the world who can help you. As I watched, the lady turned to the computer terminal next to her and began punching the keys of the console. I shook my head sadly. The whole world is becoming computerized.

I figured I had a few minutes to kill, so I window-shopped all along the fifth level, finally taking up a position directly across the arcade from the travel bureau. I wanted to light a cigarette, but this is the New Age and smoking in public places is a heinous offense, punishable by stoning and shunning, so I just leaned against the window of a high-priced haberdashery and waited, content to know that I was polluting no one's air. People-watching. For a shopping center located right in the middle of the downtown district, the clientele of the Old Arcade was surprisingly upscale. There were a lot of precious little gift shops and boutiques to spend money in, places that catered to the impulse buyer who perhaps couldn't live without a jar of English marmalade or a home espresso machine or a Hummel figurine of a little milkmaid. There was also a trendy clothing store that sold safari clothes to intrepid explorers who wished to stalk the wilds of University Heights dressed like Stewart Granger.

I walked over to the balcony railing and leaned against it, taking in the view of the main floor of the arcade. It wasn't really high as high places go, but because of the openness of the architecture and the glass ceiling, the effect from seventy feet up was a bit dizzying. At the Euclid Avenue entrance I could see Buddy, nervously pacing back and forth in front of the door, looking around for some sign of me or Pursglove. I felt like a young mother who had deliberately ditched her kid in the crowd to get a few moments of peace. I was four floors above him, so I made no effort to get his attention. Besides, I was just as glad to be doing this particular number solo. I went back to my post against the men's store window. I didn't much look like an advertisement for the English tweeds displayed just behind me.

After about fifteen minutes Pursglove came out of the travel bureau, putting a large envelope into his inside jacket pocket. It looked like an airline ticket folder, but at that distance I couldn't be sure. He stood near the railing for a moment, conducting a nervous surveillance. When you've been doing what I do for a living long enough, you get to where you can spot fear at a glance, and Leonard Pursglove's demeanor was definitely wary. He began walking around the gallery toward me, so I started moving, too, always keeping him in sight, always maintaining the distance between us. He detoured into another store, and I kept walking around the balcony until I reached it. It was a luggage shop. Apparently Pursglove was going somewhere.

Through the open doorway I could see him examining some of the less expensive luggage, hefting it and looking at the seams to be sure they wouldn't fall apart under the rough treatment they'd get from airline baggage handlers. I figured he was going to stay put for a moment or two, so I went back around the gallery to Arcade Travel.

The redheaded lady looked up from her paper shuffling. "Hi," she said a little too brightly. "Can I help you?"

I grinned weakly at her. "Maybe," I said. "I thought I saw a friend of mine walking out your door a few minutes ago, but I lost him in the crowd. Was that Leonard Pursglove?"

"Yes," she said. Her smile lost a little wattage.

"Damn!" I said. "We worked together on an ad campaign. I haven't seen him in ages, and I don't know how to get in touch with him. Did he give you a phone number, by any chance?"

"No," she said, "he paid for his airline ticket in cash. But I really couldn't give out a phone number anyway."

"Sure, I understand," I said. "I'll just have to try and find his number someplace." I snapped my fingers. "But he must be going out of town if he was in here seeing you. When's he coming back, do you know?"

"I'm afraid not," she said. "He bought a round trip ticket to San Francisco, but he left the return date open."

"Well, I guess I'm out of luck, then. Hey, sorry to have bothered you."

"No trouble at all," she said, and dismissed me out of hand. If I wasn't going to buy a plane ticket or book a cruise, there wasn't much profit in talking to me.

I went back around the balcony to the luggage shop. Pursglove was still in there. From my vantage point in the doorway

I could see he had selected three suitcases—not a three-suiter, a small valise, and an overnight bag, the set one might expect a man to buy when he was going on a trip. These were the largest cases in the shop. If he was heading for San Francisco, he wouldn't be traveling light.

He gave the clerk a wad of bills and fidgeted while waiting for his change, as the clerk attempted to make small talk. Then Pursglove tucked one of the cases under his left arm, picked up the other two by the handles, turned around—and looked right at me. His eyes opened wide in surprise. It wasn't the look you give a passing stranger in a shopping mall. He knew who I was. He got his composure back a lot quicker than most people would have, looking away, up at some of the briefcases on display on the high shelves, at some of the wallets and key holders in the glass display cases. Anywhere but back at me. Casually, slowly, he came toward the door and through it, walked briskly past me and turned right, heading for the elevators. There weren't very many shoppers up on the fifth level, none within about thirty feet of us, and I heard his heels clicking on the floor. I took a couple of steps after him, and then all of a sudden he spun around, the whites of his eyes showing and his perfect teeth bared in a snarl, and swung the case in his right hand. It didn't weigh much, so he was able to complete the move pretty quickly, and it took me by surprise. The leather-reinforced corner of the case caught me right across the bridge of the nose, and the fourth of July went off behind my eyes, complete with cherry bombs and whistlers and an explosion of red and yellow sparks. The canned music they were piping into the arcade all at once became discordant in my ears, as if they had started playing the tape at a slower speed.

I staggered backward, and then he threw the other two suitcases at me, one at a time. The first hit me in the face. It didn't really slow me down much, but it hurt. The other caromed off my arms, which I had thrown up to protect myself, and went bouncing over the balcony railing, dropping seventy feet and seriously beaning a porter with a broom and dustpan who was cleaning the litter off the floor on the main level below. By the time I got my bearings back, Pursglove had sprinted off down the gallery toward the stairs. I went after him, stumbling over one of the suitcases and trying to stanch the blood that was spurting from my nose like beer from a tapped keg. Somewhere a woman was yelling something I think had to do with us. The world turned into a fun-house mirror.

Pursglove was wearing leather-soled loafers, and they slipped on the tile floor as he ran, slowing him down a few steps. He gyrated his arms wildly to keep his balance. Since I had on my rubber-soled deck shoes I didn't have that problem, and I remember thinking that was probably why people called policemen gumshoes. It all happened very quickly. But out of shape as I was, I was still an ex–football player, and Pursglove was a sedentary copywriter and I was able to catch up with him by the time he got close to the far end of the fifth level. I stopped him with the kind of tackle I hadn't used since I left Kent State.

I heard the breath *whoosh* out of his lungs as he fell, but he still had enough left to wriggle over onto his back and kick both feet up and out at me, catching me in the chest and knocking me backward. Then he kicked again, wildly, and one of his pointy shoes dug into me about four inches below my navel, far enough below the belt to give me a moment's pause. A sharp pain shot through my lower abdomen and I rolled away, grabbing hold of the railing to haul myself to my feet. Whoever had yelled earlier had gotten the whole place excited, and now almost everyone was looking up at us. The world loves a good show; I felt like an aerial act.

Pursglove was up now, too, and starting away. I lunged after him, and he turned quickly and smashed me across the face with the back of his hand. The force of the blow, combined with my having walked right into it, snapped my head back and sent me reeling against the balustrade. I hit it with the small of my back, and the pain rocketed up my spine.

My feet went out from under me, and my upper body out over the railing, and for one crazy moment I hung suspended above the arcade floor, a human teeter-totter, bucking crazily to get most of my weight on the safe side of the balustrade. And then Pursglove was on top of me, forcing my upper body back into bare space high above the arcade floor. He fought dirty, shoving, scratching at my eyes with his fingernails, pushing, trying his best to drive my genitals up through the top of my head with his knees, doing his best to tip me over the edge. My face was pointed straight up, and the summer sky blazing through the glass roof seemed to engulf me in its blue glare. The gargoyles that lined the periphery of the gallery at regular intervals grinned pitilessly down at me. I hammered at Pursglove's head with my fists, an artless street brawler, not caring much for the style of it but just trying to inflict enough injury to get him off me so I could get my feet back down onto something solid. One of my punches connected with his ear; he gave a loud yelp and backed off a step or two, his face contorted in pain. I wondered if I'd broken his eardrum.

I struggled upright, my feet hitting the floor with a clunk, and spit out some of the blood that had run from my nose down into my mouth so I could breathe. A wave of nausea wracked me. Pursglove stood there moving his head from side to side, trying to get the bells in his ear turned off, while I tried to get my equilibrium back. Then he made a low growling sound, extended his arms in front of him, palms outward, and ran right at me. Dizzily I stepped aside like a drunken matador, and he spun by me, his elbow jarring me in the chest. He hit the balustrade, teetered crazily there for a moment that seemed like a decade, and went over, emitting a long scream that was cut off abruptly by the sound of shuddering impact down on the main level of the gallery. Some three hundred shoppers had paused in their comings and goings to watch him fall.

All of a sudden there were a lot of people screaming.

I'm not sure, but I think I was one of them.

The nurse on duty in the first-aid office dabbed peroxide on the scratches on my face and stuffed a wad of cotton up my nose to stop the bleeding. She told me that in her considered opinion the nose was not broken but suggested I see a doctor as soon as

212

possible to get some X rays and make sure. It sounded like a good idea, but I didn't have the time. First I had to talk at length to Marko Meglich, who had been summoned by the security officer at my behest and who verified that the man who had fallen from the fifth gallery of the Old Arcade was indeed Leonard Pursglove, that he had landed on his head when he fell, fracturing his skull and breaking his neck, and that he was as dead as his costaffers of *North Coast Magazine,* Jay Adams and Dan Mulkey and Nettie Shane. Marko wanted me to come with him down to headquarters and make a complete statement, but I begged him for the evening to myself so I could rest and maybe start to feel better, and since the clerk at the luggage shop had thought it peculiar that anyone in this day and age should pay for such a large purchase as three suitcases in hard cash and as a result had watched Pursglove leave the store and had verified that he had attacked me first, I was allowed to leave.

My chauffeur, Buddy, had been waiting for me by the Euclid Avenue entrance all that time, had seen the fight and the fall, and was making clucking noises at me like a mother whose toddler has skinned his knee as we walked to the garage where he had left the car.

"You gotta be more careful, Milan," he said. "You could of got killed."

I knew that.

"See, if I'd of been with you, you wouldn't of got hurt."

I knew that too. But I also knew that I would have had a hell of a time explaining Buddy to Marko Meglich, and then Marko would not have been as generous with the information he had for me, especially about the savings account passbook that Leonard Pursglove had in his pocket when he fell, and I wouldn't have known a lot of things that I knew now. So a sore nose and a few scratches on the face didn't seem so bad.

There was a pay phone near the entrance to the garage and I stopped and made some quick phone calls. It was hard to talk with the cotton in my nose, but I managed somehow. I always manage, somehow. And then I gratefully allowed Buddy to drive me home.

19

It was about six o'clock by the time Buddy and I got back to my apartment. The rush hour traffic had been bad, driving had been heavy going, and I was glad to get out and stretch my legs, glad for the brief gulp of fresh air before we went upstairs to my apartment.

The living room was empty, hot-looking despite the humming air conditioner, with the late afternoon sun baking the buildings across the street and reflecting its warmth through my windows. I crossed the room wearily and took my holster off and dropped it into the top drawer of my desk.

"Want a beer, Milan?" Buddy said.

"You'd better bring three."

"Three?"

"Three," I said.

When he came out of the kitchen with the three cans of Stroh's, I said, "Sit down, Buddy."

He put two of the cans on the desktop and went and sat on the sofa. "What's up?"

"Buddy, I want you to sit quietly and listen," I said. "Just like you've been doing all through this. Promise?"

"Sure, Milan, if that's what you want."

"That's what I want."

I got up and went to the bedroom, opened the door and said, "Come on out, Greg."

Gregory Shane, née Harry Sweet, née Harvey Schoenstein, came out of my bedroom wearing a pair of my blue jeans and one of my shirts. He'd picked one of my few expensive ones. I don't know why he had commandeered my clothes, but this didn't seem to be the time to carp about it. Buddy stared at him as if I'd trotted out a gilled and web-footed mutant from the Okefenokee Swamp.

"Buddy Bustamente, Greg Shane," I said.

Neither man made any move to shake hands. Neither man knew what the other was doing in my living room. I wasn't sure either.

Greg said, "Who's this?"

"An interested party," I told him.

Buddy said, "This is the guy we've been looking for."

"Yes," I said, "but he's been the wrong guy all the time."

"Huh?" Shane said, at sea.

"He didn't take any money from your boss, Buddy, so just relax."

Shane said, "What boss? Who's his boss? What are you getting me into here?"

"He works for the people that own the Lake Shore Hotel, Greg."

"Jesus," he said, "for four hundred bucks they send a hit man?"

Buddy said, "Who you calling a hit man, asshole?"

I said, "Nobody's getting hit. Just sit down and drink your beer. We're having company."

Shane chose the chair opposite Buddy. They regarded one another like rival gunfighters who had coincidentally showed up in Dodge City on the same day.

"Milan, we're not getting anywhere sitting around and looking at each other," Shane said.

"We're where we need to be, Greg."

"Milan," Buddy said, "I think I ought to take this guy to see Mr. Gaimari."

"I'm telling you, he hasn't done anything to Gaimari."

"What am I," Greg said, "a piece of meat you can pass around so everybody gets a hunk?"

"Both of you, please shut up," I said.

"I don't want Mr. Gaimari should get mad."

I went and stood between them. "You shut up," I said to Buddy, "and you shut up," I said to Greg. "It's all going to be explained soon."

"What soon? My wife is dead, someone's trying to kill me, and you're giving me stories!" He headed for the door. "I'm getting out of here."

He was stopped in mid stride by the ringing of the doorbell. To me it was the welcome sound of a cavalry charge sounding from over a far hill. I can be a pretty gracious host sometimes, but Greg Shane and Buddy Bustamente in your living room can cause premature gray hair, ulcers, and eventual heart problems due to stress.

My doorbell has a somewhat raucous tone, and Shane was whirling like an out-of-control dreidel. I sat him back in his chair and went to answer the door.

"What's this all about, Jacovich?" Richardson Hippsley-Tate said when I opened it. He was wearing the same gray three-piece suit I'd seen him in before, or its identical twin, I wasn't sure. "I was in an important meeting when you called."

"Come on in, Richie," I said.

I led him into the living room. Buddy and Greg stood up when we came in. Polite. For a moment everyone was frozen in a strange tableau. Four big husky men, like a pro wrestling re-union, looking at each other with suspicion and unease, wondering who was on whose side and which of us had the wherewithal to destroy one or more of the others. You could have cut the tension in that room with a pizza slicer.

"Richardson Hippsley-Tate of the Lake Shore Hotel, Greg Shane of *North Coast Magazine*," I said.

Richie Hips stiffened. "Jesus, you found him. Good work."

"And this is Mr. Bustamente."

The two men nodded warily.

"Everybody sit down," I said. I went and sat behind my desk, Shane and Buddy sank back into their seats, and Richie Hips took the only other chair in the room.

"You owe me forty-two thousand dollars, Shane," Richie said.

The color left Greg's face. "Forty-two. . . ? You're crazy. I took four hundred dollars from you! And I'll pay it back, every fucking penny."

"Forty-two grand," Richie Hips repeated.

"This is my party and I want everyone to be quiet while I do the talking," I said. "Do you want something to drink, Richie?"

Richie pointed his finger at Shane. "I want him and I want my forty-two thousand dollars, and that's all."

"You think you're gonna squeeze me for that kind of money," Shane said, "you've got another think coming, my friend."

I spread my hands on my desk. "Chill out, everyone. First of all, let's get up to date. I found Leonard Pursglove today. And he had an accident. He's dead."

Richie and Greg looked startled. For Buddy it was old news. Greg said, "What happened?"

"He fell off a balcony," I said cryptically. "How doesn't much matter."

"What matters is that this bastard is a crook," Richie said, pointing a finger at Greg. "He owes me money."

"Shut up, Richie," I said mildly. "You're right. Greg is a crook. He was bilking a bunch of small businesses by selling them ads in a magazine that didn't exist. He's done it before, in California, and he was doing it again."

"I told you—" Greg began.

"Shut up, Greg."

He subsided, hurt. Buddy leaned back in his chair and laced his fingers over his belly, just under the white patent leather belt. If Buddha had been a button man for the mob, he would have looked like Buddy Bustamente.

"But Shane is a small-time crook, Richie. Forty-two thousand dollars is way out of his league."

"*What* forty-two thousand dollars?" Shane said.

"The big crooks in this story were Dan Mulkey and Leonard Pursglove. When Greg hired them to work on this magazine, this scam, they decided it was too penny-ante for them. So they came up with another idea."

Shane glared at me. "What are you—"

"Greg thought these small advertisers were getting nicked for a couple of hundred apiece. That's the money he was getting from Pursglove and Mulkey. Some of them, like Peter Kazakis at the Kukla restaurant, really were just advertisers. But some of the others, like Merlys Mercer and Judd Cowper and Alex Malleson and Earl Faggerty, for instance, as well as Edna Warriner and Vivian Truscott, were being blackmailed."

Greg said, "That's a lie! I wasn't blackmailing anybody, I was trying to get a magazine started."

"Greg, you told me yourself you're a lousy businessman, and that you hired Mulkey and Pursglove and Adams to run your business for you. But you were too dumb and too naive to realize that your marks weren't the only ones being screwed. Your big problem isn't that you're a crook, but that you're a stupid one. And you hired two other crooks who were smarter than you were. You didn't even bother to check them out; you would have found that Dan Mulkey lost his last job because he was taking kickbacks."

Buddy said, "Milan, you're losing me here."

"Shut up, Buddy," I said. "Let me tell it."

He shrugged and sulked.

I said, "Mulkey and Adams were giving you the ad revenue, but they were banking the extortion money themselves. It came to a fairly tidy sum, too. About seventy thousand dollars."

They all looked at me blankly. "When Leonard Pursglove went off the gallery at the Old Arcade today, he had a savings account passbook in his pocket showing a balance of seventy-two grand and change. About three thousand of it was deposited over the last six years. The rest of it started coming in just about the time he started working for *North Coast Magazine.* There's one big deposit of forty thousand. That more than likely came from the Lake Shore Hotel."

Greg was stunned. "Those fucking bastards! They cheated me!"

"Actually it was you who gave them the idea in the first place—or rather, your wife."

"Nettie?"

"You wanted a big Cleveland celebrity for your first cover," I said, "and Vivian Truscott seemed to fill the bill. But when you started talking about her, Nettie remembered that she knew her in Vegas, when both of them were working the casinos. Either you or she mentioned that to Pursglove, and so they blackmailed her into giving them an interview. And while they were at it, they leaned on her for some money, too, to keep them quiet about the fact that the first lady of the news was a former Las Vegas hooker. That was so easy they decided to work the same scam again by digging up dirt on some other people, too. Mulkey and Pursglove between them knew most of the people in town, and where a lot of bodies were buried. From the amount of money in Pursglove's account, probably a lot of the other advertisers were being squeezed in the same way."

"I had no idea, I swear it!" Greg said.

"Probably not. You got your ad money, all right, Greg," I said. "But it wasn't enough for you to start up your magazine, so you did the same thing you did in California—you ran. Hid out. Another small-time scam that didn't work for you."

Buddy said, "Who did the killings, Milan?"

"Well, one can't be sure," I said, "but here's how I figure

219

it. Pursglove was putting the money into his account for himself and Mulkey. When Greg and Nettie folded their nonexistent magazine and split the scene, that meant the game was over for Pursglove and Mulkey, too. So Pursglove decided he'd double-cross Mulkey and keep the money. Mulkey threatened to blow the whistle, and Pursglove killed him."

"What about the fat guy?"

"Poor Jay Adams thought he was going to be editor in chief of a magazine. He had his suspicions about Mulkey and Pursglove, and once Mulkey was dead he knew he was right. So Pursglove had to get rid of him too. And then he figured he'd do it all, so he killed Mrs. Shane as well. And Greg, you were next. Guys don't carry their savings account passbooks around for the fun of it. He was going to withdraw all the money and head out of town. San Francisco, for starters, although I don't know what his ultimate destination was."

Greg was crying again.

"You accused me of selling you out," I said. "I didn't, but as I told you, it was because of me that he found you and Nettie. He was tailing me and he saw you coming out of my apartment the other night and followed you back to Madison, found out where you were living. He's the one that took a shot at me on the street, too. Because I was getting too close to him, asking too many questions."

Shane stood up. "This is crazy!" he said.

"Greg, when you came here the other night you said you had heard I was looking for you. Who told you?"

"Vivian Truscott," he said. "She called Nettie—they were old friends, like you said—and told her you'd been to see her."

"The question then seems to be, who told Leonard Pursglove that I was poking around?"

Shane shook his head. "It wasn't me," he said.

"Sit down, Greg." He did. "If it wasn't you, then only one other person knew about my involvement. And that was the one who hired me."

We all looked at Richardson Hippsley-Tate.

"I don't think I like what you're saying, Jacovich."

"It's the only thing that figures. Greg and Nettie were in hiding; Pursglove couldn't have found out about me from them. Mulkey never knew about me, because he was dead before anyone knew I was involved. And Jay Adams wouldn't have told Pursglove—he hated his guts. You were in on it from the start, Richie, you and Pursglove. That's why you gave him such a ridiculous sum of money for an ad. When the crunch came you were going to blame it all on Shane and let him take the fall for it. He'd pulled this magazine con before, and no one would believe him. You're an old hand at blackmail, Richie. From the Victorian Inn days."

His body jerked as if he were on a string and someone had yanked it. "I don't know what you're talking about. Come on, Jacovich, you're supposed to be working for me."

"Sure," I said. "You're pretty dumb too, Richie. Did you really think the people you work for, D'Allessandro and Gaimari, were just going to sit still for a forty-two-thousand-dollar sting? When they found out they'd been taken, supposedly by Shane here, they told you the money was your responsibility. By that time Shane was gone, and you got scared. You cried to them, and because of my past association with Gaimari he suggested you hire me—at your own expense—to find Shane and get the money back. You knew he didn't have it, that he didn't know anything about the blackmail business, but you figured Gaimari wouldn't believe him and you'd at least be off the hook. That's why you paid me in cash instead of with a hotel check. But Pursglove didn't give a shit about you and your problems, and when he heard I was looking around he decided to get rid of all the people involved who could blow the whistle on him, and to get out of town. San Francisco first, and then probably somewhere else, away from the long arm of your bosses. And he decided to take me out too, before I found out what was going on. He was no professional killer, though. He could walk in and kill Mulkey and Adams and Mrs. Shane because they knew him, they were sitting ducks. But he wasn't quite good enough with that gun to hit a moving target like me."

"You're blowing smoke," Richie Hips said.

"When Pursglove saw me at the Old Arcade today, he panicked. Trying to kill me in public was pretty stupid, but he lost his cool and tried it. He died trying. That leaves you, Richie."

Hippsley-Tate was on his feet and moving toward the door. "That'll never fly in court."

"It won't have to," Buddy Bustamente said. Those quick hands of his had moved without any of us seeing them, and he was pointing the .32 revolver from his ankle holster right at Richie's middle.

"Put that down, Buddy," I said.

"This's got nothing to do with you, Milan."

"Yes, it does, Buddy. I figured something like this when we got home here today, and you saw Shane and didn't do anything about it. Gaimari set me up to get at Richie Hips. He never really trusted him, he told me so. If he'd just wanted to find Shane he wouldn't have bothered me at all. But he and old Giancarlo D'Allessandro probably suspected Richie was running a game on them, and they didn't like it—they wouldn't like it no matter who did it, but when it's one of their own people they tend to get really upset. And knowing Richie was my client, they sent you along with me to make sure that when I got Shane, they'd get Richie. I was the stalking horse all along. I don't like being used."

"Sorry," Buddy said. "I really am."

"Jesus Christ, let me out of here!" Shane said, leaping to his feet. "I don't want to die."

Richie Hips was sweating freely; dark crescents appeared at the armpits of his gray suit. He wiped his face and said to Buddy, "Look, we can make a deal."

"You got nothing to deal with," Buddy told him. "Come on." He stood up, his gun still trained on Hippsley-Tate. Now everyone was standing up but me.

"Buddy," I said, "I can't let you do this."

"Don't try to stop me, Milan," Buddy said. "I like you and I don't want you to get hurt."

"I don't want anyone to get hurt, Buddy."

He gestured at Hippsley-Tate with his gun. "Let's go."

"Sit down, Buddy," I said.

"Stay out of it, Milan."

"I'm in it, Buddy. Sit down and put that thing away."

"Don't make me hurt you, Milan. You're my friend. I don't want to hurt you."

"Buddy, please." I opened my desk drawer and took out the .357 Magnum, still in its ballistic nylon holster.

He wheeled on me. His eyes were flat, dead, two chocolate drops in his pasty face. The muzzle of his .32 looked like the mouth of a cannon pointing at me. "Don't make me do it, Milan," he said.

"Buddy," I said, and he cocked the .32.

I blasted a hole through the end of my holster and shot him in the right eye. What was left of him was dead before he hit the floor.

20

I was well on my way to being drunk again. I'd naturally spent a good portion of my evening at police headquarters, which was becoming a habit I was getting damn sick of. I was damn sick of the whole thing. When I got home I fell into a troubled sleep, and in the morning when I woke up I started on the cognac again.

Richie Hips was in custody, and the mob lawyers were having nothing to do with him. He'd broken the code and he was on his own, taking a fall for blackmail and conspiracy. Victor Gaimari, of course, came out of it with his skirts pristine. Guys like him usually did; it was the way they always set things up. Like any good general, he stayed behind the lines and took battle reports, but he never got close enough to actual combat to have to worry about his own ass. He hadn't done anything illegal as far as the law was concerned. There was no way of nailing him for ordering a hit, because he was claiming that Buddy Bustamente had been acting on his own. He and I both knew the real story, but it's a peculiarity of the American justice system that real stories don't matter much in a court of law. That's why the jails are full of cheap hoods and the country clubs are full of rich ones.

Greg Shane was booked for fraud and was out on five thousand dollars bail, paid for by Victor Gaimari. Victor was quite a grandstander, and that was his way of letting me know what a nice guy he really was. We all knew that the moment Shane was on the streets he'd be on a plane somewhere, but nobody really cared, not even the cops.

Earl Faggerty was back on the outside. As much as Marko Meglich might have wanted to throw away the key on him, he was no murderer. My observation that the brake fluid he worked with every day contained some of the same chemical elements as gunpowder residue, coupled with the fact that Faggerty had been in custody when someone took a shot at me on the street, gave him a ticket out. And true to his word, or to my word, Marko was ignoring Faggerty's hot-car activities, with the proviso that Earl go and sin no more. Preferably in some venue other than Cleveland.

On a slab down at the coroner's office with a tag on his toe, was Buddy Bustamente less what he'd left in my living room, which I had just finished cleaning up. I vomited four times during the process, until my stomach was empty. But that didn't stop the dry heaves. I hadn't checked the paper for the baseball scores, I hadn't had my morning coffee, I hadn't even opened the curtains to let the sunshine into my apartment. I just drank. I didn't know what would give out first, me or the cognac. I kept staring at the place on the floor I had just scrubbed with ammonia. It had bleached some of the color out of the carpet. I'd have to get a new one.

I had a lot of changes to make.

The more I drank the clearer it was to me that there were more similarities between Buddy and me than differences. Both of us came out of immigrant families, both of us grew up in ethnic neighborhoods and had survived because of size and strength. But somewhere along the line he took one turn and I took another. I became a football player and then a cop, and he became a life-taker. And now he was dead and I was drinking alone and hard at eleven o'clock in the morning, and the booze wasn't making things fuzzy the way I hoped it would. Each gulp brought clarity, the very thing I was trying to avoid.

Buddy Bustamente's wasn't the first human life I'd taken. But the others were faceless men in Viet Cong uniforms whose names I didn't know and couldn't have pronounced if I had. I'd gotten medals for those.

The doorbell shattered the silence, and my nervous system along with it. I made a note to get a new doorbell, one that bing-bonged like the Avon lady instead of buzzing like a smoke alarm. Heaving my bulk out of my chair to cross the room and open the door seemed like a challenge that was hardly worth the effort. I didn't peek through the fish-eye to see who it was, because I didn't really care.

"Hello, Milan," Mary said when I opened the door. She looked hard at me, at the unshaven face and the bleary red eyes, but there was no apparent disapproval. She put her hand on my cheek, and I felt the stubble rasp against her hand. Then she brushed past me and into the living room, where she stared sadly at the almost empty cognac bottle and shook her head.

I closed the door and lumbered in after her. "You're supposed to be at work," I said. It wasn't terribly gracious of me, but for a guy carrying more than a pint of Courvoisier under his belt, it wasn't too bad.

"I took an early lunch hour." She turned to me. "I heard what happened last night. Mark Meglich called and told me this morning. He thought you might need a friend."

"Mark ought to mind his own damn business." I plopped down onto the sofa with no grace at all.

"Milan, I'm so sorry. It must have been awful for you." She sat down next to me, her hand cool on my arm.

"It wasn't my best day."

She squeezed my arm a little, and it felt good. I said, "You were right, Mary."

"About what?"

"About . . . everything. You're right, this is no way to live."

She stared at me, her blue eyes brimming.

"I'll figure out something else to do. This . . . costs too much."

"There's a price tag on everything," she said.

"Yeah, but sometimes the price is too high. I'm going to quit, Mary. So you won't have to worry all the time anymore." I looked away. "If you still want me."

She sniffled. "I want *you*, Milan. I've thought it over a lot the last few days. I love you and want you because of who and what you are. What happened last night—that was too bad, but it was *right*, too. Because someone else might have been killed, and you were there to stop it."

"I'm not God."

"Sure you are," she said. "You, me, Marko, Lila—we're all God, all a part of God. That's what God is. Not a guy with a white beard sitting up on a cloud and hurling lightning bolts. God is people."

"I don't *want* to be God. It's too big a responsibility."

"No, silly, that's why we're here. And the only way we can be worthy of that responsibility is to be who we are, and to rejoice in it."

I turned my head to face her. It required the kind of effort that made me dizzy. "How can I rejoice in killing another human being?"

"You can't," she said. "It's a terrible thing, and you're going to have to live with it. But you can know that you have certain standards that you live by, and you did what you had to do, because you thought it was right. Moral. No one can fault you for that, Milan."

I slumped back against the cushions, wanting to burrow my ass so far into them that I disappeared from my own sight. A neat trick, never been done before in all of history.

"I asked you to quit the other night because I was scared, because I'd never seen anyone waving a loaded gun around before. I was wrong to ask you that. All your life you've fought for what you believed in—on a football field, in Vietnam, on the police force. And you're still doing it, in your own way. You have to, because that's what you're made of. That's who you are."

"Pretty sad commentary," I mumbled.

"No, you don't understand," she said. "I told you once that I was attracted to you because you weren't like all the other guys I knew. You were special. Well, you're still special, and I wouldn't have you any other way. Don't quit. If you do, then you won't be you anymore."

"What about you?" I said. "You said you didn't want to live in fear—"

"I've thought about that, too. And I realized we all live in fear, unless we learn to overcome it. Hey, I could get scared every time I hop on the freeway. I could freak out whenever I had to do a sales job on some high-powered business type I hoped would buy time on the station. But I can't be afraid, because deep down I believe in myself. Milan, you're the most genuinely decent human being I've ever known, and I love you—the way you are, for who you are. And I believe in you, so I won't be afraid anymore. Now don't leave me out here twisting in the wind, believing in you all by myself."

I reached for my bottle but she snatched it away from me. "That's about enough of that," she said. "Self-pity isn't very attractive, you know, so knock it off!" She marched into the kitchen, and I heard the rest of the cognac gurgling merrily down the drain. The bottle broke as she dumped it into the kitchen trash.

"I have to get back to work. Because I believe in what I do. It's time for you to get back to work too."

She stood in front of me and held my face in her hands. "Take a shower," she said, "and shave. And brush your teeth, because your breath smells like a graveyard. I'll be back here tonight after work with a couple of steaks and some baking potatoes. We'll have dinner and then we'll go to bed and we'll make the most wonderful love, Milan, the way we always do. Because I believe in us together, too. With all my heart." She bent and kissed me on the mouth, and then straightened up. "Don't forget about brushing your teeth," she said.

The door clicked quietly behind her and I was alone again. I just sat and stared. I'd had too much to drink and there was no magic wand I could wave that would instantly get my act together. My first instinct was to make some coffee, but I knew that coffee doesn't do a hell of a lot to sober up a drunk. And that's what I was.

The phone rang. I was going to let the machine get it, but somewhere in the night I had turned it off and forgotten to reset it. I thought to let it ring, but the bell was jangling my nerves too badly. As I picked up the receiver I made a mental note to get a phone that bing-bonged too.

"Dad? It's Milan."

I rubbed a hand over my face. "Hey," I said.

"Hey," he said.

"What's happening?"

"Guess what."

"What?"

"Guess."

"You're getting married," I said.

"Come on!"

"What, Milan?"

The teenage cool struggled with the little boy in my son, and lost. His voice cracked as he announced, "The coach called this morning. I made the frosh team."

I felt veils of pain and confusion lifting, as if a cool lake breeze had come and blown them away. "Milan, that's great."

"Yeah," he said.

"I'm proud of you. Really proud."

"Yeah."

"When do you start practice?"

"Two weeks. I get fitted for a uniform Friday."

"You'll look terrific," I said.

"They probably won't let me wear your old number, though, 'cause you were a lineman and I'm a wide receiver."

Something inside my chest swelled up so big that it hurt. "You wear your own number, Milan—and be your own guy. When you graduate they'll probably retire that number, you know?"

"I'm sure," he said.

"Look, any time you want me to come to watch you practice, I'd like to. But only when you're ready. And I won't give you any pointers or anything. I'll just watch. It's been a long time since I've watched a team practice."

"Okay," he said.

"Hey, that's the best news I could've gotten, Milan. Congratulations."

"Yeah," he said.

We talked for another minute or so, and then he told me he had to go and we hung up. I sat with my elbows on my knees and my head down and allowed the paternal pride in me full reign. When I finally lifted my head my cheeks were wet and my nose was running.

I went into the bathroom and regarded myself in the mirror. I wasn't pretty at the best of times, and this wasn't one of those. I blew my nose rather violently a couple of times into some toilet paper, and then splashed cold water on my face and neck. It didn't improve my appearance any, but it made me feel better.

And then I brushed my teeth.